TIME THIEF

TIME THIEF

Bill Andrefsky

Piscator Productions
Pullman, Washington

This book, *Time Thief*, is a work of fiction. Names, characters, places, institutions, and incidents are the products of the author's imagination or are used fictitiously. Any resemblance to actual events, locations, circumstances, or persons, living or dead, is entirely coincidental.

Piscator Productions
Pullman, Washington

Manufactured in USA

ISBN 9798990578005
ISBN 9798990578012 (eBook)

To my brother Walt, and to the memory of my father

ACKNOWLEDGEMENTS

Thanks goes to my long-time editors Marilyn Bender and Louise Davison. This project was a bit different than the textbook projects I've asked of them, but the challenge was embraced.

I had a great group of "early readers" who provided comments, encouragement, editing, and advice. I thank each, and every one of them with my most sincere gratitude. Thank you again Barbara Couture, Rick Williams, Doug MacDonald, Dave Dolezilek, David Payne, and Noreen Golfman. I must especially thank Karyn Hardy who reviewed all versions of the manuscript and because of her subtle comments, I left major sections and entire chapters on the cutting room floor.

On the technical side, I thank Erin Thornton for helping me better understand the possibilities of isotope analysis, and to Biddy Bender for literally pointing out the potential of Bryozoan research.

PROLOGUE

SNAKE RIVR CANYON, WESTERN NORTH AMERICA
TERMINAL PLEISTOCENE

The village elder, Kamiakan, stood remembering his youth. As a child, he played and explored the caves and rock shelters found along the Great River next to his winter village. Sometimes he would construct small huts from willow branches and cattail reeds as hiding places in the back of the caves with his brothers and cousins. As with most children, he became intimately familiar with the area surrounding his home. He traversed every rabbit trail and deer path as they progressed through the cliffs and boulder fields of black basalt surrounding his home range.

The hunting and gathering lifeway are the oldest of all human economic strategies. Hunting and gathering was tested by humans for over hundreds of thousands of generations, and no other economic strategy had come close to that test of time. His extended family and the other villagers would trek from the Great River each year as the winter thawed and begin their annual cycle of migration through the uplands and mountain valleys, where they hunted and gathered the food and medicinal resources that became available seasonally. Then autumn brought these various extended families back to the sheltered and warmer river bottom. Every year, the returning families would repair and rebuild their shelters, settle in and sustain one another for the cold season. This was Kamiakan's life, the life of his parents, and their parents, and their parents for as long as anyone knew.

Kamiakan stood at the rim of the canyon overlooking the winter village and observed the rolling hills spread out toward the single isolated peak in the distance. The autumn sun was bright but there was a refreshing chill in the air. He could see the white snow cap at the very pinnacle of the mountain. One of Kamiakan's first memories as a child was the white ice cap on that mountain. At that time, the ice sheet extended down the mountain and across the rolling hills and came within a half-day's walk of the canyon rim. Then, slowly at first, but progressively each year, the ice and snow receded, giving way to open lands that were immediately pioneered by thick grasses.

As he stood looking over the rolling-grassland he recalled the immense grazing herds. Those herds had all but disappeared, following the receding ice field into the distance. There were still groups of beasts, but for the most part, the massive herds had moved away and the creatures that remained were different. The massive grazing elephants were gone, replaced by smaller browsing elephants. Bison with shortened horns grazed in place of the giant long-horned bison.

Kamiakan turned from the distant mountain and looked toward the canyon bottom. His village was positioned deep within the protected canyon walls at the confluence of the

Great River and a smaller tributary. Above the village on the steep rocky faces were rock shelter and cave openings. The mouths of craggy caves and rock shelters brought to his mind, the year, decades before, when he discovered the secret of the caves. He had returned to the one special cave where he had played as a child. He was surprised to find that the small toy hut he played in as a child was exactly as he had built it. He remembered carefully weaving the reeds between the willow branches. He recognized the cordage he had twisted and twined together from cedar bark. He examined the hut carefully. It was almost as if everything in the cave was in a state of suspended decay. The hut features were exactly as he had left them decades before. The woven lattice of reeds was fully preserved. It was then that he realized the cave had provided protection from decay. Over the next few years, he used the cave as a place to preserve medicinal plants and dried meats for later use. Over the following years and decades, Kamiakan built racks and rock-lined pits in the caves to expand storage capacity and encouraged others in his village to use the preservation powers provided by the dry caves.

Kamiakan's musings were interrupted by the sounds of children laughing and playing. He smiled knowingly as he watched two village children scurry up a hillside toward the rock shelters and caves. As the boys disappeared around the edge of the canyon wall, Kamiakan followed along listening to them yelping and laughing as they worked their way up the canyon. Even though Kamiakan was old, his legs and his heart were strong, and he easily kept up. The boys rose higher up the black basaltic slopes and Kamiakan happily followed along, stopping every now and then to view the brilliant kaleidoscopic vegetation as it glittered in the afternoon sunlight.

There was nobody in the village as old as Kamiakan, but his hearing and sense of smell were as sharp as they had been in his youth. First, he smelled it. The heavy musky odor of digested vegetation. Then he could hear the occasional snapping and crunching of branches. He picked up his speed, leaping from the top of one boulder to another, heading for the location of the two boys. He could not see them yet, but he could see where they were headed by the bent grasses they walked through as they made for the cave entrance. Suddenly, he heard the high-pitched scream of a baby elephant. Kamiakan increased his pace, taking longer leaps as he recklessly advanced from one boulder to the next. As he emerged up over the rim of rockfall in front of the cave he saw the boys standing in front of a steep rock wall that had a circular divot carved into it. In the divot stood a baby mastodon, accidentally trapped between the wall and the two boys. The calf cried in pure fright. It attempted to move left and then right but it had nowhere to go as the boys were blocking. The young elephant repeated its shrill bawl, over, and over again.

Kamiakan ran forward, shouting at the boys to get away from the calf! Before he reached the boys, the mother cow came running around the base of the rock face. She was huge, standing taller than a grown man at the shoulder with a thick trunk that furiously curled and uncurled. She had two log-like tusks that came to slender tips. The dark gray skin with sparse black hairs and deep wrinkles allowed the cow to blend into the basalt rock. When she saw the boys between her and her calf, she spread her flat ears sideways and bellowed a deep roar. She became increasingly more animated, shifting her weight from one front leg to the next, rocking her body.

The two boys froze in panic at the sight of the massive, angry creature.

Kamiakan flew in and grabbed the boys, one under each arm, and yanked them away from the calf, but the mother's trunk came down on Kamiakan's shoulder and knocked him off his feet. Kamiakan twisted and hit the rocky slope on his back with each boy cuddled on his chest. The force of the blow propelled him down the talus slope headfirst. Within a few feet his momentum was stopped, but the mastodon was instantly upon them. She raised her front leg and brought her enormous foot down. Defensively, Kamiakan raised his own foot and kicked. This shot the three farther down the 60-degree slope. His kick had quickly put some distance between the cow and Kamiakan and the youngsters. Fortunately, the cow elected to grab her terrified baby and lead it away from the melee. The humans abruptly stopped at the base of the talus slope. The boys wiggled out of Kamiakan's arms and jumped to their feet to escape but stopped when the elder did not rise. They shook his shoulders and coaxed him saying, "Ancient one, you must get up before the beast returns." The boys could see blood coming from Kamiakan's head. They looked at each other and ran to the village for help.

The death of the legendary Kamiakan spread quickly throughout the canyon and far into the forested mountains. The winter village only housed about a hundred people, but thousands lined up to bid Kamiakan a safe journey into the next world. They stood quietly while the four elders presided by custom over the burial of Kamiakan. He was placed in an excavated pit under a ledge, laid on his side with his elbows and knees flexed in the fetal position. He lay on the thick hide of a giant short-faced bear. Each person walked forward to the burial pit, and many placed something into the pit as they said their farewells.

On a pole scaffolding next to Kamiakan's place of rest hung a feathered cape. The cape was constructed of light leather with the outside covered in thousands of bird feathers. The feathers were attached in overlapping rows from bottom to top to shed water much like roof shingles. Each row was made from a different species of bird. There were tail feathers from gosh hawks, wing feathers from stellar jays, back feathers from green herons, and countless other species. One of the elders walked to the scaffolding and gently lifted the waterproof cape and spread it over the body. Another placed a woven matting of rushes over the cape. Then a progression of younger adults, female and male, each carrying a basket of heavy sand walked to the graveside and ritually poured the sand to cover the matting and fill the burial pit.

The four elders held hands and looked out into the gathered crowd. Most were direct descendants of Kamiakan or related by affinity and all the people seemed extraordinarily healthy. This was due in no small part to the deceased, who had discovered how to preserve foods for longer periods, thus eliminating the feast and famine cycle experienced by most hunting and gathering populations. He was also among the first to understand and promote that stored foods would allow most of the village residents to stop their annual migrating and instead leave for only short periods of time to gather resources and bring them back to the winter village location. With a constant source of food in one location, the people could invest in more permanent structures and equipment. Instead of making portable tools for constant residential relocation, he convinced them to make more permanent tools, equipment, and housing to insure their sustainability.

The elders held on to each other with their wrinkled hands. Their long gray hair fluttered with the occasional gust of wind. The two women and two men exchanged looks wondering if life would go on normally, or if it would drastically change for the worse. Kamiakan was that special person who could see change in the world, and adjust accordingly, to make life better for everyone. For as long as they could remember he brought his wisdom to the council of elders and the village prospered. His wisdom came from insights gathered from a long, inquisitive life. The elders wondered if the death of Kamiakan marked the end of an era.

Kamiakan had outlived all his siblings. As he aged, he saw his children grown and pass away, and their children as well. The elders could remember the time when Kamiakan would tell them stories of the giant beasts and ice-covered mountains that had long ago disappeared. These four were his remaining great-great grandchildren.

CHAPTER 1

PULLMAN, WASHINGTON
CONTEMPORARY

The town of Pullman, Washington, is located on the far eastern edge of the state, about as far away from Seattle as you can get and still be in Washington. Pullman is geographically situated in a unique landscape of continuously rolling hills formed originally by giant dunes of sandy loam and is known as the Palouse. The dunes were created at the end of the last Ice Age when the glaciers retreated after they had ground up the bedrock into fine sediment. The westerly winds blew the sediment eastward onto the Palouse, creating giant rolling hills. The dunes are now stabilized and are cultivated with winter wheat and legumes. The Palouse region tops the world in the production of lentils and is called the "Lentil Capital of the World" by locals and visitors who attend the National Lentil Festival in Pullman each summer. Just seven miles away is the border with Idaho and another town, Moscow, Idaho. Both towns, relatively small and isolated, each have a population of about 35,000 people and home to large state universities, the University of Idaho in Moscow and Washington State University in Pullman.

Dr. Samantha Riley eased into a comfortable padded chair on the back deck of her modest house in Pullman. Her relatively small back yard was a jungle of Pacific Northwest trees: western red cedar, tamarack, red fir, and white pine. The sparse patches of lawn poking up in sun lit pools were uncut and overrun by seeding grasses. She had just completed a fifteen-day session teaching an undergraduate archaeological field school with three of her graduate assistants. She was a fourth-year assistant professor whose work had been at a series of archaeological sites throughout the Snake River canyon and up in the headwaters of the Snake, St. Joe, and Clearwater rivers for the Army Corps of Engineers and U.S. Forest Service. This year she had decided to collapse a six-week field season into two fifteen-day periods with a four-day break in the middle. During the four-day break, she and her graduate assistants planned to drop off some of their collected artifacts at the university and to resupply food and gear, before heading back out to the Idaho mountains east of the Palouse. They were excavating a site where camas roots had been gathered in bulk by Native people around 4,000 years ago. She and her team of students had just arrived in Pullman to begin the break, and Riley had just taken her first real shower in fifteen days. In her mind, portable sun shower bags didn't count as real showers.

Samantha Riley was five feet five with dark blue eyes and an athletic figure. She was an attractive woman but also had the appearance of being plain. Her shoulder length frizzy blonde hair was out of control, as it had been most of her life. It was now almost an Afro and she thought maybe she'd cut it before going back into the field.

Riley had grown up in a small agricultural town in North Dakota and had worked in her father's auto parts store during summers. She graduated at the top of her high school class and moved to the "big city" of Grand Forks, where she completed her undergraduate degree in anthropology at the University of North Dakota. After graduating, she worked as a "dig bum" going from one southwestern archaeological project to another, before starting her master's degree in forensic archaeology at Northern Arizona University. She liked the Flagstaff area and decided to work on her Ph.D. there. Unfortunately, they didn't have a Ph.D. program in archaeology, but Riley knew what she wanted to specialize in, and did her doctorate in biochemistry with a focus on isotope analysis. She wanted to use these skills to investigate human diet, disease, and lifeways in the archaeological past. After a protracted academic stint, the Archaeology Department at Washington State University offered her a real job with salary and benefits.

Samantha Riley loved her job and enjoyed the faculty and students at the university. However, like many remote campuses in rural areas, the position was often a dead end for single faculty members hoping to find companionship. Almost all the faculty at the two local universities arrived with partners. The few single people she had met during her tenure in Pullman were single for very good reason. Samantha's close friendships from Arizona had all gradually evaporated because of long distances, and she wasn't quite ready to enter the electronic world of online dating. Like most truly dedicated academics in the pre-tenure phase of a career, all her waking hours were filled with work-related duties: collecting research data, pulling together publications, preparing lectures, reviewing grant proposals, mentoring students, and negotiating the departmental minefield of egos and territoriality. Actively pursuing an amorous relationship demanded time and attention. Samantha had no spare time.

Riley's cell phone buzzed. It was lying face up on a wooden side table between two chairs on the deck. She glanced at the caller ID from her sitting position and noticed it was from the department. "Riley here," she answered.

Joe, the departmental secretary exclaimed, "Wow, I found you! A call came in for you from the Army Corps office. Jonathan Higgins is looking for you and left this number."

"Thanks, Joe. The crew just arrived in town today for our midsession break. I have Higgins' number and will give him a call."

Riley put the phone down and took a deep breath. She was exhausted and gave herself a few minutes of placid repose. She picked up her cell and pressed Jonathan Higgins' direct line.

Higgins answered immediately. He had been instrumental in getting permission for Riley to do most of her work on the Snake and Clearwater rivers and he was even able to provide some funding for excavations. Although much of her work was funded by tuition recovery for the field schools, and a small grant from the National Science Foundation to do isotope research, the Army Corps funding was helpful.

"Hi, Jonathan. What can I do for you?"

"Dr. Riley, I need your help. This morning, I got a call from the Whitman County Sheriff's office. It seems that a family was boating on the Snake River and stopped at a large sand dune for a picnic lunch. The parents reported that the kids were crawling through the dunes and found a dead person."

"Well, this sounds interesting," replied Samantha. "I'm not sure how I fit into this one, but I suspect you will enlighten me, eh," her North Dakotan dialect slipping through.

"The parents checked it out, and sure enough, there was a fragment of a human skull and scattered bones emerging from the dune. To make a long story short, the family called the sheriff. The sheriff called me. I called the Tribe, who told me to get the human remains out of the dune before boaters begin to dig around and cart off ancient family members. So, I'm calling you. We need to act quickly on this. Can I count on you, Dr. Riley?" pleaded Higgins.

"Well, you sort of caught me at a good time and a bad time," replied Riley. "I've just trained a group of field school students and I'm sure they can complete this work with my graduate assistants. Unfortunately, we have been busting our butts for the past fifteen days, and I've just given them four days off. I have no idea where they are. We're supposed to reassemble at my lab next Thursday morning."

Higgins' voice sounded desperate. "We need to get someone out there as soon as possible. Desecration of indigenous sites, particularly human remains is a particular problem in this region. There could be other boaters and collectors scouring the beach as we speak. Yesterday would not be too soon."

Jonathan Higgins was a trained archaeologist with a master's degree from one of the best universities in the U.S. However, he had never conducted fieldwork except for the required two-week field school as an undergraduate. He reflected on those two weeks as living hell; fighting off mosquitos, battling sweaty conditions, and rummaging in the dirt. He had happily found his niche working as a mid-level manager for the Army Corps for the past twenty years. He enjoyed, even loved doing bureaucratic work, pushing paper behind a desk in administration. Many agency archaeologists in Higgins' situation would have fielded a crew themselves and taken care of the eroding human remains. Jonathan had no desire.

"Okay, Jonathan," replied Riley. "No promises but let me make a few calls and I'll get back with you in a few hours. Do you have any Army Corps boats at our disposal, if needed?"

"Our boats are at your disposal, Dr. Riley. Just let me know when and where you need them," responded a relieved Higgins.

Riley hung up and called her most senior graduate student, Jennifer Henderson, who was also her project director for the field school. No answer, so she tried calling Jennifer's office number. Again, no answer. Riley called the two other graduate students working on the field school project, David DeRue and Katie Pollock. Neither answered. She then called her first-year graduate student, Claire Anderson. Claire was not working on this summer's field project and was doing tests in the isotope lab instead. Claire answered on the first ring,

"Hi, Dr. Riley. What's up?"

Riley could hardly hear Claire because of loud music and voices chattering in the background. "Claire, have you seen Jennifer or David around? We just got in from the field a couple of hours ago and something's come up and I need to talk to them."

"Well, sure, Dr. Riley. I'm looking at them right now. We are all down here at Rocky's having drinks."

"What do you mean, we're all down here?" asked Riley.

"It looks like the entire field school is down here," laughed Claire. "And from the looks of it, nobody even went home to change clothes. Everyone has dusty jeans and dirty bandanas on, some are wearing cowboy hats, and they all seem to be having a great time."

Oh great, thought Riley. "I hope they aren't driving university vehicles and parking them in front of the bar."

Rocky's was the local watering hole for faculty, students, and many locals. There was usually a lunch crowd, but things didn't get going there until after dinner. Mid-afternoon was normally quiet, and it seemed the archaeologists had taken over the bar.

"Claire, can you put Jennifer on? Her phone doesn't seem to be working."

Jennifer came on the line. "Hi, Dr. Riley. You found us. I was just getting ready to give you a call to let you know you should come down to Rocky's for a beer, but my cell phone's dead."

"Thanks, Jennifer. Listen, I've been asked to do an emergency excavation to help the Tribe and the Army Corps recover some human remains eroding out of a sand dune. I don't expect anyone to participate, given our schedule over the past fifteen days, including you and the other graduate assistants, but I'd like to take any volunteers who want to help excavate these remains. Can you talk with the students and let them know? I'll be mounting a two or three-day emergency volunteer excavation. If anyone wants to participate, they need to meet at Woods Hall at eight tomorrow morning. That should give us some rest before going out again. By the way, ask Claire if she can make it, too. Call me this evening and let me know how many and who's planning to go, okay?"

"Alright, Samantha. You know I'll be there, right? I'll give you a call later this evening," replied Jennifer. "Hey, you should come down for a beer."

"Thanks, Jen, that would be great, but I'd better begin getting gear together for a water transport excavation," replied Riley. "I'll talk with you later today."

Riley punched in Jonathan Higgins' telephone number and let him know they would have an excavation team ready to go in the morning. Riley asked Higgins for details.

"Where shall we meet the boats, Jonathan?"

"Great," replied Higgins. "You should meet the Army Corps personnel with boats at the Central Ferry boat ramp. Do you know where that is?"

"I certainly do. We can be there around 9:30 a.m. We'll need at least two boats. In the meantime, can you send me a letter or email attachment in lieu of a formal contract for these services? I'll need something to cover the students for insurance purposes. I assume you will want a preliminary report soon after we're done?"

"I'll get a PDF ready and send that along later today. We can use your standing contract to cover the permitting piece of this and consider this a separate workorder on the contract. The budget will follow your standard rates in the contract, right? And it certainly would be nice to have some kind of short report noting what was found as soon after you get out of the field, if possible," suggested Higgins.

"I can't promise anything fancy. I must get the team back out to Helmer to close out the field school. Most of the students will be flying back east right after the field school ends, so I have very little flexibility with schedules. But I can have a two pager with details along with an executive summary for you before I go back to Idaho. A more comprehensive final report will come later. I hope that will work. If that isn't enough, I'm not sure I can commit to this project," cautioned Riley.

Higgins couldn't hide his delight. "That is perfect, Dr. Riley. I owe you another favor for all you've been doing for us here in the district. Also, I'll call the Whitman County Sheriff. Maybe they can send someone out who knows the exact location of the remains."

"That would be helpful, Jonathan. We'll still conduct a comprehensive survey of the immediate area, map everything in, and do a quick excavation if we find any in situ remains," explained Riley. "We should have the fieldwork piece wrapped up in two or three days."

"Great. Call or text if you need anything. I'll alert the Nez Perce that you are on it," said Higgins, as he hung up.

CHAPTER 2

SOCHI, RUSSIA

The morning fog was swiftly vaporizing as the summer sun began climbing the eastern horizon over the Black Sea. The temperature was still cool, as cool as the inside of a cave, but within a few hours it would feel like the inside of an overheated sauna.

If Russian oligarchs were stratified in a hierarchy, Nicholai Utkin would be in the highest stratum. His story was like many others, but his success was greater than most. His march to power came soon after the collapse of the Soviet Union when commerce, industrial production, agriculture and food, science and technology all came to a virtual standstill. Nobody understood how to make the transition from government-owned and operated to private ownership and operation. The initial crisis came with food. Stores had no suppliers and food quickly ran out. The little food that existed was sold to the highest bidders and very few people had money because there was no infrastructure to keep businesses and industry moving forward. Workers and managers alike were not getting paid. The first minor breakthrough in the distribution of food was a growing black market. These new capitalist managers quickly recognized the chain of production, supply, and demand. Of course, most of the black market leaders were the original managers and bureaucrats who had worked in the government and the military and had been responsible for overseeing both large-scale and small-scale production and distribution.

Before the 1991 Soviet collapse, Nicholai Utkin was a mid-level bureaucrat responsible for administering several small drug manufacturing and processing plants on the outskirts of St. Petersburg. The processing plants that he was responsible for also occasionally produced and packaged opioid medication when the central government needed to increase supplies. When the top-ranking military and government officials began to bring order to the broken industrial sector, they relied greatly upon people like Utkin to retain personnel, make sure production was back online, and allow no interruption in the distribution of goods. Utkin understood that the transition to capitalist enterprise was not "business as usual." He realized that his position as manager of several small production plants could be leveraged if he did not permit outsiders to control his profit margin and if he could expand his operations quickly.

Utkin's mercurial success began by building an armed security team that allowed him to control operations and people within his plants. It was an easily defensible and perfectly acceptable position, given the anarchy throughout the country. With his security force and salary skimming from his workers, he was able to gradually divest regional competitors of their production and distribution facilities. He soon began the production of opioids exclusively in one small plant, and then used his growing distribution network to move the product into the Russian underground. His opioid production and distribution quickly financed his takeover of the major pharmaceutical manufacturers and developers across Russia. When he encountered roadblocks, whether government officials or competitors, he had ways to eliminate such problems. Within a decade of the Soviet Union collapse, Nicholai Utkin was one of the wealthiest men in Russia. He included Vladimir Putin among his friends.

Utkin strolled slowly but deliberately across his estate grounds in what was formerly Alder, Russia. Alder was part of a relentless creeping expansion of the city of Sochi, whose most recent growth came just prior to and after the 2014 Winter Olympics. He paused and looked out across the water with a searching expression. To his right and slightly behind him was a man wearing a dark leather jacket followed by three Irish wolfhounds. The giant gray-haired dogs nipped at each other as they loped along, but every now and then they would stop and stare off into the distance with their ears perked and nostrils twitching. Sometimes the dogs would glance ahead and other times they would all turn in unison, making sure nothing was entering their domain from the rear.

Utkin's question was direct. "Are you absolutely positive the report from St. Petersburg University is accurate, Comrade?"

"There is no mistake. I had a detailed conversation with our contacts at the university myself. Both samples produced the same results. There were minor age differences, but both archaeological specimens were well over a hundred years old when they died," replied Boris Mirsky.

Nicholai Utkin had hired and trained Boris Mirsky over a decade before when Utkin needed more "experienced muscle" to help expand his underground opioid market into Europe and the United States. At that time, Mirsky was skinny, twenty-five and the leader of a gang of hooligans in Minsk, Belarus. Utkin had heard the story of an orphaned boy who grew up on the streets of Minsk and had created a small criminal empire there. Mirsky was streetwise and could speak four Slovak languages when Utkin first met him. He needed such a person to reinforce the most lucrative part of his empire. Nicholai trained Mirsky to operate in the larger public sphere, air travel, civil manners, fine dining, and he even learned to speak and write English with some amount of sophistication. Mirsky was inquisitive, resourceful, and bright. But more than anything else, he could read and manipulate people. Over the years, he became Utkin's trusted servant. When all else failed, Utkin could depend upon Mirsky to conclude what needed doing.

Utkin's pharmaceutical network had tentacles that reached into every research university and private sector corporation to scan documents, reports, and rumors related to staying healthy and young. Within his empire, he quietly began a secret Centenarian Project. The Centenarian Project initially involved taking blood samples and analyzing them from volunteers over a hundred years old. The project objective was to better understand how some people lived to be of such a great age. The blood sample analyses revealed very little, and the study progressed to the examination of human body parts from centenarians who had passed away. To obtain these human organs, Utkin's team resorted to grave robbing. With no promising results from this effort, Utkin gradually shifted the focus of his tests and experiments. His latest investigations used living people who met his sample needs. The Centenarian Project had progressed beyond seeking volunteers and robbing graves. Utkin kidnapped and imprisoned whomever he needed. After reading the St. Petersburg reports, a welcome surprise, he quickly had Boris Mirsky move his team to Vladivostok to secure the samples.

"All of the specimens are housed at the university in Vladivostok. I have already contacted the people that we need to get access to the specimens," said Mirsky. "Soon they will be at our facility for more detailed study. It was not easy, but I have persuaded one of the archaeology faculty there, Dimitri Kozlov, to work with us. He controls access to the specimens and will join our existing team of scientists."

"Excellent," replied Utkin. "I'll have the financial division begin modification and expansion of our chemical plant in Vladivostok to accommodate a state-of-the-art research laboratory. We'll use this new facility to house our Centenarian Project. Make sure we have access to everything we need."

Nicholai Utkin was of average height and build with pale green eyes. He was always clean shaven with never a hint of stubble on his chin or lip. He had a full head of dark hair, and walked erect, often with his hands clasped behind his back. His face was smooth skinned, without a wrinkle. He didn't look a day over fifty, but he would turn seventy-four that year. Utkin was a health fanatic and used every potion, lotion, and drug to look and feel younger than he was.

The Centenarian Project had become an obsession for Nicholai Utkin. Of course, there was the potential to make a great deal of money, but more importantly, the project had the potential for discovering a path for prolonged life, his life.

Utkin would stop at nothing to get what he wanted. With his pharmaceutical research and development labs and production facilities, he felt he was the one person who could discover the secret to a longer life. Until now, all leads and ideas of his team on the Centenarian Project had turned up nothing but disappointment. The trail had left no easily recognizable directions to follow or investigate. But now there were samples that might help crack the secret. Finally, there was something.

Utkin's estate in Sochi was spacious and comfortable but he spent little time there. Traveling between his various holdings, he spent most of his off-work hours aboard his luxury yacht, *Krasivaya Ptitsa.* His captain and crew kept the *Krasivaya Ptitsa* circulating between the Mediterranean, Aegean, and Black seas. He would fly to it at every opportunity.

"Boris, I am counting on you to follow every lead that develops. The power and resources of my empire are behind you. Do not fail me, comrade. We are on the verge of something extraordinary. Report back to me frequently."

CHAPTER 3

PULLMAN, WASHINGTON

Jennifer Henderson was leaning on the front fender of the university pickup truck behind Woods Hall checking her watch, yet again. She pushed off the fender and paced a short circle around the lot wondering where DeRue and Pollock could be. It was getting late and neither had arrived at the stipulated time. She was just getting ready to settle back into her leaning position on the fender but heard voices coming from around the building. Jennifer craned toward the sound, then sagged back toward the truck. They were the voices of a groups of students on an early morning jog, not David or Katie. She slid her cell phone from her back pocket and checked for messages before sending a less than polite text and was interrupted by a shout.

"Hey, Jen, we brought you coffee." The voice of David DeRue called out.

"Where have you guys been? I've been hanging around here almost half an hour."

"Sorry, Jen," said Katie. "I overslept and Dave woke me up pounding on my door. Guess I should have left Rocky's earlier."

"We stopped at the coffee shop on the way over and brought you a tall one," said David. "Just the way you like them."

Jennifer took the cup. "Thanks. How should we get started here?"

"How many students volunteered?" asked David.

"All of them," said Jennifer. "Claire too. I assume this is going to be a commuter project. We'll leave from here and return every day, so there is no need for camp and cook gear."

"That will make the load lighter, but we'll lose hours with the drive time," replied David. "I gassed up the pickup trucks yesterday but didn't get to the vans. We can back the trucks into the loading docks and inventory the gear. Dr. Riley tagged the field equipment we'll be taking. It looks like survey, mapping and excavation gear."

"I thought she said this was going to be a two or three-day effort?" questioned Jen.

"I think it's a small area so the survey and mapping should only take a day at the most. We may not even need the excavation gear if the remains are a simple surface scatter," said David. "The students should be drifting in soon."

"How about this," began Jen. "I'll organize the packing with the students. I think Samantha is briefing Claire on excavation procedures and they won't be here until the last minute. Why don't you and Katie drive the vans to the motor pool and get them fueled while I get the trucks packed."

"Good plan," replied David.

Jennifer paused, looking at her colleagues. They were all good friends, but she and Katie had particularly bonded, and had a droll-humored relationship.

"And Katie, you look like crap. Why don't you go and get washed up a bit before showing up at the motor pool."

Katie smiled and gave Jen the middle finger. "Jen Hen strikes again," said Katie.

When David and Katie returned with fully fueled vans, the small lot behind Woods Hall was cluttered with backpacks, duffle bags, and students. Nobody was dawdling or milling around. The area was teaming with controlled activity. Jennifer Henderson was orchestrating the vehicle packing and making sure all students had their personal gear in good order. The two loading dock rolltop doors were open and the university pickup trucks were backed to each loading ramp.

"You guys know the drill, right? Put all the heavy equipment in first, excavation foot lockers, shaker screens, coolers. Then all the mapping equipment and boxes of paperwork." It was second nature for Jennifer to get a project "out-the-door" on field day. She had done it so many times working in the private sector before beginning graduate school. She thought about other last-minute things a new field school student may not automatically realize. "Don't use your field school notebooks. This is a separate project. Everything gets curated differently, including your notes. Use the new notebooks for this job. This is not the field school project."

It took about forty-five minutes for the team to transfer all the gear Riley had marked on the loading docks. Samantha Riley and Claire Anderson came down from the lab upstairs just as the team was loading the last transit and tripod. They were each carrying a duffle bag with sterile hazmat suits, latex gloves, face masks, and various kinds of sterile packaging containers. They deposited their bags into the vans and Riley looked over to Jennifer. "Are we ready?"

Jennifer gave a thumbs-up as the team gathered around. She asked, "How do you want to divide up? We've got two vans and two pickup trucks."

"Why don't you and David each drive one of the pickups. Two people max for each truck. Katie and I will each drive a van. Claire stays with me so I can continue briefing her on excavation protocol during the drive." Riley surveyed the faces listening to her. "Everyone else find a seat with a belt, let's roll." There was an immediate call for "shotgun" and a scramble for the vehicles.

The drive to the river took less than two hours including a short coffee break at a convenience store halfway to Central Ferry.

CHAPTER 4

CENTRAL FERRY, WASHINGTON

The caravan of gray university vehicles turned into the gravel driveway at Central Ferry throwing up a dust cloud as they sinuously crept to the launch area. They were met at the boat ramp by the county sheriff and two Army Corps River Rangers who would oversee piloting the eighteen-foot skiffs for Riley and her team. As Riley stepped from the van, she could hear Deputy Kowalski briefing the river rangers on the location of the human remains. Kowalski, talking loudly, assumed an air of authority, gesticulating and pointing as he talked. As Riley walked up, he turned his attention to her.

"Well, hello, little lady. You must be from the university. Go-Cougs!" He pointed across the wide span of the Snake River toward an enormous set of sandy terraces on the other side. "It's hard to tell from here but that hillside has a big ole bench on it down by the water. That's where the boaters found the remains."

Riley extended her hand to Kowalski. "Samantha Riley, but you can call me Dr. Riley. But you cannot call me little lady, eh." She introduced herself to the river rangers who identified themselves as Ashley and Jake. Both were smiling at her exchange with Kowalski.

Riley looked back at Kowalski. "Deputy Kowalski, were you the officer on-scene when the boaters reported the human remains?"

"Well, yes I was, Miss, uh, Dr. Riley."

"Was there a body eroding out of the dune or are we dealing with a scatter of disarticulated bone fragments?" asked Riley.

Deputy Kowalski paused, "I have a topographic map here with the location of the remains marked." He handed Riley the map. "I can't stay, but I've put my contact number on the map. Give me a call if you need help finding the remains and I can guide you to them if need be."

Riley scanned the map and looked at the Deputy. "I think we should be able to find them. You seem to have the location marked precisely here. Were you over there?"

The Deputy looked at Riley and measured his response. "The boaters brought a few of the bones over. I recognized them as human and had them take the bones back to the dune before I called the Army Corps."

"So, you saw the boaters put the bones back on the dune at this location?" said Riley, pointing at the map.

"That's the location. It's on the other side of the river in Garfield County. My jurisdiction is Whitman County."

Riley nodded her head. "I'll call you if we need your help."

Kowalski was walking toward his marked SUV. "Sounds like a plan," he shouted over his shoulder before climbing in and driving off.

Riley turned from the retreating vehicle and looked across to the other side, studying the terrain. The sandy hillside was almost a mile long and sloped from the water's edge straight back up the canyon wall for about a quarter of a mile. The entire dune area was formed between two rocky ridges that zig zagged down like fences all the way to the water. The ridges originated from a layer of basalt caprock almost another half mile further up the canyon. There was a break in the basalt caprock located directly above the dune area. This created a notch that the wind would find and follow over the caprock and down between the two ridges. The notch and ridges provided a natural chute for the wind and whatever it was carrying.

For the most part, the prevailing westerly winds carried loess and fine sand particles from as far away as the center of the Columbia Basin, almost two hundred miles to the west at the base of the Cascade Mountains. From where Riley was standing, the dune feature looked out of place. The entire basalt canyon wall was dark colored and covered with jagged rocky ledges and ridges. Then, emerging from the black canyon was an isolated hillside of cream-colored sand and windblown sediment that appeared to be cascading down and tumbling from the dark canyon barrier to the river's edge. This was clearly a special place in the otherwise rugged rocky canyon.

The operation began almost immediately after the departure of Deputy Kowalski. Riley introduced the river rangers to her four graduate students and briefed them all on the various team duties each graduate student would guide.

The two river rangers ferried the crew and gear to the far side of the river multiple times. Each one-way trip across took approximately fifteen to thirty minutes, depending upon the number of people and gear. Ashley and Jake were professional boat operators and made sure everyone wore appropriate PFDs and secured the equipment so it would not shift during the passage across.

Riley assigned a survey crew of six students to David DeRue to go over in the first run to begin the survey immediately. As usual, she briefed her graduate student before sending him off. "Be sure to put in a datum marker as high up as possible before you begin the survey. It will make things easier when the mapping team gets there. We'll need good provenience on everything eroding from the dune."

"Should I establish true north-to-south transects or should we follow the shoreline contours?" asked David.

Riley thought for just a second while glancing at the terrain. "Set them true north-south. We don't know how extensive the site will be or how far it might extend from the existing shoreline. Everyone should have a calibrated compass."

David organized his survey team along the edge of the water with five meters spacing and had everyone take compass bearings for true north. They each marked their starting and ending positions with yellow pin flags and followed their compass heading until they hit the canyon wall. The survey team then shifted westward, and each walked a transect directly south until hitting the edge of the river. DeRue had the survey team set color-coded pin flags at every artifact and bone found as they systematically swept over the steep dune area. In addition to scattered bone fragments and isolated artifacts, David's team quickly found an exposure that contained what appeared to be an eroded human skull with intact skeletal vertebrae. Thirty minutes into the survey, the eastern margin of the dune was speckled with variously color-coded pin flags.

Jennifer, Katie, Claire and Samantha were transported over with mapping equipment. David DeRue met them when they hit the shore. "What do you have for us?" asked Riley.

"So far, we are getting eroded fragments of bone and stone tools scattered across the lower edge of the dune," replied David. "All bone is pin flagged in blue. Artifacts are flagged red. There is a small pile of bones that appear human piled on the beach to the west. I believe those must have been the specimens collected and returned by the boaters."

"Anything else, so far?" asked Jennifer.

"So far, we have one possible in situ specimen on the far eastern edge of the dune about halfway up. Looks like a human skull just starting to get exposed by erosion. In addition to the blue flag, it's marked with white pin flags," informed David.

"Okay, Jennifer and Katie, get your team set up to begin mapping and collecting. Claire and I will examine the in situ specimen," said Riley. "If David's assessment is right, that's where we'll begin excavations."

Jennifer and Katie worked with two other students and began setting up the laser guided total mapping station over a datum point that David had marked with his survey team. They tied it into a USGS survey point about half a mile upstream. The students held the prism-topped mapping rods while Katie and Jennifer instructed them on what features to mark so the position could be quickly shot with the total station. The mapping team's job was to record the location of artifacts and scattered human bones that DeRue's team had marked with pin flags. After each pinned location was recorded, the person with the mapping rod collected the item, bagged it, and gave it an inventory number. Katie recorded the number in the data collector within the total station next to each shot taken.

Riley and Claire's crew and excavation equipment took two trips to make it over. Their team of students laid out excavation units over the area where David's survey team had found the in situ skull. The remains were definitively human, but until it was excavated a bit, they would not know if it was an isolated human skull with vertebrae or a complete skeleton, and perhaps a burial, exposed by erosion. Riley wanted Claire to stay with the excavation crews because she had taken her undergraduate degree in human anatomy, and she was specializing in human osteology. Claire would help with the identification of anatomical parts as they were uncovered. Riley and Claire instructed their team to fence off the excavation area with yellow caution tape. All the students working directly in the excavation zone were required to wear white hazmat suits, taped-over surgical gloves, and face masks. Those on survey and mapping would do the same if they came into the fenced-off area. It was hot work but there were enough students on the team to take breaks and cool down.

The survey, mapping, and excavation teams were in sync. Riley and her graduate assistants had trained them well. They worked with confidence and pride, knowing that their efforts were called upon in an emergency and that the Army Corps and Tribe were depending upon them to help preserve the eroded remains. The river rangers stayed with the boats and watched, mesmerized by the efficiency of the team. After a few hours, Riley checked her watch and noted that the team was well ahead of schedule.

The archaeologists had a late start to their day but had an early lunch break shortly after arriving on site. By 4:00 p.m.

they were still working hard. All the isolated bones and artifacts that had eroded out of the dune were mapped and recovered, but the excavation team in the fenced area was still meticulously troweling and brushing away debris to expose the partially covered human remains.

As the overburden was gradually removed in successive degrees, more of the remains were exposed and the excavators' excitement increased. First, the long bones of the legs materialized. These were folded or bent at the knees and the knees were tucked into the chest. It was a textbook example of a flexed burial. The skull was ever so gently exposed and proved totally intact and articulated to the spine with the face looking east toward the rising sun. With each scrape of the trowel something new appeared and was photographed.

One of the students yelled through her facemask. "There's something solid here! The person is holding something in each hand! Someone look. Look at what I've found here!"

The students who had finished the survey on DeRue's team ran up to the caution tape and peered over.

Riley came over. "Don't try to pick them up. Leave them in place and begin brushing outward to expose the shape of the items."

"Look, there's more!" exclaimed the students. They look like huge flint tools. Look at all of them!"

"These over here, are all painted red!" said another student as he slowly exposed more tools.

Everyone crowded around the taped-off burial area, including the two river rangers, who couldn't resist and hiked up the slope from the water's edge and stood with the students watching the burial being systematically uncovered.

"No," said Riley. "They are not painted. Those are covered with red ochre. We often find this at ancient burials. Ochre was spread over the body and any burial offerings. It is one of the great mysteries from all over the ancient world," explained Riley. "Nobody knows why red ochre was used, but it was often found in human burials from Asia to Africa and South America to Europe. Claire, be sure to get some samples of the ochre. It is usually diagnostic of specific geographic locations."

Another student working near the feet of the burial suddenly exclaimed, "What's all this stuff? This black stuff is all clumped together and slick like grease. It's all around and under the skeleton!"

Riley dabbed some of the material with her gloved finger and rubbed it with her thumb. "It's organic. It's an offering or maybe clothing. Claire, be sure to get a good sample of this and take multiple samples if the color or texture changes. There may be multiple items here."

Some of the students began talking loudly with each new find. They sensed the excitement in the air. Were they on the verge of uncovering a human that might make history? Maybe from the Pleistocene?

Jennifer glanced from her mapping duties looking at the students crowding the excavation area. She turned over the total station mapping to Katie to finish any individual shots that needed mapping and walked over to where Riley and DeRue stood outside the taped-off zone. Jennifer was the most experienced of Riley's doctoral students, having worked in the private sector for three years before coming back to school and finishing her master's degree with Riley and now working on her doctorate. She was a tall woman with wavy dark hair and a perpetual smile. Her good looks, field experience, and sharp wit easily made her a leader.

"Hey, you two," she called out as she walked up the dune trail toward the burial excavation. She stopped and surveyed the excavation team. "Wow, you forensic types go all out with the sterile equipment. I've never seen an excavation team in full hazmat gear."

Riley knew of too many cases where archaeologists had to spend extra years to gather new samples that were not contaminated by DNA from the excavators. "We just need to be cautious with intact human remains," replied Riley. "Especially this one."

"What's so special about this one?"

"I'm not absolutely sure yet, but I have a few preliminary observations." Riley began her quick field assessment as some of the other students and river rangers listened in. "You see that relatively hard band of sediment along this terrace of the dune? That band at one time extended out past where we are currently standing. This person was buried underneath that hard sedimentary structure. It was almost like a rock overhang when he, or she, was laid down. That hard layer protected this individual from decay and massive decomposition. Over the past several thousand years that band has become more and more exposed to the elements. Recently, in the last couple of decades, as our climate has been drastically changing, it became so permeated with snowmelt and water that it collapsed, leaving our friend here with no more protection from the elements."

Riley continued, pointing toward the burial area. "See the volcanic ash in the wall profile of the excavation unit? I think that's Mount St. Helens ash. That volcanic ash created a seal and made this a very well-preserved burial from the end of the last Ice Age. We know very little about the biological heritage of the oldest people living on this continent, so this one is special. We need to make absolutely sure this one is not contaminated by our DNA."

Jennifer peered over at the exposed burial. "What's the plan? Looks to me like we have another two or three hours before we'll have this unit completed. Unless it gets complicated and then it could take longer."

David added, "We'll still have to get the gear to the boats, ferry across and pack the vehicles. All before the drive home."

Riley considered the comments. "With all the volunteers, we've made great time. I'd hate to have to tarp the site overnight, drive back to Pullman, then drive back here again in the morning just to do an hour or so of final excavation. Let's put in an extra-long overtime day and get this wrapped up before dark. We're just about at the point where we can do a plan view map and photos and then pull the skeleton. I'd like to keep the skeleton as fully articulated as possible and even keep the underlying sediments with the bone material, just in case we have some decomposed organics preserved under the skeleton."

Jennifer Henderson agreed. "We can slide some of that heavy duty aluminum foil under the remains and pull the entire skeleton. Maybe we should cover the location with plastic after pulling the burial, in case we need to return and grab some additional sediment samples for a particle size analysis."

Riley nodded in agreement. "We should make a few changes. Let's double the screeners, have two people writing bag labels only. Jennifer, put on some hazmat gear. You and

I will help with the troweling and take notes. You'll enjoy this because there are a bunch of huge bipointed stone tools buried with this fellow that you can't see from here," Riley added.

Stone tool analysis was Jennifer's specialty, and she quickly looked back at the burial hoping to see one of the tools. "Hey, are those big dark things the stone tools? Can't tell for sure, but those are the largest bipoints I've ever seen. They sort of remind me of those Sluiceway bifaces from Alaska. How many have you guys found?"

"You'll have plenty of time to fuss over them. Let's just get them out of the ground, eh?" responded Riley. "We can have Claire do the photos. David, why don't you talk with the river rangers and see if they are willing to stick this out for a few more hours. You and Katie can work with the rangers and transport half the crew, the artifact boxes, and any equipment we don't need to the other side and begin packing the vehicles."

The original plan was to commute each day from Pullman to Central Ferry until the job was completed. They had not planned to keep a crew in the field through dinner. But now they were ahead of schedule and would possibly work until dark. Riley considered the situation.

"David, there's that little general store and café at the campground on Deadman Creek Road about twenty minutes from here. Why don't you take someone with you when you get across and buy whatever food they might have available. Cobble together a dinner for twenty. If we get out of here late, I'd like to get everyone fed before we hit the road." Riley handed David the university credit card. She paused, then handed him a couple of twenties. "Might as well pick up some beer to wash down dinner for those of legal age."

DeRue took the card and cash. He had been Riley's logistical go-to person in the field for the past two summers. David was one of those people who always found a way to "MacGyver" a project, no matter how big or small. With minimal instruction, he made sure the final project was accomplished, even when no plan existed. Samantha Riley knew that David would find something to make the entire crew feel they were well served.

"I think the rangers are in, even if it takes all night. They've been yakking it up all day in this nice weather. Those two live for water work like this, and they seem pleased to not be at the shop in Walla Walla. I'll go over and have a chat with them, just to make sure they don't mind staying," replied David.

It was close to nine at night when the last of the gear was packed into the vans and trucks. The river rangers had just pulled out with their boats in tow after sharing a hodgepodge dinner with the team. In David's patched-together meal there was something for everyone. They all seemed in good spirits on the drive back and the time went fast as they talked about what they accomplished and what they imagined the results of an exciting day's dig might be. They also had two days left of their original four-day break before heading back to the field to close the season.

CHAPTER 5

PULLMAN, WASHINGTON

The lab reflected a sense of organization and purpose, but also a lot of light. It doubled as both an osteological/forensic lab and an isotopic lab, complete with layout tables, fume hoods, chemical cabinets, microscopy stations, data monitors, and sample processing machinery. In the center of the room were three active worktables with the human remains collected from the field carefully arranged by anatomical parts.

There was evidence of three individuals. Two were represented by disarticulated broken and decayed bone fragments that had eroded from the sand dune. As of yet, these were of an undetermined age and may have been from a later interment that had been exposed for years. The third individual was a completely intact human skeleton. It had only been partially exposed by erosion but would probably have eroded out over the next winter and following spring runoff. Samantha Riley gingerly held a mandible under the flood of florescent light, peering through a ten-power self-supporting magnifier. Her attention passed carefully from one molar to the next, examining the wear patterns. Riley laid the mandible down and studied the cranium without lifting it. She rolled it first to observe the facial front and then the cranial top to examine the fused sutures and fractured bone. She planned to spend a few days in the lab conducting the initial analysis on the intact skeleton. Jennifer would oversee getting the students back out to the field school site in North Idaho. The team had left for the field earlier that morning. Riley would follow, after the initial lab work was completed. Claire was already prepped and would be working in the lab with her.

Claire had minimal field experience. She came straight from her undergraduate program to start graduate education with an interest in archaeological forensics. Riley normally preferred graduate students with more field and lab experience, however, Claire's letters of recommendation were unusually glowing. Her application package portended a potential superstar with grades and GRE scores off the chart. These were not necessarily the criteria Riley relied on as the most important for admission. Riley had invited her for an interview and after talking with her for twenty minutes, decided to recommend her for acceptance into the program with full funding. Claire's personality, archaeological insight, and communication skills won Riley over.

"Claire, call up Pullman Regional Hospital and see if we can get an MRI on some long bones scheduled for today or early tomorrow."

Riley had a standing contract with the hospital for MRI work, so it wouldn't be too bizarre a request. Claire asked, "They'll want to know what for?"

"Tell them we'll need a dozen very high-resolution MRI thin sections from each of two femurs. They should be in sequence about two millimeters apart. The femurs must be rotated to show the osteon structure of the bone. It would be great to get them in today so we can do the counting tonight or in the morning."

Riley assumed there would be a DNA study conducted on the remains at some point, but that would probably be for a later time after consultation with Native communities. Like any good forensic archaeologist, Riley had already made sure the recovered human remains were not contaminated by the excavators. She also had to assure that the laboratory and hospital personnel handling the bones used adequate protection. She was quite sure that the one intact burial with the complete skeleton dated to the end of the Pleistocene by the context of its location in stratified layers of sediment. It was found below a volcanic layer that she recognized as "Mount St. Helens J." It was an eruption from the same vent as the 1980 eruption that covered most of Washington State and southern British Columbia. The earlier ash eruption occurred 11,200 years ago, so the burial was at least that old and probably older. She wouldn't know for sure until she submitted an Accelerator Mass Spectrometry (AMS) radiocarbon sample for dating. Riley planned to have Claire begin some trace element analysis on the volcanic ash sample, using a portable x-ray florescence gun to make sure it was from the St. Helen's vent.

Riley sat at the largest table to examine the intact skeleton and positioned lights for better observation. She had her extraction kit opened, along with a carton of sterile sample tubes and sealable bags, and indelible ink pens for labeling. Riley determined the intact skeleton to be male, but there were some odd characteristics about it that she had noticed as it was being removed from the field. Several bones appeared to have been broken but then healed. She now could confirm these to include a tibia, two ribs, and several finger bones. There was no pattern to the breakage, so each break and subsequent healing probably occurred at different times. She did notice a head trauma that showed some skull fracturing that was not healed and could represent the cause of death. Either he lived a long life, and the injuries were just an accumulation of accidents over a lifetime, or he was a very clumsy person. She suspected the long life because the man's teeth were heavily worn down. Teeth do not replace or repair themselves so that older individuals usually have more worn molars than younger people. This man had very worn molars. Interestingly, he was not missing any incisors. Usually older individuals, particularly individuals that lived in prehistoric times, lost a tooth or two or many because of accidents and dental disease. The skull showed no evidence of dental disease, at least from initial observation. His other bones showed no signs of osteological degeneration, such as arthritis or osteoporosis, also often found with older individuals. Here was a very healthy, very old man, who lived at the end of the last Ice Age. Riley couldn't wait to begin some more detailed analyses.

Because of Riley's ongoing field school project in North Idaho, she wanted to run some tests immediately and submit some samples and then get back to the field to close out the project. The age at time of death was her first concern because the macroscopic evidence was showing some interesting contradictions. She would apply an old technique, Osteon Lamellae Analysis (OLA), developed by one of her undergraduate professors. However, as originally developed, it was a destructive type of analysis requiring human long bones to be sliced and thin sectioned onto glass slides. The thin sections would then be microscopically assessed for relative amounts of various structures that change at known rates during the life of an individual. The change in these structures ceases at the time of death and can provide an estimated age at the time of death. The primary concern Riley had in this case was that she did not wish to perform a destructive analysis, respecting the heritage values of contemporary Native peoples. Because of these concerns, she had developed a modification to the OLA technique by "taking" thin sections from long bones using very high-resolution MRI imaging. It was important that the MRI images be taken at extreme resolution to view them under magnification to make accurate counts of various osteon structures. Another advantage of using the MRI was that many samples could be taken to calculate the average proportion of lamellae structures, thus eliminating the possibility of a sampling bias.

The AMS radiocarbon dating was a more difficult thing to conduct. It is a destructive technique. She decided to request permission to run a human bone sample. In the meantime, Riley decided to submit an AMS sample for dating of the carbon found directly below and above the skeleton. She suspected they were remains of clothing or some organic offering, such as plants, flowers, or some other materials that were placed at the time of burial and created a thin layer of greasy carbon material above and below the human remains.

Riley used a sterilized set of forceps and removed two carbon samples from below the skeleton and put each into its own small glass vile. She then used another sterilized set and removed two carbon samples from above the skeleton. She decided to send the four samples overnight to a private radiocarbon lab in Miami. She had Claire complete the paperwork for AMS dating and pay the expedited processing fee.

Samantha elected not to use the National Science Foundation lab at the University of Arizona because sometimes they just took too long to return a date, even though they were a fraction of the cost. Riley examined the carbon film below the human bone again and decided to pull two additional samples and marked them to be sent to the evolutionary ecology lab at UC Davis.

"Claire, I have the AMS samples. Can you grab them and get them into the shipping package and have Joe call for pick up as soon as possible? There are two samples marked for Davis, too. Send those to the DNA lab there. I think those sediment samples might help identify what kind of organic material was under the burial."

Claire collected the samples Samantha had deposited into the labeled vials. "Done," she said, as she walked out of the room.

"Thanks, Claire," Riley called as she continued studying the skeleton. The cranial fracture did not occur post-mortem, and it showed no evidence of healing. It appeared to be blunt force trauma over a broad surface, so it probably was not a club or some other kind of weapon that caused the injury. It looked more like an injury that might be caused by a fall or some other kind of accident.

Claire returned and announced, "Looks like we're going to have a long night, Dr. Riley." Samantha raised eyebrows above her facemask. "Hospital just called and can take the skeleton today at noon."

Riley nodded, "MRIs will be quick. We'll be done before 5:00 tonight with the counting and we'll know exactly how old this guy was when he bumped his head for the last time. Let's begin wrapping this guy up for transport to the hospital. I'll drive him over and wait for the MRIs."

"I'll go with you," replied Claire. "We can review the schedule for various analytical procedures while we wait."

As predicted, the MRI was fast, and they were able to take the skeleton back to the lab by two in the afternoon. Riley asked Claire to put the skeleton next to the other two boxes with bone fragments in the climate-controlled storage room, known as the "vault." "Here's the key to the vault," said Claire and handed Riley the key when she was finished.

Riley clipped the key to her key chain and looked directly at Claire. "I'll be heading out into the field in a day or so. Nobody is to have access to these remains if I am not here," said Riley. Claire nodded her understanding.

They split up the MRI imaged thin sections, and each had a thin section up on their laptops and were soon recording counts and locations of bone structures. They tallied them on coding sheets on a desktop computer as they went along. Minutes transitioned into hours as their counting continued. Both Claire and Samantha recognized how important the work was, but both felt the weight of the monotonous process. The counting required absolute concentration so that structures were not overlooked or counted twice. Within a few hours all the thin sections had finally been viewed, counted, and entered. Riley had written a short equation just for this technique and now downloaded the tabulated data into the program. The computer instantly computed and listed the individual's age at the time of death, along with standard error and confidence interval.

Neither smiled. "I thought we were ahead of schedule," noted Riley. "Looks like you were right, and we are in for a long night."

They each began looking through the analytical sheets to see which of the thin sections were entered wrong. There appeared to be no outliers for either femur.

"We should have known that outliers weren't the problem. The standard error is too small. This is a narrow range for all the thin sections. We are going to have to recount," said Riley.

They both looked at each other and then back at the desktop analysis. The age at time of death for the Pleistocene man was one hundred and thirty-eight years old.

Before recounting, they ran the analysis again and then they ran the analysis by individual input just in case either were recording measurements significantly different from each other. With no change in computed age at the time of death, they began the tedious process of recounting the osteon lamellae structures on each MRI slide. This time, however, they traded slides. After several more hours, they were ready to download the tabulated counts into the program again. With a keystroke, the computation was complete. The age at time of death was again one hundred and thirty-eight.

Claire was tired and wondered what Riley had planned for them next. "Wow, what could be wrong with the data?" she questioned sadly.

Samantha Riley looked at her and said, "I'm not sure, but maybe nothing."

"What do you mean, Dr. Riley? There must be something wrong with the data--or maybe the technique? Yeah, this method of analysis was originally developed and confirmed on specimens with an upper age of eighty years old. It was never evaluated for people that were much over a hundred because people don't live that long. So, that's probably what's going on here."

"That could be true, Claire," replied Riley. "However, the technique uses an algorithm that extrapolates the relative proportion of bone structures all the way out to a count of zero. If there are recognizable structures in the bone section, we probably have an accurate estimate of age at the time of death, and all our bone sections have concentric lamellae structures present."

"So, what could be causing the age estimate problem?" continued Claire.

"We'll have to reconfirm everything to determine that," said Riley. "On the other hand, we may not have a data or computational problem. Instead, we may have a unique hundred thirty-eight-year-old who lived at the end of the Ice Age."

Claire looked confused and said, "But that would be, that would be...." She paused, and slowly cracking a huge smile, continued, "that would be one of the most amazing discoveries ever made in archaeology."

The two women, mentor and mentee looked at each other as they digested the ramifications of their discovery. Simultaneously, they stood and gave each other high fives and loud whoops. "You should get some rest, Claire. I'll draft a three-page summary report for the Army Corps and get your feedback on it in the morning. This is unbelievable but we should let them know, with the full understanding that this is preliminary. We will begin renewed age testing immediately. After you have a look at my report and before we send it to the

Corps, I'll circulate it to the archaeology faculty for any comments and suggestions. I don't expect much, since no one else on the faculty works in forensics, but it is important for me to make sure everyone has been briefed on this before we send this out. It could create some negative press very quickly. Anything abnormal in this field of study is generally thought of as heresy. I can leave your name off the report, if you wish?"

"No way, Dr. Riley. I'm sticking with you on this one."

"Okay. Let's meet back here at eight tomorrow morning and discuss it all again."

By the next morning, Samantha had a finished report ready for Claire to review. Claire went through the three- page document and suggested no changes except a few typos, attached it, and sent it back. Riley spent the rest of the morning double checking the report and added additional context. She emailed it to the archaeology faculty in the department under a confidential heading. She was sure to let everyone know that comments were expected by the end of the day because she needed to get it finished and head back to the field.

By the end of the day, only one person had submitted any comments, Dr. Maddington. Professor Peter Maddington was one of the old-timers in the department. He was a senior faculty member and enjoyed reminding everyone of his long and self-proclaimed illustrious career. His comment congratulated her on making sure she had emphasized the fact that the analysis was preliminary and would need to be reviewed. "After all, people don't live to such an age," lectured Maddington in his reply. "This report pretty much reveals spurious analysis and/or immature scholarship," he had concluded.

Riley was irritated by her senior colleague's comments, but not devastated, having lived most of her graduate and professional life within the world of peer review.

Worse however, was that word was already getting around from the email she had sent to departmental faculty, even though she has marked the file confidential. Samantha had begun receiving notes from colleagues around the country asking for more information about the burial. Some comments were from friends who wanted to congratulate her on the spectacular preliminary findings. Others questioned her results without seeing any kind of a technical analysis. Amazing how word travels in this discipline, she thought to herself.

That evening Riley pushed the send key for the report to Jonathan Higgins in Walla Walla. In her cover note, she asked for permission to run a bone sample for AMS dating and let him know that she had submitted carbon samples from above and below the remains. She also suggested that it would be appropriate once she returned from the field to conduct traditional carbon isotope analysis to determine something about the individual's diet. In the meantime, she would have one of her graduate students recount osteon structures found in the MRI thin sections, conduct an oxygen isotope scan with non-destructive laser ablation, and if time allowed, begin evaluating the volcanic ash samples for trace elements using x-ray florescence analysis. She suggested he call her in the morning with any questions as she planned to be traveling by the afternoon.

CHAPTER 6

WALLA WALLA, WASHINGTON

Jonathan Higgins' clothing and mannerisms displayed an orderly, even tidy personality. His office was arranged symmetrically with a desk in the center, exactly halfway between two windows, with two evenly spaced chairs facing the desk. His desk held a stack of papers and mail neatly positioned in the center. His desktop computer was directly behind him in the center of a narrow rectangular computer stand.

Higgins swiveled from the computer. After carefully reading the report attached to Samantha Riley's email, he picked up his telephone and asked his secretary to call Samantha Riley at her university office number. He needed to talk to her as quickly as possible. The last time the Walla Walla Army Corps District dealt with an ancient human remains case was a couple decades ago from Clarkston, also in Washington State. That case turned into a national debate, complete with a string of lawsuits, television news crews, and a couple of televised documentaries. There were no winners in that case and all parties suffered from a real lack of understanding when cultural heritage mixed with scientific inquiry. Higgins was right in the middle of that fray.

Riley read the incoming caller identification on her desk phone and picked up. "Thanks for calling back this morning, Jonathan. Your reactions to the report?"

Higgins, being polite as he usually was, replied. "You seem to have found another unusual archaeological discovery on Army Corps managed property." He jokingly said. "I think I'll regret calling you for help. You know what my motto is, no press is good press."

"Jonathan, I want to emphasize that these age results are still preliminary and need to be evaluated and perhaps confirmed with other methods and evidence," responded Riley. "I tried to keep this as confidential and contained as possible, but I felt I had to circulate the draft to my departmental faculty colleagues. Since yesterday evening, I've been bombarded by emails about the report. I had no idea that any of my departmental colleagues would leak this to the professional community," apologized Riley.

"Even if the report was circulated by someone from your department, it clearly comes across as a preliminary draft that begs reanalysis. Thanks for getting it to me so quickly, given your schedule. I need you to know that I've gotten a few calls from some of the local tribes asking why they weren't contacted about the burial. There are some very concerned individuals out there."

"I thought you had gotten permission from the Nez Perce to move forward with the salvage."

"Yes, I did. But every tribe has a different opinion, and as you know, any individual in a tribe may have a dissenting opinion. I called the Nez Perce Tribe because they were the closest Native American Nation to Central Ferry and the burial was on treaty ceded, Nez Perce lands. They rightfully gave the go-ahead to recover the remains to protect them from looters. Now, other tribes in the region are contesting the Nez Perce authority to have given such approval. Some are even suggesting that we should have put into place some kind of guard to protect the burial. They suggest we should have left it in the ground."

"I didn't put it in the draft, Jonathan, but that burial would have eroded out by next spring or over the winter if it weren't retrieved. It was originally placed under an overhang, but the overhang has since washed out. It was just a matter of months before the skeleton would have washed down to the river, become disarticulated, and probably decayed away. I can emphasize the geomorphological context in the final report. That should help," said Riley.

"Yes, that should help," Higgins responded. "But you understand, I can't give you permission to do anything else with the remains until I have a more detailed collaboration with the tribes and other interested communities. I'm sure the scientific community will be at my door shortly, demanding access. No radiocarbon analysis of the bone, or any destructive kind of isotope analysis on actual human remains, okay?"

Riley could almost feel the stress coming from Jonathan as he recited the dos and don'ts. She knew that Higgins had been caught in the middle of the last fiasco associated with human remains and he could not afford a repeat with this one. Having worked with human remains from North America during her entire career, Samantha Riley anticipated the restrictions. "Of course, I figured that. I have always respected the position of descendant communities in my investigations.

As much as I love pursuing the scientific details, I think it is equally important to understand how materials are perceived by heritage citizenry. I don't have to remind you how often heritage values are overlooked in the name of science."

"As noted, the Nez Perce had requested this excavation," repeated Higgins.

"I did send out some nonhuman carbon samples for AMS dating and DNA work. Those were associated with organic stains directly above and below the skeleton. Again, they were not human remains," emphasized Riley. "Also, I had some nondestructive laser ablation scheduled for some tooth and bone samples. You know that I'm heading back out to the field this afternoon, so if there is nothing else for now, I'll sign off, Jonathan. You have my cell number. The reception is not great in that section of the national forest, but I'll check text messages every day or two. I'll talk with you when I return."

"I don't anticipate any problems with the sediment samples," replied Higgins. "I hope you have a productive and safe conclusion to your field school project, Dr. Riley. After that I may need your help communicating the results of your research to the various groups when those results start coming in."

"My pleasure, Jonathan," said Riley, and ended the call.

As word began circulating in the Native communities about an ancient burial, the Walla Walla District Office got progressively more inquiries from Native American representatives who felt they were not properly notified regarding the excavation at Central Ferry. Most of those calls were directed to Jonathan Higgins. He was able to assure callers that the burial was safe and protected, now that it was no longer subject to erosion or open to boaters or looters who might desecrate it.

The situation, though not out of control, was quickly becoming complicated, with different tribal nations taking different positions on burials, in general, and burial protection and excavation, in particular. Higgins knew better than to side with any one of the tribes. That was one of the problems with the Clarkston Mummy case. The tribes were initially given complete authority over the ancient remains, an almost universal practice. Yet the law, as written, required documentation of Native American affiliation before the federal agency could relinquish control. Some of the lawsuits in that case indicated that the remains were not demonstrated to be of Native American origin and, as such, at that time, did not fall under the Native American Graves Protection and Repatriation Act or NAGPRA, as it was commonly known. Much had changed since the Clarkston Mummy days, but Higgins could feel the pressure mounting in this case. He felt trapped between the different tribal factions, the potential for scientific investigation that would surely come, and his employer who preferred not to be caught in another high-profile case. It took years for Higgins to recover from the Clarkston Mummy fallout. It ruined his marriage, and he could feel his blood pressure rising again. Several calls had already gone straight to the District Commanding Officer, Colonel Blankenship.

Higgins' secretary tapped on the open door and peeked into his office. "Jonathan, Colonel Blankenship would like to see you in his office. Immediately!" Higgins rose from his desk concerned and uneasy. He exited the main entrance of the building and walked to the building next door. The Walla Walla District Office was composed of a series of buildings spread out over a small campus. It was a short distance to the District CO building. Colonel Blankenship's secretary showed Higgins into a waiting room. After a brief five-minute wait, he was ushered into the CO's office.

Following their standard handshake, the Colonel pointed to a chair with an open palm. "Have a seat, Higgins."

Blankenship was not one for small talk, and he went straight to the issue at hand. "I've been getting calls from a few of the local tribal council leaders asking about the excavation of some human remains on the Snake River. I'm not sure what to tell them. Maybe you can enlighten me on the matter?"

Higgins briefed the Colonel on the call from the county sheriff's office, his conversation with the Nez Perce cultural resources director, and how he contacted Washington State University to recover the remains before looters began their own excavations.

"What you're telling me sounds straight forward. What's the big deal? Why are tribal leaders so upset?" asked the Colonel.

"As you know, each native tribe is a separate nation with its own governing council. Each tribe has different religious and political policies, particularly as they relate to burials," replied Higgins.

"Why not just turn over the remains to the tribes?" queried the frustrated Blankenship. "Isn't that required under Federal statute?"

Higgins peered up at Blankenship, thinking about how he had done that same thing the last time and was figuratively crucified. "We are the stewards of this resource, Colonel. Ultimately, it is our responsibility to follow the law and to follow proper ethical procedures, and the law and ethics may not agree. Furthermore, which tribe do we turn the remains over to? What if the remains are not culturally, biologically, or politically affiliated with any of the tribes that want them? I think we should act with caution on this issue and make sure we follow the law to the letter."

"Are you telling me this could blow up into another Clarkston Mummy case?" asked the Colonel.

"I certainly hope not," replied Higgins. "We have been very careful with all aspects of this case, beginning with Native American consultation through contractor excavation procedures. However, you should also know that the recovered human remains in this situation are very unusual."

"Unusual? This entire thing is unusual, Higgins. I manage lock and dam construction and re-engineering. What could make this case more unusual, Higgins?"

"Well," began Higgins. "There was a preliminary assessment done by our contractors at Washington State University, and it seems that burial was a man one hundred thirty-eight years old."

"So, the person died in the eighteen hundreds," replied the Colonel. "Why is that so unusual?"

"No, the person probably died about thirteen thousand years ago at the end of the Ice Age. That is significant, in and of itself. The initial report also states that he was one hundred thirty-eight years old at the time of his death. That is the unusual part."

The Colonel looked at Higgins in disbelief. "Are you fucking kidding me, Higgins? How can that not be a mistake? Are you making recommendations and decisions based on obvious errors? One hundred and thirty-eight years old? Higgins, are you out of your damned mind?"

"True, the report is preliminary, but the initial tests have produced this very extraordinary result. You need to know this before the press, or someone else, begins asking you about it," replied Higgins.

"Damnit, Higgins, this has all the earmarks of a super clusterfuck! Isn't there an outfit in D.C. that's supposed to handle these kinds of things?" demanded Colonel Blankenship.

"If you are referring to the Interagency, Natural, Human and Cultural Resources Institute, my recommendation is that we don't get them involved at this stage. I've never worked with them before and, with all due respect, sir, they seem to be focused on military research and program compliance. I'd hate for some outsiders to come in and blow this thing up in our faces."

"Higgins, the Corps hires civilians like you to aid, but damnit, we are the military, and from where I'm sitting, this thing is about ready to blow up in our faces right now. There could be an explosion before the day is over. I want you to bring that group in immediately, before this thing gets out of hand. Do you understand me, Higgins?"

"Absolutely, I'll make some calls as soon as I leave your office, sir." Higgins stood up, "Is there anything else?"

"Yes. Send me a short summary sketch and some contact information on this Interagency organization. And keep me updated on the situation. I don't want this District to be blamed for another Clarkston Mummy screwup. Not on my watch."

Higgins left the office and began weighing the advantages and disadvantages of asking for assistance from the Interagency Institute. Certainly, there was a chance that outsiders, who had no experience with local tribes and researchers might fumble the project. But the upside was that Washington D.C. would have to absorb a great deal of the blame if the project were fumbled. Higgins felt better. His career couldn't afford to take the blame for another major miscue. Yes, let someone else take the responsibility. He would start by checking the Interagency Institute's web page to get the profile report for Blankenship. That would provide him with some background before making the call.

CHAPTER 7

ST. MARIES, IDAHO

Without a sound, the boat glided slowly through the sparse patches of wild rice, coming almost to a complete stop. The fisherman nimbly stepped from behind the windshield onto the bow. He began rigging his fly rod, pausing every few seconds to study the water. The rod was an ultrafast 8-weight with matching line and reel. There was nobody else visible or audible on the chain-lakes, but he did pass several chattering and honking flocks of geese, and a range of duck species flushed and keened from the water when the boat had sped along. An occasional deer and moose were positioned along the shoreline during this early morning run. He selected a large fly and attached it to his wire leader tippet. The fly had silver flashing and red dyed bucktail hairs tied onto a barbless hook. These were laid over a five-inch thin strip of white rabbit fur, hence the fly's name, "bunny bug."

Deak Allen began stripping line from his reel onto the floor of the boat bow and then flipped the bunny bug out toward the weedy edge of the lake. Before it hit the water, he loaded the line with a backward raise of his arm. Just as the line extended out behind him, he pulled sharply down on the line and loaded it with forward motion. The coil of line in the bow began flying up through the rod eyes and the bunny bug landed twenty-five yards away, at the edge of the weed line. This technique, known as the a "double haul," was often used for heavy fly gear or for saltwater fishing that demanded long casts in strong winds. The water was so clear that he could watch the streamer sink. Allen began stripping the bunny bug back toward him. With each pull of the line, it streaked through the water, the hair compressed and lying flat. When it stopped at the end of a pull the rabbit hair would decompress and fluff out, which created a pulsating motion through the water. The few strands of silver flash tied into the steamer simulated fish scales flashing in the water.

Just as the bunny bug came to rest at the end of the pull, it disappeared in a giant swirl of water that bent the rod. He let the remainder of line play out as the fish headed away from the boat. The fish was now "on the reel," but it kept taking line and his spool began to sing as the drag continued to release line down to the backing. The fish broke the water surface several times during its run. The ginormous fish was extremely powerful but was beginning to slow down and then stayed deep under water, swimming along the bottom. Meticulously, the fish was guided back toward the boat, using the rod tip to coax the fish left or right as it seemed to take an interest in each and every piece of cover on its reluctant swim toward the boat.

After almost fifteen minutes, the northern pike was steered near the boat. Suddenly, it rushed the boat, breaking the water surface. Still full of energy, the fish was downright furious. The pike became gradually calmer and ceased shaking its head trying to toss the fly from the corner of its mouth. Allen reached down with a pair of heavy forceps, careful not to get too close to the razor-sharp teeth. The barbless hook was effortlessly clamped, twisted, and extracted from the pike's toothy gape. The pike spun and leapt out of the water and smacked it monstrous tail before flashing back into the depths of the lake. Deak Allen's face and shirt were soaked, but he smiled. The pike was massive, close to four feet in length. It had to have been forty years old. "A rare fish," he said to no one.

Allen was on vacation in North Idaho after returning from a four-week field assignment in Nangarhar, Afghanistan. Allen was an archaeologist with the Interagency Natural, Human, and Cultural Resources Institute, part of the Department of Defense. Originally, the "Interagency Institute" or "Institute," as it was referred to, was housed in the Army Corps of Engineers. However, the Department of Defense separated it because there were many other entities in the government that needed similar help with policy and problem solving that related to the mitigation of impacts from large government projects, such as canal building, road construction, and military campaigns. In addition to the Army Corps of Engineers, the Institute worked closely with the Office of Naval Research, the U.S. Army Research Laboratory, as well as specific federal research installations. The Institute helps facilitate successful execution of research and applied projects through a team of highly trained field agents with expertise in those specific areas.

Relevantly, the Institute was called upon to help train U.S. employed civilians and combat forces to recognize and protect important natural and cultural resources, as in the Nangarhar region. Allen had been assigned the project and now all he needed to do to close the project was to compile the final report.

His graduate school mentor and good friend had offered the use of his small fishing cabin at the mouth of the St. Joe River where it emptied into Idaho's Lake Coeur d'Alene. One of the Allen's favorite escapes was fly fishing. The cabin was in Heyburn State Park, the oldest in Idaho, and was one of a few privately owned structures within the park. The cabin was situated halfway between two very different towns, Plummer and St. Maries.

To the east, Plummer is in the middle of the Coeur d'Alene Indian Reservation with tribal headquarters in the town. The culture of the town is distinctly Indian. The town to the west is St. Maries, a lumber mill town in an age of mechanized lumbering. The change in technology has left many in the town longing for the good old days of lumber jacks, chain saws, and unlimited forests. The two towns could not be more different.

Allen's friend and mentor, Walt Steward, along with his wife, Windy, were away for most of the summer aboard their 66-foot fishing yacht, cruising the waters off British Columbia and Alaska. They cruised the North Pacific every summer and sometimes ventured over to east Asian waters. Walt had helped Deak Allen get his first position out of graduate school with the Army Corps because of several federal government contacts he had over the years. Even in retirement, Walt occasionally consulted with federal agencies, as an expert witness on archaeological and heritage management lawsuits and property claims.

From the cabin, Allen could fish for cutthroat trout in the wild and scenic St. Joe River or for northern pike in the shallow waters at the southern end of the lake. He relished catching both using fly tackle, and he had an assortment of rods to match the task. The best way to fly fish for pike is to cast from the bow of a boat facing weed beds that drop off to deeper water. Cutthroat fishing requires a drive up the St. Joe canyon, where wading through the river and casting into pools and eddies works best.

Allen had to drive through St. Maries to fish the upper reaches of the St. Joe. He spent his first day and a half of vacation exploring and fishing "The Joe," as the locals called it. It was a gorgeous drive into remote North Idaho and the St. Joe is one of the blue-ribbon cutthroat fisheries in the United States. The clear cold waters of the St. Joe are composed of slower flat sections with ripples and eddies, as well as fast narrow sections that cascade over rapids. In places, it runs slow and deep along rocky canyon walls. These changes provide fish and insect life excellent locations to reproduce and grow healthy.

Allen had caught and released numerous cutthroat trout in the twenty-inch range on his first day of vacation. But today he had Walt's boat on the water and was casting large streamers for northern pike. His friend had left a custom-made, welded-hull aluminum boat for him to use. A map of the southern end of the lake had been left on the kitchen counter. It pinpointed the cabin location and had several areas circled in red with the word "pike" written nearby. Deak had brought the map with him on the boat and had just released the monster pike caught near the first circled area on the map.

Allen began noticing that this southern end of the lake contained numerous gelatinous globs like fish egg sacs. They appeared to be clusters of single-celled organisms that formed a colony. These colonies were attached to subsurface plant stems or directly onto submerged sticks or rocks. If he had seen one or two of the globs, he probably wouldn't have even paid attention. However, in the area he was fishing, he had already spotted half a dozen of the gelatinous clusters. Some were quite large, the size of a cantaloupe and others as small as a golf ball. He used his cell phone to photograph them, thinking that someone would know what they were. The river emptying into the lake and the lake itself were pristine. What a contrast to where he had just been for the past month.

He decided to move to the next spot circled on the map. As he began to negotiate the boat into deeper water, he spotted another boat headed in his direction. The boat pilot waved his arm and yelled, "Walt, how are you doing?"

When they were closer, Allen stepped into the bow from the cockpit and the man, wearing a ranger uniform, said, "Oh, sorry, fella, I thought you were someone else."

"Walt is letting me use the boat while I stay at his place."

"Fair enough," responded the uniformed man. "My name is Rick and I'm the ranger here. I manage Heyburn Park and the waters around the park. I assumed you were Walt because I know his boat."

"Hello, Rick. I'm Deak Allen and I have the great privilege of using his boat. Walt, Windy, and I go back a few years and I'm enjoying this amazing part of the world at their courtesy. I've been casting for pike near the lily pads over there and have found some giant fish."

"Those species of lily pads are known as water potatoes by the indigenous people in this area because their roots form tubers that are easily harvested in autumn when the lake is no longer being filled by snow runoff. Your friend Windy collects them by the bushel in the fall. Apparently, she's been a wild food nut her entire life. She's always picking berries in the mountains around here, and she collects with the Tribe during their fall ceremony, too. And, yes, the pike like to hunt those edges. Do you know that the Coeur d'Alene Tribe has put a bounty on those fish? You can turn in a fish head or the entire fish for five dollars each, no limit."

"I didn't know that. That sounds like a quick way to eradicate fish from a body of water."

"The Tribe manages the southern third of Lake Coeur d'Alene and they've been trying to eliminate invasive species of both plants and animals. Northern pike were introduced into this lake about fifty years ago in the 1960s by some bucket biologists and they have, at first gradually, and now quickly become the apex predator in the lake. The Tribe and the park would like to bring the wild fish population back to its natural equilibrium."

"That can be an uphill challenge," replied Allen, as he looked across the lake's shoreline.

His eye caught a glimpse of one of the gelatinous sacks just under the surface in shallow water. "Rick, you sound like a wildlife biologist. Can you tell me what that is?" pointing to something below the surface. "I've seen several of those in this part of the lake."

The ranger peered in the direction of Allen's extended arm and looked closely into the water. "That is a Bryozoan. Those and their kind are among some of the oldest animals on earth. That animal species is a freshwater organism that has been in the Pacific Northwest since way before people were here and probably much earlier. The Bryozoan population fluctuates over time. In the past few years, it has been increasing in this part of the lake. Most people never notice them because they are so like fish or frog egg sacks, and they just blend into the shallow water diversity of interesting but unknown plant or animal life. Over the past decade, with warmer temperatures and less rain, we've been getting more and more forest fires in the upper watershed, and there seems to be a correlation between defoliated upland run off areas and the increase in the Bryozoan population. However, correlation does not equate to cause. In the past couple of years, I've noticed an increase in Bryozoans, as well as the size and health of the predator fish populations in the lake."

"I'll vouch for the size and strength of the pike here," grinned Allen. "I just released a fish that had to be well over forty inches long and had the girth of a man's leg."

"Well, I've got to be going," said Rick. "If you see Windy before I do, please tell her that some of her photographs of the park have been selected to be featured in next year's park pamphlet. She was one of the photo contest winners. It was a pleasure to meet you, Mr. Allen."

"The pleasure was mine, Rick."

The ranger's boat crossed the lake and pulled toward the river channel and disappeared around a bend in the forested river.

CHAPTER 8

Allen's mind easily settled back into the water world around him. He searched his fly box for a different color as the late afternoon shadows began to stretch. Allen felt the vibration of his cell phone in his pocket, pulled it out and glanced at the screen. It was a text message from his office in D.C.

Allen reported directly to the director of the Interagency Institute, Brigadier General Orlando Ortega. Ortega was the founding director and driving force behind the Interagency Institute. As a colonel, teaching economics and humanities in the United States War College in Carlisle, Pennsylvania, it appeared that his career would top out there, even though he was a West Point graduate. Then the ground fighting in the Middle East began and he took a deployment in Bagdad. He witnessed the massive destruction of human heritage in the Tigris and Euphrates River valleys, the cradle of human civilization. Ortega made a name for himself advocating for human and environmental protection in the war zone. He became one the few ranking military in the field whom local leaders trusted. His efforts earned him a star and he was offered the opportunity to build the Interagency Institute.

General Ortega's secretary in Washington sent Allen a text outlining a brewing problem in the Walla Walla Army Corps District Office. Because Allen was in the region, Ortega wanted him to stop by the District Office and see if he could act as a go-between for the Corps and the Native tribal representatives who seemed to be at odds over some recent actions on the part of the Corps.

Allen had had nearly two days of good fishing, but he would have liked to fish for a couple more days. He devised a plan. He would fish for the rest of the day, leave for Walla Walla early the following morning, make the three-hour drive, be there by nine and maybe get back to the cabin for the evening hatch. However, he would make another call first.

Deak Allen was assigned to multiple field projects, but like most senior field researchers in the Institute, he was lead on only one or two at a time but briefed on a half dozen others. The Afghanistan project was behind him and was ending with his report. The senior researchers for the Institute had special assistants who could make necessary arrangements when the leads were in the field, sometimes for two hundred days a year. Allen's special assistant was Jack Mills. Jack not only managed schedules and transportation, but also acted as logistics and research coordinator, and all-around troubleshooter. By now, Deak Allen and Jack Mills had worked together for over two years, and each had a good sense of the other.

Mills picked up immediately when Allen speed-dialed his number. "Hi, Jack. How bad is the situation in Walla Walla?"

Jack had it covered. "Well, the District Commanding Officer thinks it could be politically explosive with the indigenous community. The regional cultural resources specialist, a Jonathan Higgins, doesn't agree, but he was also the person who was involved with the Clarkson Mummy fiasco. I think they need outside guidance."

"I'm going to call them to set up a meeting tomorrow morning," replied Allen.

"You want me to do that, Deak? I can set that up."

"No, I'll handle it. I'm sending you a couple of cell phone pictures of a colony of single-celled organisms called Bryozoans. Seems this thing might be associated with some aspect of global warming. Have someone over on that project look, and get me some information on these things, okay? Text me the Walla Walla number, too."

"Will do. Have fun in Walla Walla." Jack hung up the phone.

Allen punched in the Walla Walla contact number from Mills' text. The call was answered, and he was transferred to Jonathan Higgins. Allen introduced himself and told Higgins he could be in Walla Walla by 9:00 the following morning. Higgins said he had no other appointments and that would work.

"What can you tell me about the situation?" asked Allen.

"We have some human remains that a couple of different tribes are claiming as their own. They are not on the same page. There are also some interesting technical issues related to the remains that you'll want to know. I can go over all of this in the morning when you get here," said Higgins.

"Are the remains there in Walla Walla?"

"There are not. We had a contractor, Washington State University, do the excavation, recovery, and initial analysis for us, so the remains are still in Pullman. I'd like to talk with you about how we should handle that, as well."

"I'm sure we'll have time to cover that. Higgins, give me an idea of the extent of the collection. A couple of cubic feet or a couple hundred?"

"One intact skeleton with burial remains and a scatter of bones and some stone artifacts. Can't be more than about three cubic feet," replied Higgins.

"Okay, sounds like we have a plan. I'll see you at nine tomorrow," said Allen.

Early the next morning Allen was sitting on a comfortable chair in the bedroom listening to the day slowly yet progressively begin. He heard a raven's distinctive vibrating cluck, then the distant almost laughing call of a pileated woodpecker. There was the garbled call of a red-necked grebe followed by its splash and dive. He stepped from the bedroom just as the sun's first rays were cracking through the clouds over the eastern mountains. Allen made coffee while getting dressed and walked out to the deck with a cup of strong black French Roast. The lake in front of him was coming to life. Fish were probing the smooth lake surface as they grabbed insects. Kingfishers were on the hunt and loons were piercing the early morning light with their morning calls. He filled a travel mug with coffee, grabbed his daypack, laptop, and reluctantly walked to his rental for the drive to Walla Walla.

CHAPTER 9

WALLA WALLA, WASHINGTON

Ultimately, the drive to Walla Walla was longer than Allen expected. He arrived at the Army Corps District Office a few minutes after nine and found his way to Jonathan Higgins' secretary on the lower floor of the building. "Excuse me, I have a meeting with Mr. Higgins this morning. I believe he is expecting me."

Higgins' secretary was stereotyped out of the 1960s. She appeared to be in her early forties or maybe middle thirties. She wore heavy dark-rimmed glasses, red lipstick, with red hair pulled into a tight bun on the back of her head. Wearing a dark mid-calf skirt and white blouse, her name tag/badge hung directly in the center of her chest. The woman looked up with an expression that could have been efficiency or slight bother. "I assume you are Deak Allen from the Interagency Institute?" She paused, seeking a verbal response.

Allen nodded.

"Let me see your identification and I'll log you in."

Allen passed over his credentials. She registered him and passed back his identification without making eye contact. "Please follow me," she instructed and walked down the hallway with her high heels clicking loudly.

After pleasant but somewhat cautious introductions, Allen and Higgins got down to business. Higgins quickly summed up the scenario of the boaters finding remains while picnicking, through the Nez Perce request for excavation, to the excavation and preliminary analysis of the burial by Washington State University, and the subsequent flurry of phone calls from various Native nations. He also gave Allen a copy of the preliminary report produced by Samantha Riley and gave Allen a few minutes to digest the report.

"I suggested to the Colonel that we move slowly on this project and not make any rash decisions without full consultation with all current and potential stakeholders," informed Higgins.

"That's a wise move. You have the Nez Perce support for your actions for an immediate salvage recovery due to the imminent danger to the burial either by looters or erosion." Allen had the urge to make a few recommendations to Higgins regarding how he might proceed with "official and unofficial" interactions with the various stakeholders, but he didn't want to infringe on Higgins' responsibilities. "I'm sure you are in the process of formulating a plan for working with the tribes?" sought Allen.

"As I've indicated, nothing was done in this situation without tribal input and guidance from the Nez Perce."

"I absolutely understand that," said Allen. "If you don't mind, might I suggest that it could be beneficial to bring other regional tribes into the loop on this project, especially since a few others have expressed an interest?"

"Do you have a particular strategy in mind?"

"You are the one who knows the situation and the tribal personalities the best in this area, Higgins, so I defer to you on best strategies here. I can only make some gross suggestions that may or may not be helpful in this case. For instance, it might not be a bad idea, and I'm sure you've already thought of this, to call a meeting of all the tribes who feel they have a claim to the remains and give them a briefing on the status of the remains. This would give them firsthand knowledge of what has taken place from the very beginning, and it would emphasize their inclusion in the process," suggested Allen.

Higgins though about it. "Yes, that's a very good idea and, actually, I hadn't gotten there yet. How shall we handle the age of the skeleton and the issues that may arise from that?" inquired Higgins.

"All of that is hearsay at this point, and I don't believe the Army Corps should propagate any rumors of either an incredibly old individual or one that lived an incredibly long time ago. The radiocarbon dates have not been returned yet, so we don't know when the burial occurred. And the age of the individual at the time of death needs to be confirmed. Again, it's important to deflect any questions related to those issues. Those analyses are preliminary. They are just speculations, at this time. I'd put your efforts into establishing lines of communication with any of the tribes or researchers who have a real stake in the remains," suggested Allen. "I would like to talk with the principal investigator who excavated the remains for you and view them myself before making any kind of longer-term recommendation about what we can and should do with those remains. Was that a Dr. Riley at Washington State University?"

"Yes. She's a forensic archaeologist there, but she is currently out in the field in North Idaho finishing up a field school. You might give her office a call and find out when she's planning to return." Higgins dug through his desk for the note pad with contact information. "Here's her department telephone number, her direct office line, and I have her cell number as well. My guess is that she won't be back for another week or so."

"We need to move a bit quicker than that. Do you know where her field camp is located? I should probably have a face-to-face meeting with her in the next day or two."

"The closest town is Helmer, Idaho, but you could spend months looking through the forests in that area. That region is dissected with mountains, valleys, and temporary logging roads. I believe her office has the exact location and can provide you with a map to her camp. I suggest you call that number, and they can probably send you a PDF copy of the map."

"That's a good idea," responded Allen. "You wouldn't have a map of that area we could look at right now, would you? I'm staying at a friend's place outside of St. Maries and I wonder if that might be in the neighborhood."

Higgins spread a U.S. Forest Service map on his desk, and they located both Helmer and St. Maries after a quick search. They were able to trace a series of back roads that linked both the towns and Higgins estimated that they were about sixty to ninety minutes apart. "Looks like you might be able to make it back to St. Maries and then leave from there to Helmer."

"Excuse me for a minute. I'm going to call the WSU department right now." Allen left the office and stepped into the hallway. Joe, the departmental secretary, confirmed that Riley had gone back into the field about a few days earlier and he agreed to attach a map with the location of the field camp to an email.

"When do you think that you'll be visiting the camp? I would like to give Dr. Riley some advance warning that you intend to visit the camp," Joe thoughtfully remarked.

"I'll spend some more time here in Walla Walla then return to St. Maries. I'll probably head to Helmer tomorrow."

"Great," said Joe. "I'll give Dr. Riley a call and let her know that you plan to visit the camp tomorrow. Who do you work for again?"

"You can tell her I work for the Department of Defense."

Allen spent the rest of the morning working with Higgins on both a press release and some talking points for the face-to-face meeting with tribal representatives. "The tribal meeting may take several days to materialize, so I would suggest that you call each of the invitees and let them know there will be a press release and give each a personal briefing on the press release," suggested Allen. "Be sure to note who you talked with, as part of the press release, to develop a sense of buy-in from as many of the tribes as possible. This entire thing is preliminary, and it's moved forward because of thc pending destruction of the human remains. Again, any speculation on the age of remains is unconfirmed. At this point we still plan to have Washington State University do the initial descriptive analysis, but there will be no destructive techniques performed."

Higgins liked the direction of the planned contacts and press release. He had intended all along to include all stakeholders in the operation, but for one reason or another, he hadn't expected the excavation to unfold in the way it had. "Thanks for all your help with this, Dr. Allen. I think this will be good for our working relationship with the tribes."

"My job is to help in these kinds of situations. The difficult job falls on your shoulders. You are the one who must make this work now, and into the future."

Allen had arranged a lunch meeting with Colonel Blankenship to review the strategy with him and to brief him on the broader picture of the Interagency Institute's mission. He was also to give the Colonel a hearty hello from General Ortega as both men had intersected in Iraq.

Blankenship had the lunch catered in his conference room. Higgins asked his secretary to walk Allen to Blankenship's office. She got up, nodded to Higgins and looked at Allen. "Please follow me." They walked to the CO's building, and she handed Allen off to the Colonel's secretary.

Allen was shown into the conference room, where lunch had already been delivered. After sitting and waiting for five minutes, the inner door opened and a tall man in an Army officer uniform walked into the room and extended his hand. "Robert Blankenship."

Allen shook hands. "Deak Allen, I'm glad we're able to meet."

"I reviewed the mission of the Interagency Institute," commented the Colonel. "It sounds like my old friend Ortega has developed a much-needed unit in the DOD."

"As everything becomes progressively more global, our work is getting increasingly more valuable," said Allen.

Blankenship looked at the food, grabbed a plate and invited Allen, "Please help yourself."

"One of my contacts in D.C. said the Institute was wrapping up a training mission in Afghanistan. That sounds a bit outside of the Institute's range of responsibilities."

"That was my assignment, Colonel. We generally don't do field training. Often, we work at the planning stage of projects, and stay with a project through the implementation stage. However, our government has been getting some significant negative press from the United Nations and from within the states, so someone thought we should at least do some in-field training to preserve natural and heritage resources when possible."

"I also heard that you were once in the Army Corps, Dr. Allen?"

"That wasn't too long ago, Colonel. I came over from the Corps when General Ortega formed the Institute and began assembling a team of researchers. How long have you been in Walla Walla?"

"As you probably know, the Corps brings in a new District CO every two years. I've been here for eighteen months. Don't know where I'll be assigned after this one."

The two men reviewed the case at hand in detail, and then discussed some of the other projects the Institute was involved with before ending.

"I just want to thank you again for providing some guidance on this ancient skeleton matter. Higgins informed me that it may be one hundred thirty-eight years old at the age of death. Could that be right?"

"That would make this guy the oldest person to have ever lived if it were true. It would also be one of the most significant finds ever made," said Allen. "I don't have to tell you, once the age of this skeleton is confirmed, you will be getting national and international press."

Colonel Blankenship was a hard man to read. He pushed his chair away from the table. "Be sure to give my best to Orlando. Thanks again for assisting with this project."

Blankenship stood up and extended his hand. Allen walked next door and met again with Higgins to give him some idea of what direction he would be taking in the project, and to thank him for his willingness to work collaboratively with the Institute. Higgins and Allen came away from their meeting on a positive note, both feeling that the burial situation would not spiral out of their control.

It was just after 2:00 p.m. when Deak Allen waived goodbye to Higgins and pulled out of the Corps parking lot. He calculated that he'd get back to the cabin by six that evening and might be able to get in an hour or two of fishing. He planned to send General Ortega a preliminary report of his activities the following morning and then make the drive to the Helmer area to meet with Dr. Riley. The map he had received from the department was well marked, but there did appear to be a lot more forest service roads on the map Higgins had shown him than on the map from the department, so he wasn't too sure exactly how long it would take him to make the trip to the field camp.

CHAPTER 10

VLADIVOSTOK, RUSSIA

Vladivostok, Russia, is situated east of China, north of the Korean peninsula, and west of the islands of Japan. Most vestiges of the city's ancient Chinese past have long disappeared. The town square architecture now hints at originating during the Russian cold war era. The remainder of the city's buildings are home to a modern industrial port city of half a million people and include the Far Eastern Federal University.

Boris Mirsky was in Vladivostok putting the final touches on securing the ancient human remains for the Centurion Project. Things did not go as he had planned. The curator of collections at Far Eastern Federal University, Professor Dimitri Kozlov would not release the collections to Utkin Chemicals and informed Mirsky that such a request was unprecedented and ridiculous. He was ushered out of the building and off campus.

Academic protocol regarding archaeological remains was alien to Mirsky so he resorted to his tried-and-true methods. He found Kozlov's home and kidnapped his wife, demanding cooperation and the human remains.

Tom Rackerman, a classic Ivy League faculty member, sat with his hands folded neatly in front of him. He said nothing while waiting, biding his time, allowing others to make their comments first. He unlocked his fingers, straightened his bow tie, then locked them again on the table in front of him, without saying a word. An American archaeologist from the University of Pennsylvania, he had funding to work collaboratively with Russian government archaeologists at the Federal University. He had been invited to Vladivostok by his old colleague, Dimitri Kozlov. He was now sitting in a conference room at the university with Kozlov and two other scientists discussing the latest results reported to them from human bone samples they had sent to St. Petersburg University over a month before.

The human remains were not complete but the excavators, two of whom sat at the table, had recovered a mandible with intact dentition, part of the cranium, two femurs, a tibia, and assorted bone fragments. The bones had been scattered from animal activity or ancient looting, but the samples they recovered were well preserved because they were found deep within a cave under roof fall.

Radiocarbon dating indicated that the individual had lived at the end of the Pleistocene, approximately 13,000 years ago, in a relatively temperate climate. Rackerman was there to help interpret the ancient stone tools found at the site. He worked primarily in Alaska and wanted desperately to find the migration link between Asia and North America. He believed similarities in stone tool technologies were the key to explaining how and when North America was colonized. It was exceedingly rare to find human remains from the Pleistocene, and these presented a new opportunity to help make the argument of an Asia-to-Alaska migration over the Bering Land Bridge at the end of the Ice Age. The problem was that Rackerman, and the Russian archaeologists, feared the samples were contaminated.

Dimitri Kozlov, the senior scientist at the Russian university was confounded by the lab report from St. Petersburg. "The report unequivocally states that the individual was one hundred and twenty years old at the time of death. This is ridiculous. It is impossible for a person today to live that long, and it is preposterous to think a person living then could live to be of such old age. Am I not, correct?"

Rackerman agreed with him in theory. But he badly wanted to have a site that was not contaminated and could provide a good comparative sample to the materials he was getting from Alaska. He was not as interested in the human remains as he was the tool technology from the site. However, since reviewing the report the previous evening, he had given the rare finding a great deal of thought. "Gentlemen, I am no osteologist," began Rackerman. "I can only go by what the dating experts at St. Petersburg decide. However, given what they have said, I ask myself how can an individual live to be so old? That is the important question for me."

Kozlov spoke, "What is your answer or speculation on that question, Tom?"

"The Ice Age was a unique and extremely harsh time. Undoubtedly, not all human populations were as successful as others. There had to be a great deal of selection. I see no reason why some successful Ice Age people could not have had a slightly different genetic composition that allowed them to survive bitter cold conditions and perhaps to have lived slightly longer than other people," explained Rackerman.

"Do you really believe a person can live to be of such an old age?" asked Kozlov.

"Dimitri, as I have said, I can only follow the data from those who are experts. I have no idea if a human can live to be a hundred and twenty years old. But if someone did live to be such an age, I would certainly ask how and why," replied Rackerman.

Rackerman stood, as he remembered hearing about another anomalously old burial just reported via email rumors in the United States. He tried to remember where the burial was from. Rackerman looked over at Dimitri and the two other Russian scientists sitting around the table. "Rumor has it that there's a recent burial excavation in the U.S. that was supposedly of an individual who died at a similar age. I don't believe there is a formal report or publication. I recall seeing some email comments related to the burial a few days before I arrived here in Vladivostok. Apparently, it has caused quite a ruckus. I seem to recall it was associated with someone from the archaeology program at Washington State University."

Dimitri perked up, "That is quite interesting, Thomas. Don't you know anyone there you can call and get some details? At this point, any additional information that might help explain the report we have from St. Petersburg would be extremely helpful." Kozlov paused and waited for Rackerman to respond.

Rackerman sat back down. "There is a fellow there whom I've known casually for quite some time. He is a very productive scholar who seems to always know what's going on in that program. In fact, I have his number right here in my cell phone. Peter Maddington. He specializes in geoarchaeology. If I get through, I'll put him on speaker phone."

Rackerman had good cell service at the university and was able to get through. Within two rings Peter Maddington picked up. "This is Dr. Maddington."

Rackerman identified himself and after some pleasantries, Rackerman asked, "Peter, I seem to recall a report that someone in your vicinity has recovered a human burial with a very old person. Does my memory serve me correctly, or am I thinking of some other program?"

Maddington almost laughed, "Oh, that is what one of our new young faculty members contends. What a bunch of baloney. I heard her say that the person was almost a hundred and forty years old at the time of death. Why would any serious scholar even entertain such a preposterous idea?"

"Well, Peter, I couldn't agree with you more," confessed Rackerman. "However, we just got a report back from St. Petersburg that indicates we have a person who died at the age of a hundred and twenty. I just wanted to check and make sure I had heard correctly about this crazy dating. Who is the person who reported the skeletal age?"

"You have a hundred twenty-year-old individual from Alaska?" asked Maddington.

"No. No. I'm over here in Vladivostok. It came from a cave in the highlands near here."

"I see," replied Maddington. "What time range did you say your specimen dated from?"

"I didn't, Peter, but the radiocarbon dates are coming back around the end of the Pleistocene."

"What a coincidence. I believe the skeleton from here is about the same age. Maybe there was something special in the water at the end of the Ice Age," joked Maddington.

Tom Rackerman laughed. "I'm sure. Maybe they were all drinking out of the Fountain of Youth. So, who was it over there that reported the skeleton?"

"Her name is, uh," Maddington paused. "It was one of the junior faculty members. She is really out of her league here. I'm sure she contaminated the sample when she excavated it. If you need any information about the sample, just give me a call. I'm essentially in control of the research around here," lied Maddington. "I'm thinking about having the skeleton sent down to the Barry Baldwin Forensic Laboratory at the University of Tennessee. Have them do a more professional analysis on the skeleton to put this gossip to an end."

"Okay. Thanks Peter. I thought you might have the most up-to-date information on this issue. Hey, were there any stone tools associated with this find?"

Maddington paused trying to remember Riley's report. "I'm sure there were but you know how it can be, I was primarily interested in the geology and didn't have time to really focus on the artifacts. I'll circle back on that one," replied Maddington.

"Great," replied Rackerman. "I'll contact you directly should we have more questions or need additional information. Please let me know if there were any associated stone tools. One other thing. Don't tell anyone about our ancient bones until we double check this."

"Will do, Tom. I'm not one to spread rumors." Maddington said reassuringly.

Rackerman hung up and looked around the room. "There you have it, my friends, another possibly very old person who lived during the end of the Pleistocene. But, like Maddington said, this is probably a contaminated sample situation."

"I agree, Tom. However, why do we think the samples are contaminated?" pressed Dimitri. "There is no evidence of contamination, as far as we currently know. The ages seem to be anomalous because we have never heard of such old people. Not because of contaminated samples."

"As I previously stated, I am not an expert on the aging of ancient people and leave that to those who have such training," replied Rackerman.

Kozlov stood. "Now, if you will excuse me, it has been a very long day and I still have a stack of paperwork to go through before we meet again tomorrow to review some of the artifacts recovered from the cave deposit."

The four archaeologists stood up and shook hands. Rackerman said, "I'll be heading back to my hotel and will take dinner in my room. I, too, could use a good rest this evening. I'll see you all in the morning."

Kozlov hastily left the conference room and searched for anyone that might be in the hallway as he made his way to the elevator, and up to his third-floor office. He peered out of the elevator before stepping into the hallway and rapidly walked into his office, closed the door, and turned the lock. He sighed deeply. And waited, catching his breath. Kozlov went to his desk, picked up the office phone and dialed.

"Good afternoon, Dimitri. Do you have some good news for me from your meetings today?" asked Mirsky.

"How is my wife? Let me speak to her."

"She is doing fine, Dimitri. You can speak to her after we have completed our conversation. What have you found out about these ancient bones?"

"It appears that the St. Petersburg analysis is probably correct."

"Good," replied Mirsky. "What else did you learn today?"

"It seems that another skeleton was very recently found in the U.S. that may be as old or older than the individuals we have from our cave excavations. And the U.S. skeleton is also an Ice Age specimen."

"When was the U.S. skeleton found?"

"I don't know," said Dimitri.

"Is the skeleton male or female?" came the next question.

"I don't know that either."

"Is it a complete skeleton?" asked Mirsky.

"Well, I don't know that either. But I found out that the skeleton was excavated by Washington State University researchers."

"For someone with a great deal to lose you know very little about things that should be very important to you."

"The specimen from the United States was just discovered. The analysis is incomplete. There is no formal report yet," replied Kozlov.

"Who told you about the specimen?"

Kozlov hesitated, unsure how to proceed.

"If you ever want to see you wife again, you had better speak up," said Mirsky.

"The American archaeologist visiting with us, Tom Rackerman informed us about the U.S. specimen. He called a colleague at Washington State University during the meeting to confirm the find."

"What is the name of the person at Washington?" asked Mirsky.

"I don't know for sure. I believe Rackerman called him Peter Manly or Peter Mattingly," said Kozlov.

"Where is Rackerman staying?"

"He is at the Hyundai Hotel. Please let me speak to my wife. That's all I know," implored Kozlov.

CHAPTER 11

Tom Rackerman looked out over the city from his room in the Hyundai Hotel. Vladivostok had become inclement and onerous. He was eager to finish inspecting the stone tools from the Russian cave site and get back to Alaska. Perhaps one more day and he could leave this backwater city. For some unknown reason the city had grown unpleasant and no matter what he did, he couldn't shake a clammy feeling. He sensed a tension in Kozlov and that feeling had spread to him as well.

Rackerman reflected on the meeting this afternoon and wondered how an Ice Age person could live to such an old age. His seat-of-the-pants theory relating to a genetic mutation for terminal Pleistocene people was as possible as any other theory. But he felt there had to be a problem with the determination of age at time of death. Rackerman had yet to order room service dinner and paced the room wondering if he should pass on dinner and just go downstairs for libations at the bar. He was not hungry or thirsty. His mind was unquiet. He seemed unable to make a decision. Rackerman was sure of only one thing, he just wanted to get out of Vladivostok.

He picked up the phone and pressed the operator. “Room service, please.” After a minute, room service answered. “Please send up poached salmon, a green salad, and a roasted potato,” requested Rackerman. “Just oil and vinegar for the salad and extra butter for the potato.”

“Will there be anything else?” asked the room service operator.

“I think that will do. Wait! Please also send a bottle of white wine. A chardonnay will be just fine,” said Rackerman. He cradled the phone and resumed pacing.

Mirsky and his two partners moved swiftly through the hotel lobby. Without giving a look at the desk, he walked straight to the elevator and pressed the button. They ascended to the ninth floor without interruption. The three men marched with little caution, but with minimal noise, down the hallway to Rackerman’s room. Mirsky tapped on the door, and with a deep Russian accent announced, “Room Service.”

Rackerman opened the door quickly without question and was surprised to find the burly man and his two colleagues. With a look of surprise and slight confusion, he said, “Can I help you gentlemen?”

Mirsky kept his head low, not looking up at Rackerman. He began by saying, “I’m sorry, we must have the wrong room. We are looking for the famous American archaeologist, Thomas Rackerman. Do you know if his room is on this floor?”

Rackerman took the bait and smiled. “You have come to the right place, my friend. I am Tom Rackerman. What can I do for you?”

"May we come in? I, unfortunately, have some bad news about Dimitri Kozlov. He has fallen ill," said Mirsky.

Rackerman looked concerned. "By all means, come in. What has happened to my friend, Dimitri? I was just with him less than an hour ago. What has happened to him?"

Rackerman stood back and let the three men into his room, waiting to hear the news of his friend. The last man slipped into the room, closed the door, casually turned the lock, and stationed himself at the door.

Rackerman startled at the lock click and immediately looked toward the door. "Hey, what is the meaning of this?" he demanded. "Who are you guys? I have a mind to call security."

Mirsky held up his hand. "That would not be advisable." He moved casually across the carpeted room to the desk and pulled the telephone from the wall, to make a point. "I'll take your cell phone as well, Dr. Rackerman."

"This is outrageous!" shouted Rackerman. "You all must leave immediately, or your government will not hear the last of this. Do you know who I am?"

Mirsky did not immediately speak. He turned towards Rackerman, looking into his eyes as if to read his character. He then turned his back on Rackerman and paced toward the door, stopped, turned around and paced back toward Rackerman. "Dr. Rackerman, we can have a civil conversation and I will bid you good night, or you can act in a way that will leave me no choice but to make certain you never leave this country. Let's talk."

Rackerman was about to order them out of the room again but glanced at the three hefty men and thought better of it. His eyes assayed the room for an escape, but he knew there was only one door to the suite, other than the door to the balcony, on the ninth floor. "Well gentlemen," began Rackerman, "you seem to have a captive audience. Please explain yourself."

"Thank you, Dr. Rackerman," said Mirsky. "It is so kind of you to volunteer the information we are seeking. It is extremely important that there are no misunderstandings here. I need to know the truth and there can be no half-truths. I need to know who your contact is in the United States. The one who has the recently discovered ancient skeleton. I need as much information and detail as you can possibly give me. You also must promise that you will never tell another soul about our conversation. If at any time during our conversation I do not trust what you are telling me, I will become a little less civilized." Mirsky looked over at Rackerman. "First, why have you not given me your cell phone as asked? Second, do you agree to the terms?"

Rackerman slightly shook his head as he listened, not believing what he was hearing. "I don't understand. All this villainous gangster behavior and you want to know about an archaeological site?"

Mirsky stared at Rackerman. "Dr. Rackerman. I will ask the questions."

Before Rackerman could respond the doorbell sounded. The three men looked toward Rackerman. "Are you expecting someone?" asked Mirsky.

Rackerman paused, considering the situation. "I believe that is my dinner," replied Rackerman.

"Dr. Rackerman, I must ask you to follow my colleague into the bathroom for a moment." Mirsky nodded his head and Rackerman was pointed in that direction.

Rackerman maintained his position in the room, still mulling his options, but turned and went to the bathroom with his guard.

A few minutes later, Mirsky called for them to come out.

Rackerman emerged from the bathroom. His dinner was still covered on the serving trolley with a bottle of chardonnay in an ice bucket. "I don't know anything about the site. I simply called a colleague in the states today who might know something about it," stated Rackerman.

"Excellent. That is the perfect place to begin," said Mirsky. "Who is this person? Remember, I wish to remain civil tonight. Your dinner is waiting, and we have better things to do."

CHAPTER 12

HELMER, IDAHO

Camas plants grow from bulbs, much like tulip bulbs. These bulbous rhizomes, about the size of a walnut, provided the main source of starches and complex carbohydrates for the aboriginal peoples in most of the Pacific Northwest. In the past, these wild roots were harvested annually in late summer when the flowers had wrinkled and dropped to the ground. The process of harvesting the plants caused them to reproduce more densely, as some bulbs were sliced and separated causing more plants to propagate. As a result, harvesting increased the number and reliability of the wild root crops that were gathered every year. In this sense, they were almost like domesticated plants that reproduced with the aid of humans. The bulbs were baked in underground ovens, which desiccated them and reduced their weight by almost four times but preserved the bulb's starches. The lighter roasted camas could be more easily transported and stored for later use.

Samantha Riley stood, hands on hips, looking out over the site area and across the small mountain valley. Her field school had been excavating the site for close to a month. When they had started the excavations in late spring, the small valley was flooded by violet blue for as far as far as could be seen, spreading into every finger canyon and curve. Now it was gone. The lake-like violet blue was the spring bloom of camas. Camas flowers grew on thin stems about twelve inches high and they grew so close together there was no space between the plants. When the wind blew across a field of camas blossoms it gave the appearance of waves flowing across a lake.

Riley had completed her preliminary work on the Central Ferry skeleton about a week earlier and had left Claire to continue nondestructive tests. The second half of the field project was going well. All the targeted randomly sampled squares had been completed, and Riley and her graduate students had already discussed where to place the nonrandom sample units to complete the dig. All excavations and site breakdown would be completed within the next four days or so.

The cell service in the valley was spotty, but Riley had found a location on the top of the ridge about a ten-minute walk from camp and had arranged to check into the office every Monday, Wednesday, and Friday around 2:00 p.m. to collect messages and, if needed, have supplies driven to camp from Pullman.

When she reached the clearing on top of the ridge on this afternoon there were several messages on her cell phone. She read a text message from Claire Anderson that said the radiocarbon assay was called into them and was to be followed by a paper report. All dates clustered around 13,000 years ago, as anticipated from the skeleton's position below Mount St. Helen's J ash. Joe had left a voice message and then a text message warning her that a representative from the Department of Defense was planning to visit her tomorrow regarding the skeleton she and the team had excavated during their short break between sessions.

Oh great, thought Riley. That message was left on my phone yesterday, so tomorrow means today.

Before heading back down to the site, Samantha called Claire in the lab. "So, we have some good news about the Pleistocene date?"

"We sure do," replied Claire. "However, I'm just getting some of the results back from the laser ablation work, and it's confusing."

"What's up?"

"The oxygen isotope signal doesn't match the area," answered Claire. "It looks like this guy drank water primarily from North Idaho, not down there on the Snake River."

"Well, that could be explained in a number of different ways," responded Riley.

"There's more," said Claire. "Looks like this guy had eaten a lot of complex carbohydrates and CAM plants, you know, cacti. Those two things don't match well for this region and time. This is the first time I've worked with laser ablation so I might be reading this wrong."

"Sounds like I should drive back to Pullman today and check this out," responded Riley. "Oh, crap. I can't leave today because some Department of Defense guy is scheduled to visit. I'll drive back tomorrow morning. In the meantime, check the MRI data again for age at death," instructed Riley. "That's going to be the big hurdle."

Riley began heading back down the ridge but stopped when she saw David and Jennifer walking up toward her. "Thought we'd find you up here," said David.

"You two look like you have something to say."

"Lab is about ready to start but we're hitting sterile levels in many of the excavation units," replied Jennifer. "David and I've been talking about maybe having a lecture and demonstration on processing sediment samples using floatation. We've got a ton of them. We usually save them for the lab back on campus, but we could do some out here since the excavations are slowing."

"We have some nested sieves but no drying racks," said David. "I could make some temporary racks from shaker screens."

"This sounds like a good idea. David, you should do the lecture. You do sample processing all the time for your research."

"I have a power point that shows what some of the plant material looks like. We can set that up on three or four laptops spread around the tables for visuals. I think we can make it work."

"You want to do the lecture today or tomorrow?" asked Riley.

"Let's do it today along with a demonstration, then have them start processing tomorrow," replied David.

Jennifer and David pulled out their cell phones to check messages as Riley headed down the ridge.

CHAPTER 13

PULLMAN, WASHINGTON

His eyes darted around the room as he sat behind his desk without moving. Then, just a sliver of a smile materialized. He leaned back deeper into his desk chair with the look of a plump pleased cat. After having listened to Rackerman about the potential age of the ancient skeleton, Peter Maddington began pondering the possibilities of the skeletal remains collected by Samantha Riley and her team of students. Maybe Riley had really stumbled on a rare discovery. If Rackerman was also investigating an Ice Age individual of very old age, maybe Riley's assessment was correct. If those remains really were from a person who lived to be one hundred thirty-eight years old, the remains could point to incredibly important aspects of human aging. Maybe not the "Fountain of Youth," but perhaps a cure for cancer or some other life extending drug. Whoever develops this research would be world famous and even more important to Maddington, that person, if it were all handled correctly, could become very wealthy.

Maddington gritted his teeth and frowned as his mood began to change. Anger slowly and consistently built. It always seemed to be this way. He should have been the one who was contacted by the Army Corps. In fact, he thought, the Army Corps probably tried to call him first. He should have been the one to have run the burial excavation that found the ancient skeleton. After a long career of technical research, Maddington felt that he had not been given the same easy opportunities other faculty received. He would not let this opportunity pass. He had better look at this ancient skeleton before Rackerman called back with more questions.

Peter Maddington was large framed. He was wide and tall with meaty hands that emphasized poor dexterity. Maddington carried ninety pounds of body mass more than was healthy. He stood and lumbered down the hallway like a truck with a flat tire, and slowed as he approached Samantha Riley's lab and stopped in front of the door. Hearing voices in the lab, he peeked through the lab door window observing several graduate students. Maddington continued down the hallway, then circled back to his office. He waited for the lab to clear for the evening. When he returned just before five that afternoon he noticed a single female graduate student in the lab. He recognized the student as one of Dr. Riley's first year graduate students. What was her name? Oh, yes, Claire something or other. Maddington pushed the door open and assumed an air of authority.

"Where are the skeletal remains Riley emailed me about? I need to inspect them," commanded Maddington.

Claire Anderson looked up, surprised to see this heavyset man suddenly appear in the lab. When she realized it was Professor Maddington, she said, "They are in the locked vault."

Maddington spoke, "I need to examine those remains immediately to ensure they are properly stored. I need to look at the artifacts as well. Pull them for me."

Claire was not sure what to do. "But Dr. Riley explicitly said that nobody was to have access to the skeletal materials without her being present."

Maddington's expression changed instantly. "Who do you think you are?" Maddington bellowed at the young graduate student. "I am a senior professor in this program. I was the person who designed this climate-controlled compactor. I need to inspect those remains and I need to do so immediately, or I will see to it that you never finish your degree here or anywhere else."

Claire's voice cracked as she responded softly, "Dr. Maddington, I can't show you the skeletal materials because…" Claire paused.

Maddington leaned toward her, within inches of her face, "Because why? Speak up, young lady."

Claire could feel Maddington's breath on her face as his condescending voice continued to bounce off her eardrums. She could lean back only so far in her chair, and Maddington's face followed hers, shrinking the space between them. "Well, because I don't have the vault key."

"Where is it?" Maddington persisted in a gentler but still menacing manner, as he straightened up.

"I believe Dr. Riley keeps the vault keys. But I don't know where she keeps them."

Maddington stared down at Claire. "What a ridiculous way to run a lab. I'll have to bring this up at the next faculty meeting," he snarled.

Maddington abruptly turned and walked out of the lab toward his office. He remembered the email from Dr. Riley saying that she planned to go back into the field right after submitting the draft report to the Army Corps. This could be the opportune time to collect the remains if he could only get into the vault. He might even be able to make it appear that Claire had incompetently left the vault unlocked. Maddington smiled to himself as he thought about how this might unfold. As he reached his office, the telephone rang. "Hello, this is Professor Maddington."

"Good afternoon, Professor Maddington, I have just recently had a long conversation with a colleague of yours, Dr. Thomas Rackerman. He informs me that you are the person I should meet to discuss the recent discovery of an Ice Age individual."

"Why, yes, yes. That is correct," replied Maddington. "And who are you?"

"I am of no consequence, but I work for a large Russian research organization that has considerable resources for the study of people who, shall we say, live a bit longer than the rest of us. If possible, I would like to discuss with you an opportunity to join our team of consulting scientists and researchers. Of course, we recognize how busy researchers like you are, and we would certainly compensate you very well for your valuable time. Is it possible to arrange a face-to-face meeting soon?"

Maddington's eyes widened as he listened. This was just the kind of break he'd been hoping for. "Well, of course.

I am always open to new research opportunities. What do you propose for a meeting?"

The caller asked, "Do you have the skeleton?"

"Well, not with me at this moment. There are some preliminary tests being run on the skeleton and I won't have it back for a few more days," Maddington lied. "But I shall certainly be able to show you the skeleton once the tests are completed."

"I am currently in Los Angeles and can catch a flight any time. Perhaps we can have a dinner meeting in a day or two and discuss this further?"

Maddington smiled to himself, "That would be ideal. We can meet at the Red Window Restaurant in Moscow the day after tomorrow?"

"Moscow?"

Maddington continued, "Yes, there is a town near here called Moscow, just over the state line in Idaho. The restaurant is quiet, and we'll be able to discuss our collaboration without being interrupted. How does that sound?"

"I believe I can be there, say around six o'clock the day after tomorrow. That sounds fine. I'm sure I can find my way to the restaurant."

"When you say collaboration, what specifically were you hoping I might be able to contribute?"

"My organization works with researchers in many ways. It really depends on how the researcher wants to participate and the kind of trust we can develop."

"Well, of course," replied Maddington. "I am quite confident that we can develop a strong and trusting partnership. My entire career is based upon solid partnerships. And who shall I be expecting?"

"My name is Mirsky, Boris Mirsky. I so very much look forward to meeting you."

"Excellent," responded Maddington. "I shall see you in two days."

CHAPTER 14

HELMER, IDAHO

Samantha Riley had set the excavation schedule for field work to begin in the early morning. Lunch break was usually middle morning, and the crews were out of the field by two before it became too hot. An hour break period in the afternoon allowed students free time to swim or shower under primitive sun-warmed portable plastic shower bags. Alternatively, they could rest up or do whatever, until three o'clock when afternoon lab began. During lab, students processed the samples from the day, sometimes they would have presentations and occasionally a technical review of equipment instruction and use. Today they received a lecture and demonstration on processing floatation samples. While lab was going on, dinner was being cooked and served at five, after the last sample was processed and the lab tables cleaned for use as dinner tables. It took a while, but the students now worked together as a true team. They helped each other finish collection inventories, processing, whatever needed to be done before five.

Everyone was always ready for dinner by the time the last artifact bags were completed.

Dinner usually lasted about an hour. The meal was coming to an end and Riley's Department of Defense visitor had yet to show. She grinned and thought to herself that he probably got lost in the maze of logging roads.

The students were in a festive mood around the dinner tables. There seemed to be a sense that the season was coming to an end, and everyone had learned more than they had imagined possible. New best friends were made all around. A total of fourteen students had been selected and enrolled for the field school. Only a few of the students were undergraduates from Washington State University. The rest were from institutions all over the U.S., and one student was from Queensland University in Australia.

It was still three hours before sunset, but the crew looked up as they first heard and then saw a vehicle's lights bouncing and swaying back and forth through the forest on the logging road that wound through their camp. The headlights shot into the dark tree canopy and then disappeared to the ground as deep ruts guided the vehicle through a battery of obstacles. The muffler was roaring in protest as it had clearly been dislodged from the exhaust pipe. After several long minutes, the loud Subaru slowly rolled into camp and backfired as the transmission shifted out of drive and the ignition switched off.

A dark-haired man slightly over six feet tall with a mustache and two day's growth of whiskers unfolded himself from the compact Subaru. The man's face was of indeterminate age. His hair had no hint of gray but there were deep wrinkles at the corner of his eyes. He could have been twenty-six or he could have been forty-four. A lean man, he stretched his back and then stepped forward with a crooked friendly smile.

"These cars are supposed to be great off-road vehicles. I guess they work best when the terrain is flat and straight. I lost the muffler within minutes of turning into the forest."

The students around the table just stared at him and nobody responded immediately. Allen finally said, "Hello, my name is Deak Allen, and I'm looking for Dr. Samantha Riley."

"Well, Mr. Allen, better late than never. I'm Samantha Riley, and this is the Washington State University Archaeological Field Project Camp. These are my students and staff."

Beginning with her graduate assistants, she instructed each student to introduce him or herself and say what university they were from. Her senior graduate student, Jennifer Henderson, stood up and walked toward Allen with her hand outstretched.

"Hello, Mr. Allen. I'm one of Dr. Riley's Ph.D. students here at Washington State University. I specialize in lithic analysis from this region. We are just finishing up with dinner. Can I get you something?" Before he could answer, the next graduate student introduced herself and then the introductions continued.

"Wow, what a wonderful looking team of archaeologists," complimented Allen. "When I was in field school, we were so grubby and tired that any stranger coming into camp usually went in the opposite direction."

Jennifer looked at Allen, with more interest than before. "Oh, you're an archaeologist? Dr. Riley said we were receiving a visitor from the Department of Defense. You still didn't tell me whether I could get you some dinner. Are you hungry?"

Allen looked at Samantha then back to Jennifer. "Thank you very much, Jennifer, but the only thing I would like at this moment is a drink, and some time with Dr. Riley."

Jennifer spun around. "Hey, guys, let's get this dinner cleaned up," she commanded. Jennifer was also in charge of assigning camp chores among the other responsibilities she had on the project.

"Mr. Allen, why don't we sit over there. I have a couple of lawn chairs in front of my tent," said Riley. They walked over to her tent area. It was positioned close to the communal area of the camp but had a circumference of privacy that most field directors chose to build to insulate themselves from the constant commotion of camp life. "You have a distinctive name. Haven't I read something you might have written?"

"Please, call me Deak," began Allen. "I suppose you run a dry camp?"

"All dry camps have cooking and medical resources that can be called into service for special circumstances," smiled Riley. She walked the few steps to her platform-based canvas tent and returned with a bottle of Jack Daniels and two tin cups. Her athletic figure did not go unnoticed by Allen. "No ice, but we have water, if you like?" said Riley.

"You guys are really roughing it. I'll take it neat."

"So why do I recognize your name?" Riley began again.

"As a graduate student, I was joint author on a handful of papers in the journal *Science* dealing with the preserved village that was crushed in the Bering Sea ice storm in Barrow, Alaska. Perhaps that is where you've seen the name. I had a mathematics undergraduate degree, so I helped write simulations to reconstruct how the ice sheets could have been pushed up by the Bering Sea to crush the houses while everyone was sleeping."

"Oh yes, I remember now. Quite an archaeological odyssey. An entire village fully preserved in their houses. Didn't the *National Geographic* TV station run a short series on that project?" Before Allen responded, Samantha continued, "So how does a brilliant archaeology graduate student wind up with the Department of Defense?"

Allen examined her closely, and she shifted uncomfortably. Samantha turned slightly, "I'm sorry, I didn't mean to get personal."

Deak Allen responded quickly, "That's okay. Pleased by your interest. I graduated from high school at sixteen and went straight to college. After getting my mathematics degree at twenty, I found myself with a bunch of education but not many social skills, and no idea of what I really wanted to do. I was a young, lost, first-generation college graduate. I applied for OCS within a few months of graduation.

Samantha interrupted, "What's OCS?"

"Officer's Candidate School for the Army. I went through OCS and was commissioned with my first deployment in Iraq as an officer in 2005. During my second year in Iraq, my Bradley Armored Personnel Carrier hit an IED, and I spent the next seven months recovering at Walter Reed."

Samantha now looked concerned. "I'm sorry to hear of your injuries. I hope you are better now and thank you for your service."

"I finished my three years at the rank of Captain and decided to go back to graduate school, but not in mathematics.

After seeing the destruction of all that cultural heritage in Iraq, I decided to study archaeology."

Allen paused before continuing, "It was a rough job market in academia. After getting my Ph.D. I couldn't land a tenure-track position anywhere, but I was able to get a position with the U.S. Army Corps of Engineers. Not that one position is any more important than the other. I enjoyed working for the Corps. My job with them was as a cultural resource's specialist. I was stationed out of the St. Louis Corps District. They were picked to help understand how to best protect and preserve the cultural heritage in Afghanistan. They sent me because of my military background and research interests. Soon after that, the Department of Defense created the Interagency Natural, Human, and Cultural Resources Institute. The director contacted me and a handful of other folks with training in our respective areas and asked us to help build the new Institute. That was over three years ago, and I've been doing missions inside and outside of the country since then."

Riley held up the bottle, Deak nodded, and she poured another drink for both. Samantha Riley was wearing khaki pants and a tight sleeveless denim shirt. Her exposed arms were well-tanned and smooth.

Allen noticed her slender hands had short but dirty fingernails from doing her share of the field work. She was wearing two rings, one on each pinky. "If you don't mind my getting a little personal, how does an attractive young professor like you stay single?"

"I guess I put you on the spot, so I deserve the same," replied Riley. "I don't know. This academic grind just demands so much of one's life. To really excel you need to give it full-time attention and full time means everything else takes a back seat. Sometimes I wonder when life is going to begin. Then I think, this is my life and I love it. No matter what, I stay busy.

Riley, wanting to get out of the personal chat, changed the topic. "What brings you to the Northwest?"

"My job is to not only help preserve heritage sites, but to do it in such a way that new research is promoted for the benefit of all. That skeleton you helped recover for the Corps has a variety of different communities staking claims to it for all kinds of reasons. There are probably several tribal members camped out in Walla Walla right now asking to have their ancestor returned to the ground to find peace. To be honest, the age of the individual is important. The date you have determined for the time of death of this person has the potential to help us better understand human health related issues."

"I understand the indigenous claims piece. What do you mean by human health issues? Do you know something I don't? Also, I'm not sure I heard you correctly, did you say your office promotes new research? Do you fund research?"

Allen smiled again, "I think you just asked me half a dozen questions all at once. We do have a modest budget for new research but it's not proposal driven in the same way as the National Science Foundation solicits proposals. If something emerges, related to our investigations, we can pursue it by issuing fellowships and grants to researchers and institutions."

"And the human health issues?" inquired Riley.

"You must admit that a person living to be a hundred thirty-eight is quite extraordinary. Was there something about that person's diet, genetics, lifestyle, or something else that allowed that person to live such a long life?"

Riley quickly interrupted, "That age at the time of death is so controversial that it needs to be checked and verified."

"True," responded Allen. "I suspect you may have already done some of that. However, with today's new technology we can replace knees, hips, feet, pulmonary sections of hearts and a host of other organs. New genetic therapy allows us to more effectively address personal, individual health issues as they arise. What if we also find that there are external aids, such as a new drug or substance that will help extend human life? If a person living at the end of the Ice Age can live to be that old, or even a hundred and ten years old, how long will a person twenty years from now be able to live with the new technologies and the discovery of external substances? Two hundred, two hundred and forty, longer?"

"Deak, I believe you are talking fantasy stuff here."

"That may be true, Dr. Riley."

"Please call me Samantha."

"Okay, Samantha, but what was considered fantasy yesterday may be real life tomorrow. I can talk to someone on my cell phone and see them in real time when I'm sitting on a mountaintop halfway across the world. Who expected that twenty-five years ago? Your students in camp here think it's commonplace and probably have never seen an actual telephone booth before. Heck, I don't know that I've ever been inside one of them."

Allen paused. "Let's say that the average person living today has a seventy-five-year lifespan. It could be more, or it could be less, but let's say that's average. If we look at life in thirds, with the first third as infancy through young adulthood and the last third as older and aged, the middle third would be the heart of adulthood, the prime of life. At age fifty-one the person has completed over two thirds of his or her life and is living in her final third. The prime of life, if we define it that way, is over. If technology and other aids can extend the human life span to two hundred years or even one hundred sixty years, a person at fifty-one would still be in their first third of life. That person would have the entire prime of life before them, and they'd live for another hundred years or more. You have a skeleton that may help us understand that potential."

They continued their discussion covering how the skeleton had been dated, the benefits of nondestructive analysis, potential carbon isotope studies, and a variety of other topics that intersected with their relative expertise.

Riley and Allen had talked for about three hours, both enjoying each other's company.

"You certainly have a way of making an archaeological discovery sound really, really important," said Riley.

"This discovery is important, but I'm just thinking out loud with a couple of drinks under my belt. All of this is preliminary until results are confirmed and additional analyses are conducted."

Riley leaned over and picked up the bottle of bourbon. "Another?"

"I'm not sure I'll be able to find my way out of the forest here if I have another. I'm going to pass."

"We can probably scratch up another cot for you here in camp if you don't want to make the drive out."

"That sounds mighty tempting, Samantha. It's still early and I'm staying at a friend's place on the south end of Lake Coeur d'Alene about an hour from here." Allen pulled a card from his wallet. "Here is my cell number. Let's meet back in Pullman to look at those remains when you get out of the field, okay?"

"I assume your friend has dinner waiting for you?" inquired Riley.

Deak raised an eyebrow, "I said I was staying at a friend's place. He, unfortunately, is traveling and I'm all by myself." Allen stood and looked toward his Subaru.

Riley touched his arm. "Be safe out there on those roads. That muffler will attract some attention and you've had a few drinks."

Allen smiled, "It will allow me to fit right in. When will you guys be out of here?"

"Four days is the estimate right now," replied Riley.

"It would be nice to look at the collection sooner but if that's when you can make it, we can discuss a plan then. Given me a call when you're out of the field."

"You betcha," said Riley. "Wait a second. I'm heading in tomorrow morning to look at some of the results one of the graduate students is struggling with. Why don't you meet us at Woods Hall tomorrow? Can you make it in at about nine or ten in the morning? I can show you the remains, some of the other materials recovered, and we can brainstorm on how this guy lived so long?"

"That sounds like a great plan. The more detail I have on this project, the better I'll feel about any recommendations. I'll be there a little after nine, if that works?" said Allen.

"That works."

He walked over to the Subaru, got in, and turned the key. The muffler immediately exploded to life, making sure everyone was still awake. Allen backed into a small turn around and bounced the vehicle through the timber. Everyone in camp could hear him for the next five minutes as he slowly made turns and switchbacks along the narrow lumber road.

CHAPTER 15

Camp breakfast was self-serve, a la cart, and cold with hot coffee or tea. During breakfast the students also made field lunches for themselves and deposited them into the lunch cooler. The crew was ready to move from camp to the excavation units just after daybreak. Immediately after breakfast, the three graduate students gathered at Riley's tent to quickly go through any last-minute assignment changes, as they did every morning.

Riley informed them that she had to return to Pullman for a day or two to deal with some issues that had come up with the Central Ferry burial. "David, that floatation lecture and demonstration went well yesterday. Do you want me to bring some drying racks back when I return?" asked Riley.

"That would be great. Grab another set of nested sieves, too. It would help speed the processing. Jen and I've been talking about timing as we approach the end here. We think it might be productive to transition half the students to processing the float samples during lab."

"That's probably the best strategy given that we are encountering sterile levels in many of the excavation units. I don't want to start too many new units. The floatation processing now would also save weeks of lab work in the coming fall semester."

Jennifer and Katie gave Riley calculating smiles. "What's with you two?"

"You didn't tell us the Department of Defense was sending a hunk into camp," teased Katie.

"You two seemed to find a whole lot to talk about last night. We were surprised to see him leave so early. It looked pretty cozy over here," added Jennifer.

DeRue stood back and didn't say a word but couldn't wipe the grin off his face.

There was an atmosphere of raillery among Riley's graduate students. Riley was not only a mentor to her three graduate students, but also a friend. Privately, they were all on a first name basis, but deferred to formal names and titles in public. Now she feigned a look of hurt. "What? Am I not allowed to share a drink over academic conversation after hours?"

The three just smiled at her. Finally, Jennifer suggested, "Academic conversation? Okay. I bet you two have plans to meet again to discuss free radicals and other chemical attractions. We saw you exchange contact information."

"Get moving, you guys," Riley raised her voice in a play of authority. She knew her graduate students must have approved of her visit with Allen, or they wouldn't have mentioned it. "Let's get a start on the day."

The crew mobilized, some walking, others driving from the camp to the excavation area. Riley found her day pack and tossed it into the truck she regularly used to commute to and from the Helmer location. She wanted to make this a quick trip to Pullman so she could get back and close operations on the field project.

Riley savored driving. Over the years, she mastered everything from her high school convertible Karmann Ghia, to off-road 4-wheelers, to bulky one-ton pickup trucks. Coming from North Dakota she could drive in snow and slick conditions. During her years jumping from one field project to the next, she was often given the task of driving vehicles because of her expertise.

This morning, she needed to make time, conduct her business in Pullman and get back to the field camp as soon as possible with the floatation gear. She started the pickup and pulled out of camp. Riley tried to maintain a speed about five miles per hour over the posted speed limit on paved roads, and as fast as she safely could on gravel roads. She was driving faster than most but was alert for any dangers as she sped along in the early morning light. It was approximately an hour and a half drive from the site near Helmer to Pullman. Because fieldwork started at dawn, Riley had an early start. There was no traffic on the road, and she made good time. It was just before eight in the morning when she set the parking brake on the vehicle behind Woods Hall and stepped toward the back building entrance.

CHAPTER 16

PULLMAN, WASHINGTON

Every time Riley returned from a field project and walked into her lab, it felt like she was home. She was familiar with the position and location of every piece of instrumentation. She knew where to reach when tools or supplies were needed. Riley had an intimate affinity with her working space.

She flipped on the overhead lights as she passed through the isotope area into her forensic space, again flipping on more light. Claire wasn't in yet but had left a short report and a pile of notes on their conference table, so Riley began scouring over the information.

Claire walked in a few minutes before nine. "Boy, am I glad to see you, Dr. Riley."

"Yes, these results are complicated," replied Riley.

"That's not at all what I'm getting at," responded Claire. "Professor Maddington was in here yesterday and yelled at me to give him access to the vault so he could examine the burial remains."

"What? Maddington doesn't know anything about human remains and has no right to demand access to anything in this lab," said Riley.

"I told him you had the key. I didn't tell him we have backup keys," confessed Claire. "I didn't lie to him. I just didn't explain where we keep our key inventory."

"You did right, Claire. From now on, if he should approach you about this lab, tell him that I have instructed you to defer all access to me. In the meantime, I'll call him and find out what he thinks he's doing."

There was a knock on the lab door. Both Claire and Samantha turned. "Is this the right place?" asked Deak Allen.

"Hey, Deak, glad you could make it," said Riley. "This is my graduate student, Claire Anderson. She is working on the human remains from the Central Ferry project. Claire, this is Dr. Deak Allen from the Interagency Institute in Washington, D.C. He is here to…I'll let you explain. What are you here for, Deak?"

"It is a pleasure to meet you, Claire," responded Allen. "Please call me Deak. I'm here to promote new research and scholarship on government affiliated projects and to head off any potential political misunderstandings."

Riley looked over at Claire with a friendly smirk. "He is essentially calling the shots for the government on our remains."

Allen quickly responded, "That's not exactly true. I am more of an advisor to various agency personnel when it comes to natural and human resources that might get impacted by government undertakings."

"So, let's have a look at the remains," suggested Riley.

Claire opened a drawer in her desk, extracted some keys, and briefly dangled them knowingly in front of Riley. She walked over to the vault door, unlocked it and went in. "I'll pull the box and put it in the sorting area."

Riley nodded to Allen. "We call this the vault. It is climate controlled, with shelving units that slide together to eliminate aisles. More efficient storage. Most curators call these compactor rooms."

"I've seen these before," replied Allen. "Do they compact manually or are they electronic?"

"These are manual. But, like the electronic version, the aisles won't compact if the floor sensors register weight between the aisles. The entire vault is alarmed and has motion activated video cameras."

Claire called from the vault. "I've laid them out in here. Come and have a look."

They all put on surgical gloves and facemasks and gathered around the sorting table. "Pretty amazing preservation for someone buried directly in the ground thirteen thousand years ago," said Allen. "Also, no signs of osteoporosis."

Riley glanced over at Allen. "I didn't know you dabbled in osteological analysis?"

"Unfortunately, I've seen quite a few human remains in my time. This guy looks unusually healthy for a one hundred thirty-eight-year-old. How did you determine age a time of death, again?"

"We used a slightly modified version of the Osteon Lamellae technique."

"Wait a minute," inquired Allen. "That technique requires thin sections on transparent slides. I don't see any cut marks."

"No. We used high resolution MRI," corrected Riley. "It is a modification of the technique my advisor developed decades ago." She peered at Allen again with a questioning look. "So…you have some experience with forensics, too?"

"I have to be a pretty broad generalist in my line of work. I leave it to you guys to do the real science," said Allen.

"Maybe you can tell us why we are getting oxygen isotope signatures that say this guy wasn't drinking his local water. Instead, there's a match for the water signature in the St. Joe and St. Maries River drainages in North Idaho," asked Riley.

"Can I have a look at the oxygen ratio printouts?"

"Sure," said Riley.

Claire had anticipated Samantha's request and had already brought the printouts over. She handed them to Dr. Riley, who remarked, "It's okay, we can share whatever we have with Dr. Allen."

"Here you go," said Claire, and handed the file to Allen. "There seems to be quite a bit of deviation between counts. I can't explain that, but I believe that's because we were using laser ablation to get the chemical signatures. Our standard technique would require crushing bone samples and running them through chemical washes for cleaning."

"That makes sense," responded Allen. He studied the pages, flipping them back and forth as if checking numbers. "So how about this," began Allen. "Our ancient man lived in North Idaho and was visiting friends on the Snake River when he died. Or he lived part of the year in North Idaho and part of the year on the Snake River."

Claire spoke up, "If we rule out the first scenario in favor of the second, this guy would have had to bring water with him from North Idaho to drink for the entire time he was living on the Snake River to get an oxygen isotope signature like this."

Riley broke in, "Or he would have had to bring food to the Snake River grown or raised in North Idaho. And we know during the end of the Ice Age there was no domestication of either plants or animals."

"The food wouldn't have to be domesticated," stated Allen. "It only must have been nurtured from the waters of the St. Joe or St. Maries Rivers. It could have been wild plants or animals."

"None of this makes much sense, because the food would have had to be continually available while living on the Snake River and we have never found evidence of food storage here or any place else in the world this early," mused Riley.

"I wouldn't doubt the possibility of storage just because the majority of archaeologists believe storage is a relatively recent invention," said Allen. "Our profession is filled with assumptions that have turned out to be wrong. Look at how well these bones have been preserved after being in the ground for over twelve millennia. Why couldn't people have preserved food for a few months in the same climate? Now, what kind of food would he have eaten if he were getting a supply of food from North Idaho?"

"I looked at some of the other isotope data to drill down on diet a little bit," offered Claire. "Most aboriginal people in the interior Northwest have a salmon or anadromous fish diet signature. This guy was not eating salmon."

"Interesting," mumbled Allen. "This guy was living or at least buried on the Snake River, and he wasn't eating anadromous fish?"

Riley commented, “It was thirteen thousand years ago and, so far, we have no evidence salmonids were around on the Snake at that time. No salmon bones have been found in archaeological or geological samples before about ten thousand years ago on the Snake. So, it may fit.”

Claire continued, “He did have some CAM plants in the carbon isotope signature. But that is probably a mistake. This wasn’t a time we would expect to see cactus and succulent plants in the region.”

“That wouldn’t be my first expectation either,” offered Riley. “But we are talking about the end of the Ice Age here, rapid global climate change. Thousands of animal species died out in just a few centuries, and some even became extinct over a few decades. That change was probably even more accelerated with the flora. I would not be surprised to find floral retreat and replacement over the region even after a few years. I wouldn’t write off CAM plants in the diet right yet. What else turned up?”

“As I mentioned on the phone, he was a big consumer of complex carbohydrates,” said Claire.

“Hey, that might work for the North Idaho connection,” offered Allen. “Wasn’t camas root a primary food resource for people in this area? Camas roots are one of the best sources of complex carbs you can find. If he lived in that area for part of the year and collected camas for storage on the Snake, that would give him close to twelve months a year with North Idaho water and food consumption.”

“Okay, I’ll buy this as a long shot theory. But how does this get him to the ripe old age of one hundred thirty-eight?” asked Riley. “People have been eating camas as a staple for a long time in this region and they don't live even half this old."

Deak smiled with a twinkle in his eyes. "Clearly, this guy exercised, and, by any definition, he conformed to a strict paleo diet."

Claire chuckled. "Paleo diet and exercise. We better not even joke about that. If something like that got out, it would sweep the nation faster than influenza."

"Listen, I'm going to have to go back to the field to help shut the camp down," informed Riley. "I think it would be most efficient if I went back today before dark. Claire, I'd like you to run some nitrogen and strontium isotope scans. I don't suppose you've had enough time to recount the MRI slide images since we last talked?" Claire shook her head, confirming what her professor already speculated.

"Deak, I can show you the rest of the collection we recovered from Central Ferry before I leave."

"I'd like to see everything that was recovered, including any artifact and sediment samples. I also need to find some time to finish a report from my last assignment. Since I'm going to be around, I can help Claire recalculate the ratios from the MRI images."

Riley gave him a look of approval. "Boy, if you're going to volunteer in the lab, Deak, you can crash at my house instead of driving back to the lake. You'll have plenty of space and privacy to finish your report. I probably won't be back in Pullman for another couple of days."

"That would be great. I'll take you up on that offer. I might try to switch cars with the rental company while I'm here, as well. You'd think I was riding a camel down the street the way people have been staring at me and my detached muffler."

After reviewing the remainder of the collection, Riley gave Allen her home address and told him the backdoor key was under a potted tomato plant on the back deck. She also gave him her internet password. "I'll probably be back in two to four days, depending on how much work the team has completed," she said. "If you're still around then, I'll cook dinner."

Allen accepted happily. "Only if I bring the wine."

"Okay, then. See you in a few days or so," said Riley, as she grabbed her backpack and headed for the door.

Allen helped Claire in the lab for the remainder of the day. The MRI counts were checked and rechecked. Their review produced the same age at time of death for the Ice Age skeleton. After the last run, Allen leaned back in his chair and stretched. "I don't think I can make another count with these MRI slides. The only way we are going to get a different age at time of death is if we have some new MRI slides made and that still may produce the same age. My eyes are pretty much shot. This counting is grueling. I'm going to call it a day."

Claire looked up with a nervous smile. "Don't go yet, Dr. Allen. I'll pack up the materials and lock the vault, then walk out with you. Would that be, okay?"

Allen gave her a serious look. "You look concerned about something, Claire. What is it?"

"There's this guy, another faculty member, Professor Maddington, who has been trying to get access to the collection. He's creepy, and I don't want to be here alone in the lab this late. He was nasty to me the last time he came in," confessed Claire.

"I'll stay here with you as long as you need," said Allen.

Claire secured the files and shut down the computer station. She boxed up the bone samples and shelved them in the active area of the compactor. She gathered her personal belongings and then checked to make sure the vault door was locked. Claire turned to Allen and nodded toward the door. They walked out together, and she locked the lab door behind them. As they passed Maddington's office, Claire noticed that the door was open but didn't see anyone inside. Allen followed her glance and murmured, "This the guy's office?"

Claire nodded her head without saying a word and kept walking. When they were outside the building Allen asked, "Can I give you a lift? My car is over in that direction."

Claire replied, "No, I'm good. Thanks for walking me out."

"My pleasure," said Allen, as he headed to his car.

Allen stopped and grabbed a few things for dinner and breakfast, then tapped in Riley's address and let the phone guide him to her house.

CHAPTER 17

SPOKANE, WASHINGTON

Spokane, Washington, is but one of hundreds of prosaic U.S. cities in the middle to small size range. The city has a population of just under 230,000 residents, while the metropolitan area has a population of less than a million. The Spokane River winds through the downtown area. In the middle of the city the river drops and tumbles into the thunderous Spokane Falls. Though it is unremarkable in size from a nationwide perspective, Spokane is the largest city in the northern tier of the U.S. between Seattle and Minneapolis.

Boris Mirsky was somewhat familiar with this inland Northwest city. Spokane was home to a relatively large population of Russian and Ukrainian immigrants. He had visited Spokane several times over the years when making inspections of the Utkin Chemicals facility. More importantly, his visits were associated with efforts to establish a network of "Russian Mafia" drug traffickers.

He landed in Spokane on a corporate jet with his assistant, Pasha. Flying commercially would have made smuggling the skeletal remains out of the United States almost impossible. Two local contacts met him at the terminal and walked him to a pair of white SUVs that would take him to Moscow, Idaho, for his dinner meeting. Mirsky and Pasha got into the back seat of the lead SUV. Both escorts were from Kharkiv, Ukraine, and had been assigned to Spokane as part of their rotation with Utkin Chemicals. The taller of the two escorts, Alexander, slipped behind the wheel and the second man, Nick, drove the trailing vehicle.

Once in the car, Alexander reached over and handed Mirsky a small athletic bag. Mirsky took the bag and casually unzipped it, knowing the contents. The top of the bag was covered with bound hundred-dollar bills. Mirsky counted ten bundles. Next, he noted the 40 caliber Glock. Mirsky picked up the Glock and pressed the clip release. He checked the cylinder and returned the full clip to the pistol grip. He located the silencer in the bottom of the bag, along with a full second clip. There was also a two-page report. After he carefully examined the biographical sketch of Peter Maddington with an attached photograph taken from the Internet, he handed the bag to Pasha.

Mirsky greatly enjoyed working with academics, most recently Kozlov and Rackerman. He felt most academics lived in an insulated world and were easy to predict. He firmly believed that most academics didn't really care about increasing knowledge, but primarily wanted recognition as the source of that knowledge.

"Pasha, remember what I told you about academics: half want recognition for their brilliance and half aren't paid well. Peter Maddington appears to fit into both those categories," noted Mirsky as he finished looking over the file.

"This should be a quick operation," continued Mirsky. "We will buy Maddington's services and he will believe he is in charge of the research."

"How long do you believe we will be away from Spokane?" asked Alexander, the driver.

"Just make sure we have hotel rooms for two days and be ready to drive us where we need to go," responded Mirsky. "Who put together the report on Maddington?"

"Nick hired a couple of computer techs. We call them our R&D division," replied Alexander. "They track our orders, do background checks, and pull information from the Internet as needed."

"You and Nick appear to know what you are doing."

"We have been here for almost a year now. It is easier than when we started," replied Alexander.

CHAPTER 18

MOSCOW, IDAHO

The drive from the Spokane airport to Moscow was an uneventful two-hour trip. Mirsky sat in the SUV waiting for the signal to enter the restaurant. He busied himself going over materials on his laptop. Pasha interrupted, "He's here."

Nick stood across the street from the Red Window and now motioned affirmatively to the car. The signal meant Maddington was in the restaurant waiting.

Maddington had entered the restaurant and was seated alone at a table along the back wall. "Excellent," said Mirsky. "Let's give him another ten minutes to ponder his situation and then go meet him."

While he waited, Maddington scrolled through his telephone, reading and listening to messages. He had just read the message from Samantha Riley informing him that if he wanted access to the storage room in the isotope lab, he should speak to her directly and not make demands of her students. Maddington's face reddened and he slapped the table, "I'll teach her a lesson when she comes up for tenure next year."

Mirsky entered the restaurant and walked straight over to Maddington's table with both hands outstretched. "You must be Professor Maddington," said Mirsky. "I recognized you from the pictures I've seen of you on the Internet associated with your extraordinary scholarship. What a pleasure it is to meet someone of such world-famous repute. My company is eager to collaborate with the best and brightest. I am Boris Mirsky."

Maddington was radiant as he took Mirsky's hand and shook with a healthy grip. "You're too kind. It is a pleasure to make your acquaintance."

The two men ordered drinks and dinner. "So, Professor," asked Mirsky, "did you recover an entire skeleton with this unusual age? I have heard rumors, but I would like to know from you how old the person was at the time of death."

Maddington smiled a little nervously, "What have you heard about the skeleton?"

"Not much," replied Mirsky, "only that it was very old and that you were the person I should contact to begin a collaboration. Was the skeleton complete or do you only have a few bones?"

"What kind of collaboration are you thinking about, Boris? Do you mind if I call you Boris?" asked Maddington.

"Not at all. My company has authorized me to hire you to help with the skeletal investigation at our facility in Vladivostok. We have all the equipment needed for first-class archaeological research," replied Mirsky. "Provided, of course, that I gather enough basic information about the skeleton tonight to determine if it is worth our effort to make an investment. So, tell me how old the skeleton was at the time of death and if the skeleton was complete or not."

Maddington began to wish he had read Samantha Riley's emailed report more closely. "We have only conducted preliminary analyses, but it seems the skeleton was a hundred thirty-eight years old at the time of death. We believe it lived during the end of Pleistocene roughly thirteen thousand years ago." Maddington paused, thought for a moment, and then continued, "Most of the skeleton was recovered, but it has yet to be fully rearticulated, so it would be premature on my part to say we have a complete skeleton," answered Maddington.

The waiter arrived with dinner. "Can't you see we are out of wine. Bring another bottle and be quick about it," instructed Maddington.

The men toasted and began eating. "This is excellent news," said Mirsky. "We will need to transport the skeleton to Vladivostok as soon as possible to begin the analysis. When can you bring the skeleton?" asked Mirsky.

"Like I mentioned earlier, Boris, we are still conducting some preliminary analyses on the skeleton. It may take a few more days before I can get it ready for transport. Besides, we may also have to go through a complicated permitting process to move it out of the country. These things take time, you know," said Maddington.

"My company can do whatever preliminary analyses you are currently conducting, and we can expedite any paperwork since we are currently working with several institutions on burial materials similar to the one you have," replied Mirsky. "All you must do is turn the skeleton over to me and I'll handle the paperwork. I know you have a busy schedule, but we can fly you over whenever you are ready to participate."

"That all sounds very efficient but I'm not sure I can just hand over the skeleton without some kind of formal agreement with your company. How do I know that my institution will be compensated appropriately for our discovery?" asked Maddington.

Mirsky reached into his coat pocket and extracted a large expandable envelope and put it on the table. "This is an advance to cover your expenses for cancelling the analyses by whatever lab you are currently working with. We can perform whatever analyses you wish at our facilities in Vladivostok. Perhaps we can meet at your lab tomorrow to view the skeleton and arrange for transport?" suggested Mirsky.

Maddington unfolded the envelope flap to find four bundles of hundred-dollar bills wrapped in thick stacks. Maddington quickly closed the envelope and looked up at Mirsky, laying the package back on the table, but close to his plate. "I have an engagement tomorrow, but how about meeting the day after to look at the skeleton?" suggested Maddington. "I'll call you or leave a message tomorrow, to let you know where to meet."

"Professor Maddington, let me be clear. That is a down payment for the transfer of the skeleton to my company for analysis with you as a contributor. I would like to take possession of the skeleton no later than two days from now when we meet. When I take possession of the skeleton, we will begin all the needed permitting and paperwork to make the transfer completely unproblematic for you and your institution. Is that understood?"

"Of course. Of course," replied Maddington. "When you say down payment, what exactly does that mean?"

Mirsky smiled at Maddington. "One third now, two thirds when I take delivery."

Peter Maddington smiled back and scooped the envelope off the table stuffing it into his briefcase. "One quarter now, three quarters when I make delivery." Maddington quickly held out his hand to seal the deal.

Mirsky looked thoughtfully at Maddington, wondering if he had underestimated this particular academic. Then he reached over and took Maddington's hand and announced, "We have a deal. I will be waiting for your call tomorrow."

Mirsky stood up and started to leave. Maddington stopped him, "We haven't finished dinner yet."

Mirsky dropped three large bills on the table and looked at Maddington. "Like I said, Mr. Maddington, I'll be waiting for your telephone call." He turned and walked out of the restaurant.

Mirsky crossed the street and walked down a block to the car. The back door was opened, and he slipped in. Alexander and Pasha were in the front. Mirsky snorted, "I don't trust that bastard. Alexander, have Nick start following Maddington. He's up to something. Call your R&D team in Spokane and have them gather more information on this skeleton at Washington State University. Get me more background on Maddington, too. Something is not right. Where's the hotel?"

"The University Inn a few miles from here," replied Alexander. "You ready to go?"

"Let's wait for the pig to finish his dessert and follow him so we know exactly where he lives. Like I said, I don't trust him," replied Mirsky.

CHAPTER 19

PULLMAN, WASHINGTON

Maddington had put himself in a difficult situation, promising the human remains he did not possess. However, he had devised a plan and was confident he could acquire and deliver the skeletal materials. Like an annoying meddlesome neighbor monitoring the traffic on his block, Maddington had been checking the activity of the isotope lab all afternoon, waiting for Claire Anderson to leave. He walked by the lab about three in the afternoon and noticed Anderson working in the lab with a man he did not recognize. He walked by again about an hour later and noticed the lights were off and everyone had gone for the day. He checked his watch and decided to wait another five minutes before putting his plan into action. At 4:45 p.m. Maddington entered the main department office with his usual air of authority and informed Joe he needed the pass key. "I have inadvertently let my office door swing shut with my briefcase and keys inside," explained Maddington.

"I can walk up with you to unlock your office door, if you wish," said Joe. "We are just about ready to close the office."

"No need for that," announced Maddington. "I'll just be a minute or two and I'll come right down with the key." There was a sign out protocol for the pass key, but most faculty didn't follow the procedure if they were going to use the key for a minute to gain access to their office or lab. Joe handed Maddington the pass key, which was attached to a large wooden paddle painted bright orange so it wouldn't get lost or accidentally put into a pocket or purse.

"Dr. Maddington, I have an important appointment at five-thirty. I would like to have the office locked up at five sharp," said Joe.

Maddington raised his head slightly and looked down his nose at Joe. He could really care less about Joe's appointments or schedules. "Did you not understand what I said? I thought I was perfectly clear about returning the key," responded Maddington. He turned and strolled out of the office.

Uncharacteristically, Maddington took the stairs to the second floor. He walked past his office and down the hallway to the isotope lab. He examined the lab through the window, making sure nobody was inside, then unlocked the lab door, reached in, and turned the lock handle to keep the door unlocked, then quickly hastened back to the stairway and down to the main office. Maddington stepped in, handed Joe the pass key, and walked out without a word. He went back up to his office, collected some personal materials and then left the building.

Maddington returned to Woods Hall that evening about seven-thirty struggling with a heavy duffle bag and made a path straight to his office. He stood in his office, waiting and listening for any activity in the building. Hearing nothing, he stepped out of his office with the duffel bag. As quickly and as quietly as he was able, Maddington barreled down the hallway, turned and looked around, then stopped at the isotope lab door. He examined the inside of the lab through the window and, satisfied nobody was around, turned the knob and entered. Maddington unzipped the duffle bag, pulled on a headlamp, and turned it on to avoid the overhead lights. He found a pair of latex gloves and pulled them clumsily on. He rustled within the duffle, moving wrenches, a battery-operated drill and other assorted tools. Finally, he extracted a large handheld angle grinder with an attached extension cord and walked over to the compactor door. After plugging in the extension cord, Maddington attempted to insert the grinder blade between the steel door frame and the wooden door above the latch plate. The blade was just a millimeter or two thicker than the gap between the door frame and the latch plate. Maddington frowned and mumbled incoherently. He pulled a thinner blade from the duffle bag and tested to make sure it fit between the door frame and latch plate. Beads of sweat were now trickling down the sides of his face and into his eyes, as he clumsily attempted to loosen the locknut on the grinder blade. He kept dropping the wrench and it clattered noisily each time it fell. The physical activity combined with his anxiety were more than he was accustomed to. He was finally able to remove the grinder blade and inserted the new blade over the mounting spool, but again fiddled with the locking nut and wrench. In another five minutes, he had the blade seated and was ready to cut the door latch.

Before he pressed the starter switch, he heard people outside speaking loudly in the stairwell. This isn't going to work, he thought to himself. I should come back after midnight to do this, so I won't be interrupted. He put the grinder and other materials hastily back in the duffle bag and walked to the lab door and stopped to listen. There were clearly people coming up the stairway and more than likely heading to the isotope lab. He turned the lock on the door, stepped into the hallway, and closed the door behind him. As the lab door clicked shut into the locked position, he heard the stairway door open, and slam closed from around the corner.

Maddington stepped away from the lab door and headed in the direction of his office but stopped. The voices were coming toward him. He suddenly realized he still had the headlamp on, and he was also wearing the latex gloves. Maddington tore off one glove and accidentally dropped it as three people came around the corner. He grabbed for his headlamp as he stooped to pick up the glove. Maddington stood up to see Claire Anderson and two other students.

The students stopped talking as they watched Maddington flounder with removing his second latex glove while holding a flashing headlamp in one hand and a large duffle bag in the elbow of his other arm. Maddington was attempting to walk as he fussed with his equipment, all the while perspiration dripping from his face. It was an asinine performance.

"Hello, Dr. Maddington," said Claire Anderson as they approached. "Can I help you? Do you need some help?"

Maddington stopped walking. He glared at the three students without saying a word and then trudging down the hallway and quickly entered his office to calm down and collect his thoughts. Fortunately, he had locked the isotope lab door because Riley's students would know something was amiss if the door was unlocked. Of course, this also meant he couldn't get back into the lab later that night. He'd have to repeat the pass key ruse with Joe again tomorrow. Maddington had no choice but to call it a night.

CHAPTER 20

The house was dark as usual when Peter Maddington pulled his Ford Taurus into the driveway. His wife had left him ten years before in a heated divorce. Maddington literally dropped the duffel bag in the garage and carried his briefcase into the house through the kitchen door and laid it on the counter. He turned on the light and immediately noticed an open bottle of tonic water and a sliced lime on the table. "Who's here?" he called out.

A light flicked on in the living room and he heard the voice of Boris Mirsky. "You don't mind if I made myself a drink, do you, Peter? You don't mind me calling you Peter, do you? After all, we are now partners."

"How did you get in here?" demanded Maddington.

Mirsky walked into the kitchen. "That is inconsequential in the larger picture of things, is it not, Peter? I waited all day for your phone call, but you never called me. I thought perhaps you had forgotten that we had a deal. Was I wrong, Peter?"

"I was just getting ready to call you," lied Maddington. "It has taken me all day to get the skeletal remains packed up and ready for transport." Maddington could hear someone else in the living room and rubbernecked in that direction. "Is someone else here?"

"Some of my associates are here as well," said Mirsky. A tall man holding a vodka tonic stepped into the light. Maddington could see a third man lingering in the background. "You were saying something about getting the skeleton ready for transport, Peter? Is it ready for me to take delivery?" asked Mirsky.

"Not yet," replied a shaken Maddington. "We agreed that the delivery would be tomorrow. I'll have the remains ready for you tomorrow as we agreed."

"We also agreed that you would call me today to let me know where to meet you with the remains, but you never called. Where shall we meet tomorrow to transfer the remains?" As he spoke, the tall man walked to the kitchen behind Maddington and stood in the doorway. "Since we are all here, why don't we make the transfer now?" prodded Mirsky.

"We can't! I don't have them with me."

"Why don't we go and get them, then? This is a small town. They certainly can't be that far away."

Maddington rapidly pondered his dilemma. "The skeletal remains are strictly curated in a vault room that is only accessible by a timed locking mechanism. It is impossible to access the vault after hours," lied Maddington. "We will have to wait until tomorrow during normal work hours."

"Do you even know where the remains are?"

"Of course, I do!" exclaimed Maddington.

He attempted to change tactics. "These remains may be very, very valuable to the right person. They are much more valuable than the little amount that you tried to get me to accept for them. The information those bones hold may be worth millions and millions."

"But, Peter, what about our deal? You have already taken the down payment. Remember, one quarter now, three quarters after delivery." Mirsky looked over at the man standing behind Maddington and nodded his head slightly. As Maddington began to respond, Alexander delivered a powerful punch directly in the solar plexus, causing him to gasp for breath and double over in pain. His glasses flew off as he bent over. Alexander shoved him into a kitchen chair and Nick sauntered into the room with a nylon rope and secured him to the chair.

"You were about to say something, Peter. I didn't catch it," sniggered Mirsky. Maddington clamped his mouth shut and glared at Mirsky and his thugs. "Take his shoes off and tape his feet to the chair legs." Maddington tried to struggle when Nick started to pull his shoes off but quickly went limp after a sharp slap to the side of his head.

Mirsky held up a report and flipped through its pages. "Peter, there is something I don't understand. Maybe you can help me. How can you have excavated the skeleton when this report says that Dr. Riley excavated the skeleton?" Mirsky laid the three-page document on the kitchen table. "Why does the report say Dr. Riley is conducting the analysis when you told me it was you doing the analysis? Is it possible I am reading the report incorrectly? You haven't been telling me the truth, Peter."

Maddington scowled at Mirsky and remained mute. Mirsky motioned to Nick, who left, went into the garage and began noisily rustling through drawers. Nick returned with a two-pound ball peen hammer that he was slapping into the palm of his hand.

"Listen to me, Peter. I need you to talk to me. When I ask you a question, I need an immediate and truthful response. If you choose to not respond, or if I don't believe you, Nick will crush one of your toes. When all your toes have been crushed and we still have questions that need answers, we'll work on other body parts. You understand what I'm saying, Peter?"

Maddington just glared at Mirsky. Before another word was uttered, Nick slammed the hammer on Maddington's little toe and pulverized it. Maddington screamed in agony and Mirsky shoved one of his socks into Maddington's mouth. "Now listen to me, Peter. Are you listening?" Maddington nodded his head through the throbbing pain.

"That's better, Peter," said Mirsky. He reached over and pulled the sock from Maddington's mouth. "Where can I find this Dr. Riley?"

"She is currently out in the field working at another archaeological site," responded Maddington as quickly as he possibly could.

"Where is this site?"

Maddington paused, thinking, then quickly said, "Wait, wait! I have a map with the site location in my briefcase." Mirsky nodded to Alexander, he walked over and popped open the briefcase and found a photocopied map and handled it to Mirsky.

"Is this the map showing the location of Dr. Riley's work?"

"Yes," responded Maddington.

Mirsky pointed at the map. "Is this the specific location?"

Again, Maddington nodded affirmatively.

"Where is the skeleton?" asked Mirsky.

Maddington thought and replied, "I don't know." Nick slammed the hammer down again and crushed the next toe. Maddington screamed out again, and Mirsky repositioned the sock.

"The pain of your other toes will pale in comparison to the agony you'll feel when the bones in your big toe are crushed." He pulled the sock out of Maddington's mouth and repeated his question, "Where is the skeleton?"

"It's in Dr. Riley's laboratory storage vault in Woods Hall," cried Maddington.

"Why don't we go and get the skeleton right now, Peter?"

Maddington quickly blurted out, "It is locked in the vault room and only Dr. Riley has the key. She may have the key on her person, or she may store it at her home. I don't know where she keeps it. She must return the remains to the government agency soon."

"So, there is no timed lock," inquired Mirsky.

Maddington just shook his head.

Mirsky looked at Maddington with a surprised expression. "Another organization owns the skeleton?"

"It was found on Army Corps property, so it has to be returned to them," responded Maddington.

"Who is the contact person at the other organization?" asked Mirsky.

Maddington was afraid of his answer, but said, "I don't know. You have to believe me. I don't know anyone at the Army Corps."

"What kind of analysis is Dr. Riley conducting?" asked Mirsky.

"She is a forensic archaeologist with an advanced degree in biochemistry. She knows how to figure out everything from the bones. She can determine what the person ate, how he died, almost anything," explained Maddington.

"Are you not able to do these things?" asked Mirsky.

Maddington shook his head. "No."

"I see," said Mirsky. "Tell me, why should I have hired you as an expert consultant when you have no expertise in these matters?" Maddington paused for a second and Nick immediately slammed the hammer down again and Maddington's screamed through a mouth full of fabric. After a minute Mirsky pulled the sock out and said, "Answer my question."

"I did it for the money. I saw an opportunity to get rich from the skeleton, so I took credit for it. I really don't know anything about human osteology or forensic work. Dr. Riley did the excavation, and she is probably one of the leading authorities in this kind of analysis," confessed Maddington.

Mirsky stared down at Maddington with disgust. "Now it appears we are going to have to work with Dr. Riley to make sure we learn all we can about the skeleton. Isn't that right, Peter?"

Maddington began to nod his head, but Mirsky held up a finger to stop him. "That was, how do you say it…a rhetorical question," grinned Mirsky.

Mirsky strolled around the room in thought. He looked over at Alexander. "We need to find the key, perhaps at Dr. Riley's residence. He will give us the address. Then we will need to have Dr. Riley explain her analysis to us. I need to make a call from the hotel. You and Nick stay here until I contact you."

He looked at Maddington. "We have a few more…non-rhetorical questions for you. I trust I can count on you to tell the truth when asked?" smirked Mirsky.

CHAPTER 21

VARNA, BULGARIA

The city of Varna is situated on the Bulgarian coast of the Black Sea. Considered a seaside resort and playground for the wealthy, it is also a major economic, social and cultural center dating back over 5,000 years. One of the city's claims is the Varna Necropolis, with over three hundred known burials and the recovery of thousands of gold artifacts. It is the oldest archaeological site ever found in the world with treasures of solid gold. The ancient and modern city is famous for its architecture, museums, and educational institutions. However, the city is even more famous for its twenty miles of white sand beaches and its natural hot springs, which feed soothing and healing water into pools and baths along the waterfront.

Varna is also a mysterious city. Every century or two for thousands of years Varna was invaded and altered. The city reveals traces of each captor in its architecture, languages, and people. The outward appearance of celebration and waggishness hint of inward mystery.

Nicolai Utkin was on his private yacht, a favorite hobby of Russian oligarchs. The more than three hundred plus foot yacht was not the largest but it was among the most elegant. It was moored on a private pier in the center of the nightclub district along Varna's inner harbor. The beach resort city with its bar-lined waterfront promenade was his favorite destination. Utkin's boat, the *Krasivaya Ptitsa*, was always fully manned with crew, cooks, servants, and security, but his top priority was to generously stock the yacht with young beautiful, mostly scantily clad, girls.

Utkin and his guests were on the top deck near the swimming pool level. The guests were mostly business associates or friends of associates. Utkin neither met nor talked to any of the business cliental. Most were invited and received by his lieutenants. Food was being served and cocktail hour was in full swing. The chefs and food staff had rolled portable cooking stations under the covered area adjacent the pool. The bar had flowed all day, stocked with everything from beer and wine to rare Russian spirits such as starka and samogon. The food ranged from hearty hors d'oeuvre to stogania, pirozhki, sevruga and ostetra caviars. The choices were virtually endless.

Reclining by the upper deck pool, Utkin answered the call immediately when he glanced at the caller identification. He shooed away the two women lounging on either side. "Boris, I have been waiting for your report."

"Nicolai, I have discovered that the American professor, Maddington, is a liar who took credit for the skeleton discovery, but knows nothing about the research protocol we need," said Mirsky.

The lines on Utkin's forehead deepened as he listened to this less than good news. "What do you mean he took credit for the discovery? Is there someone else?" he demanded.

"Another faculty member here, a Samantha Riley, is the one who discovered the skeleton and is conducting the analysis," explained Mirsky.

Utkin had always been a "hands-on" boss who ran his organization. That practice had gradually declined over the years as he acquired trustworthy lieutenants. However, the Centurion Project required his full engagement. "We need that skeleton. It may hold the secret we have been searching for. It also appears from my conversations with Kozlov that the analysis can be very complicated and time-consuming. We need someone with the ability to guide the research," stated Utkin.

Utkin paused, "I have questioned Kozlov closely. He and his American colleague, Rackerman, speculate that Ice Age people may have had a slightly different gene that allowed them to withstand extremely cold conditions. One of the other effects of that gene might have been longer life. Neither Kozlov nor anyone else on our team have the appropriate training or expertise to guide the investigation. We need someone with experience working with ancient human biology and DNA."

"Apparently, this Samantha Riley is an expert on human bone analysis and has addressed questions related to health and diet," explained Mirsky. "She may be very valuable for our investigations. She is the researcher who determined the age of the ancient skeleton."

"Yes, an expert on human health and ancient skeletons. A perfect fit for the Centurion Project. Is she willing to collaborate with us?"

"She is currently out of the area, so I have not had contact with her. However, I plan to meet her in the next day or two. Just tonight I learned from Maddington that Riley is the one we should be working with. I am quite sure she can be convinced to work with us."

"We need Riley and that skeleton, Boris. Is that clear?" commanded Utkin.

"I shall see to it."

"Maddington could be a problem. He knows too much. Make certain he talks to nobody about us."

"It will be a simple matter to silence Maddington," replied Mirsky.

"Be sure his demise appears to be an accident," instructed Utkin.

Utkin did not wait for a reply or comment and abruptly ended the call. The Centurion Project spreading into America was risky, but the rewards would be greater than the risks. Utkin's gaze searched through the crowds gathering around the pool and the dining area from his reclined position. Finally recognizing the objects of his search, he motioned for the two young women to return. The two thralls, wearing the skimpiest of string bikinis, eagerly bobbled back to their respective positions.

CHAPTER 22

MOSCOW, IDAHO

Mirsky considered his next steps after his talk with Utkin. He called Alexander, "You must take measures to be sure that Maddington has a fatal accident tonight. Do you understand what I am saying?"

"I believe he plans to use his propane grill in his garage tonight. How foolish," said Alexander.

"Be sure to eliminate all evidence of our visit."

"There will be no evidence left. I guarantee it," promised Alexander.

"I need a copy of the map with Riley's location."

"I'll put a copy of the map in an envelope with your room number on it. It will be at the front desk."

"Excellent. Pasha and I are going to Riley's house tonight to look for the laboratory key. Also, call your R&D people in Spokane to determine who oversees the human remains from the local Army Corps office, and send me that information. Apparently, they have some authority over this matter as well," said Mirsky and he hung up.

The white SUV circled the block once from one direction and again from the opposite direction. It was just after eleven at night when Pasha nudged the curb across the street from Samantha Riley's house. Mirsky noticed a light on in the front room. He pulled out a pair of binoculars and scanned the lighted room. There was no movement inside the house. He assumed the light was on a timer but, just in case, he instructed Pasha to case the house. After about ten minutes, Pasha returned to driver's seat, still wearing rubber gloves.

"There appears to be nobody home. The front door, the one visible from here, is locked. So is the back door. It's an older house and both doors are wood framed. I saw no evidence of an alarm system," reported Pasha. "The garage shields the back door from any neighbors. That's a safe entry. There is one car in the garage."

"Good work," replied Mirsky. "We'll focus on key racks or hangers and table drawers close to the doors. Any kind of baskets or nightstand drawers in the main bedroom are also prime spots for keys. Collect all keys and we'll sort them out later. Let's be quick and quiet."

"I'll let myself in and turn off the front room light and begin there," said Pasha.

"Excellent. I'll begin in the bedrooms," answered Mirsky, as he pulled on latex gloves. "If we encounter trouble, meet back at the car."

Pasha disappeared behind the house. Mirsky followed when the lighted room was dark.

Deak Allen came around the street corner wearing running gear and getting a little exercise after a long day helping Claire. He noticed the light was off in Samantha's house and he checked his watch. The light had come on at eight while he was working on his Afghan report, and he had checked to see when the timer was scheduled to go off. It was set for midnight.

Allen assumed the bulb had died, but he approached the house cautiously anyway. He noticed the SUV parked across the street as he walked up the drive toward the back. As he approached the back door, he immediately noticed the back door had been jimmied, and was left cracked open.

Allen instinctively ducked and listened with his ear close to the open door. He could hear someone going through drawers and shuffling materials around. He pushed the door open further and carefully entered the kitchen below counter level. Slowly and quietly, he made his way toward the front room. The intruder was searching near the area around the front door, using a small pen light. Allen moved as close as possible, then silently picked up a coffee mug from the countertop and tossed it to the other side of the room. The mug sounded like a gunshot when it hit the oak floor and bounced against the leg of a chair. The intruder spun around. Deak reached over and poked his index finger into the man's back, "Make a move and I'll blow your guts out. Put your hands behind your back. But move very, very slowly, because I have an itchy trigger finger," ordered Allen.

"Don't shoot!"

"Slowly get down on your knees and then lie face down on the floor, and don't turn around until I tell you differently," instructed Allen. "Stay on the floor."

Pasha lay down facing the floor with his arms out to the side. Allen went to the lamp and turned it on. "Just what might you be searching for? Do you have a name, my friend?"

"His name is Pasha," came a voice from behind Allen. "Don't make any sudden moves."

Allen then heard the distinct slide and clank of a shell being chambered in a handgun. "And what is your name, my friend?" asked Mirsky. "Get up, Pasha!"

"I didn't catch that, Mr. ...."

"My name is Deak Allen."

Mirsky glanced at Pasha and gave a slight flip of his head. "Go start the car."

Pasha gave Allen a vicious look and left.

"What are you doing here, Mr. Allen?" said Mirsky.

Allen looked at Boris Mirsky closely before answering. "I was about to ask you the same thing, Mr. ...?"

Mirsky ignored the question. "I will ask the questions, Mr. Allen. What are you doing here?"

"I live here," replied Allen.

"That is not possible," said Mirsky. "This house belongs to Dr. Riley."

"You didn't ask who owns the house. You asked what I was doing here," said Allen.

Before Mirsky could say another word, the light turned off and the room went dark. Allen instantly lunged at Mirsky, grabbed his gun hand and smashed his head into Mirsky's chin.

Mirsky fell backward, stunned, with Allen on top of him. Mirsky clutched the gun as Allen attempted to shake it free. Mirsky continued to grip the gun and pulled it toward his body as he rolled his shoulder, bringing Allen's hands toward his body as well. Allen anticipated the move and released his grip as Mirsky rolled further over on top of his own gun hand. Allen quickly jabbed Mirsky's neck and the back of his head with the heel of his palm while the gun was covered. He then rose up to his knees and pounded Mirsky's kidneys with as much force as he could muster. Mirsky let go of his gun to free his hand and was able to spin his powerful body through the pain of the kidney punches. When he spun his body, the gun flew out from underneath him and slid across the floor.

Mirsky was under Allen, but they faced each other. The spin move had caught Allen off guard. In the millisecond of Allen's hesitation, Mirsky was able to throw a straight punch at Allen's face that knocked him backwards. Mirsky scrambled to his feet and took a step toward the kitchen door. Allen recouped and began to rise. Mirsky quickly turned and kicked Allen in the ribs, sending him back down. His move toward the door was feigned to catch Allen off guard. Mirsky scanned the room for his gun, scooped it up and headed for the door.

Mirsky ran with a hunched limp out the open door. Allen ached but he stood and followed out the door where a powerful punch to his ribs stopped him again. As Allen bent over in pain, Mirsky spat out, "Mr. Allen, you wish more?" He again kicked Allen in the chest. The kick sent Allen tumbling to the ground. Mirsky considered inflicting more damage, but instead turned and limped to the waiting SUV. The vehicle pulled out and disappeared down the street.

Deak Allen slowly staggered into the house. He went through each of the rooms to assess the damage from the intruders. Allen noticed that the thieves were very meticulous in their search and did not rip, cut, or dislodge anything in their exploration. They were targeting something very specific.

He called 911 and reported the burglary. When the patrol car arrived, Allen met the two policemen outside the house. They talked with Allen cautiously and continually peered toward the house. When they finished their interrogation, one pondered, "So, let me get this straight. You called in a burglary, but you don't live here, right? You live in Washington, D.C.? You say there was a burglary, but nothing appears to be disturbed and you have no idea if anything was taken? Do I have this correct, Mr. Allen?"

"Like I said, the intruders were in the house when I got here just before midnight. So, I witnessed the burglary. They were wearing gloves and at least one of them had a handgun."

After another few minutes of explanation and after they called in his identification, the policemen decided to take a formal statement. The officers then walked through the house with Allen. When they were finally ready to leave, they attempted to convince Allen to visit the hospital. "You should really have those ribs x-rayed," said the officer who was doing most of the talking. Allen refused and instead opted for a double scotch on the rocks after they left.

CHAPTER 23

MOSCOW, IDAHO

His life was one exhausting situation after another. It never seemed to relent. With one eye, open and pivoting in its socket like a chameleon, he pondered the events of the previous evening. Things were not going as smoothly as he anticipated. Boris Mirsky grew up from almost nothing. A blossom breaking through concrete pavement. However, he recognized that he gained strength from his struggles and losses. This was the nature of his unyielding, plodding existence. He reached over, feeling for the room phone from his bed. Mirsky pressed for the operator. "I am expecting an envelope. Can you check to see if it is waiting for me?"

After a few minutes the desk clerk called back and told him that the envelope had been delivered. "Please send it up to my room. Send up a pot of green tea as well."

Mirsky hung up and searched the nightstand for his cell phone. He pressed the speed dial number for Pasha.

"Pasha, go back and watch Riley's house. We need to know who this Allen is. If he's still at the house, follow him.

Stay with him all day and report back to me. Do not let him see you. We must be more cautious."

"I will watch from the vehicle at a safe distance."

"Do not park too close to the house. He may recognize the car from last night."

"He will not see me, Boris. I will go now."

Mirsky heard the footsteps progressively approaching his room. He peered through the peep hole just to make sure it was room service. Cracking the door open just enough to extend an arm he took the tea tray and envelope, handed the waiter a twenty, and locked the door. Mirsky flipped open his knife and slit the edge of the envelope for the map. After examining the map, he slowly reread Riley's three-page report detailing the results of the excavation and preliminary analysis. He didn't understand the technical analysis but picked up on the important aspects of the find and noticed that Riley was one of two authors. The second author was also female, Claire Anderson.

Mirsky considered the report as he sipped tea. There were three different individuals found during the excavation, but only the complete skeleton was determined to be of great age. The other two individuals were represented only by pieces of human bone. Mirsky had little formal education, but he was very aware of the value of homework. He placed the excavation report on the desk and now studied the map of the site excavation in Helmer. He memorized every road, trail, elevation contour, and detail of the area. Eventually, he checked in with Alexander.

"Were you able to effectively take care of Maddington?"

"Yes. We cleared the house, and it burned last night," replied Alexander. "Terrible accident."

"We didn't find the key at Riley's house yesterday. She must have it with her at the excavation site. Go online and find recent images of Dr. Riley. You and Nick will go get her and the key. But I want you to carefully watch her for a day."

"What if we cannot find pictures of her?"

"Call your R&D team. They will find something. Nobody must know we have her. Pasha and I will be there tomorrow, so I can have a little talk with her. Do not injure her but detain her until I arrive."

"It shall be done," replied Alexander.

"The map shows a small U.S. Forest Service picnic area about three miles from the site excavation. Bring Riley there at three tomorrow afternoon. Do you see the picnic area?"

"I have the map in front of me now. Yes, I see a picnic area marked as Boulder Creek. Is that the location?"

"That is it," replied Mirsky.

"Nick and I will make sure we find her and get that key," assured Alexander. "We will scout the area today and have her for you tomorrow."

"No mistake can be made. You must be successful and very, very cautious. Do not harm her. We will need her cooperation. Do you understand?"

"Nobody will see us," assured Alexander again.

"What have your R&D people found regarding the regional Army Corps and the human remains?" asked Mirsky.

"Oh yes, I will send you the details. The local administrator is a civilian named Jonathan Higgins. We were able to compile a comprehensive profile."

"Good, I will contact him when I get the details."

Mirsky hung up. His mind churned, anticipating future events and follow up moves, much like a chess player. And always, always, working through backup plans and strategies.

CHAPTER 24

PULLMAN, WASHINGTON

As Allen gradually gained consciousness from his coma-like slumber, he immediately began feeling the throbbing pain. His body felt like he had been dumped from a cement mixer. His ribs were the worst. There was a stabbing pain on his left side, and he thought he may have one or two cracked ribs.

He limped into the kitchen and found ground coffee in the refrigerator door. Without counting, he spooned the grounds into a French press and zapped two cups of water in the micro, soaked the grounds, waited a minute, plunged the press, and poured a cup.

After a second cup of black coffee he showered in scalding water, dressed and was ready to head to Riley's lab. He walked back through the house in the daylight to look for any clues as to what the intruders might have been after. He had no idea.

While searching the house, he reflected on the two men, particularly the second man. Allen felt certain the man was a highly trained gangster of some sort. He had great physical strength and was obviously trained in hand-to-hand combat. He picked up the coffee mug he had tossed to the floor to start the ruckus. Satisfied that the house was in order, he left for campus.

Allen parked his new rental in a visitor's lot and walked across campus to Woods Hall. It was another dry clear day for the Inland Northwest. The walk allowed him to flex and stretch his ailing body parts. He arrived at the lab a few hours before noon and found Claire working with some undergraduate volunteers. "Hey, Claire," said Allen, walking into the isotope lab.

"Hi, Dr. Allen. I mean Deak. How did your report writing go last night?"

"The report went fine, but there were some other interesting events. Is there a place we can talk privately for a few moments?"

Claire noticed that Deak was walking a little gingerly as he came across the room. "Are you okay, Deak?" she asked with concern. She quickly motioned for them to go into the compactor room to talk.

They sat at one of the small sorting tables in the privacy of the vault. "What is it, Deak?"

"Someone broke into Dr. Riley's house last night and was systematically searching for something. I had an encounter with them around midnight and was able to chase them off," he answered.

"Wow. Do you think they were kids? Probably a lot of people know Dr. Riley travels every summer and is not at home," Claire responded.

"No. These weren't kids looking for money, booze, or medications. These were professionals who were looking for something very specific. They didn't bust up the place as they were searching."

"Did they take anything before being scared off?" asked Claire.

Allen looked over at Claire and gently rubbed his ribs. "They didn't exactly get frightened off. They were armed and probably would have stayed to finish the job, but things got physical, and they left abruptly," said Allen.

"You're hurt?"

"I'm okay now. Just a few tender spots I'll have to nurse. I don't think they found what they were looking for. So, I'm wondering what they might have been searching for."

Claire shook her head slowly. "Last night was a busy night in the town of Pullman."

Allen raised an eyebrow. "Meaning?"

"Well, Dr. Riley's house wasn't the only place with unusual activity. Professor Maddington's house caught fire last night and was almost completely gutted."

"Didn't you tell Maddington that Dr. Riley kept the vault key with her?" asked Allen.

Claire nodded affirmatively.

"I guess I'd better walk down the hallway and have a talk with him. Maybe he knows something about what might have transpired at Samantha's house last night," said Allen.

Claire looked over and said, "I don't think that will be possible, today at any rate. Professor Maddington has turned up missing. Nobody knows where he is, and he isn't responding to his cell phone. You don't think he was one of the people who broke into Dr. Riley's house, do you?"

"I don't know. I don't know what Maddington looks like. Is he in his thirties?"

Claire described Maddington. "He's about your height. You know, over six feet tall, but he is heavyset. I would say he is definitely over fifty and maybe in his sixties. He wears wire rimmed glasses and has really short hair."

Allen shook his head slightly. "That doesn't match either of the intruders from last night. Hey, when I walked down the hallway, I thought I saw Maddington's office door open?"

"Maddington is kind of funny that way. He usually keeps his door open when he isn't there and then he closes it when he is. So yes, his door was open, but he isn't around," explained Claire.

Allen stood up. "Thanks, Claire. Listen, you need to be extra careful around the lab. Try to not work here alone. And report any strangers to the police. I'm going to call campus security and suggest they keep a watch on this building and lab for next few days."

"What do you think is going on?" asked Claire.

"I'm not sure, but I think it may have something to do with the Central Ferry skeleton. My suspicion is that the guys who broke into Samantha's house may have been looking for the key she keeps for the vault," suggested Allen.

"Wow. This is starting to sound dangerous," responded Claire.

Before walking out of the vault, Allen paused. "The people I encountered last night were extremely dangerous. Your best bet is to get away from any strangers looking to gain access to the skeletal remains. I have a couple of things to take care of now, so I must leave."

Deak Allen dug into his wallet and found a copy of his card. He circled his cell number and handed it to Claire. "Call me if something suspicious happens or if Professor Maddington shows up."

Allen gingerly stepped down the hallway and stopped in front of Maddington's open office door. He peeked in. "Is anyone home?" Hearing no reply, he walked into the office and picked up the desk phone and tapped in Jack Mills' number in Washington, D.C.

"This is Jack Mills. How can I help you?"

"Hi, Jack. It's Deak."

"I didn't recognize the number. What's going on?"

"Jack, I need you to get with IT and begin tracing all incoming and outgoing calls to this line for the past seventy-two hours."

"You know that could compromise any evidence, if that is what you're seeking, Deak?" offered Jack.

"Not interested in evidence, Jack. I just need some leads. I'd like to get this information as soon as possible, too."

"Hold on, Deak. Let me send it over to IT now. Meanwhile, I can brief you on the Bryozoan picture you sent a few days ago. I'll send you a PDF report, but you might want to know a few things immediately."

"I'm all ears, Jack. What did they find out?"

"That is a freshwater version of a colony of single-celled organisms. There are saltwater versions as well. These things are filter feeders and are found in shallow waters or even places that flood annually. They generally like warmer climates but are found in colder areas as well. The cold climate ones are generally the freshwater varieties If you see them in your water, it is a sign that the water is healthy."

"Can they live out of water?" asked Allen.

"Technically, no. But they do go into sort of a state of hibernation. For instance, if there is a long draught, the colony can shed some seed like structures and, when conditions are right again, those seed like structures begin making new colonies."

"Thanks for the update, Jack. I look forward to reading the whole report."

"No. There's more, Deak. It is believed that these organisms may provide a cure for cancer and there are a few researchers working on this right now."

"That is an interesting twist."

"Get this," continued Mills. "The leading scientist in the world on Bryozoan research is at the University of Montana, less than three hours from where you are. Walt Steward's cabin is a short drive to Missoula, and if you want, you can speak to the world's leading expert on the Bryozoan/cancer connection."

"Do you have his number?" asked Deak.

"His name is Professor James Ross. My contacts say he prefers to be called Jimmy. He's in the Department of Molecular Biosciences." Mills finished by relaying the phone number and a few other facts about Dr. Ross and his Bryozoan research.

"Do you want me to call and set up a meeting for tomorrow?" asked Mills.

"Thanks, Jack, but not tomorrow. I'm still playing with some loose ends. Tomorrow won't work. How about trying to get something in three days from now? That should give me a chance to finish things and then make the drive over to Missoula. Are there any updates from Walla Walla that I haven't been looped in on?" asked Allen.

"Nothing from Walla Walla. Hold up a second, Deak. I'm getting a message on my computer screen with results from the telephone trace. Man, this confirms that landlines are a thing of the past," replied Mills.

"What do you have?"

"I'll text the details over to you, but there were only two calls in seventy-two hours. Both were incoming. The first was from a cell phone originating in Vladivostok but owned by an American named Thomas Rackerman. The second originated from a cell phone in L.A. owned by a Russian corporation, Utkin Chemicals."

"Interesting. Text the sheet to me with the details," replied Allen.

"Got it. Anything else?" asked Mills.

"Not now. Wait. Can you dig a little deeper on Utkin Chemicals, narrow the telephone user down to a specific individual? Also, can you put together a short bio sketch on Thomas Rackerman. I've heard that name someplace, but I can't place it. One other thing. I can't seem to put the finishing touches on the Afghanistan report. It's about seventy-five percent complete. I'm going to work on it for the rest of the day and then send you a preliminary draft. Can you go through it for me, Jack?"

"Send it whenever you can. I'll talk with you soon." Jack hung up.

CHAPTER 25

HELMER, IDAHO

Samantha Riley's field tradition was to be the last person off site at the end of the season dig. Much like the captain of a ship going down, she wanted to make sure everyone else was safely away and the site was properly closed. Her graduate students had already completed their final checks and had the gear and students loaded for the trip back to Pullman. She called Jennifer Henderson over for a private conversation. "Jen, I realize I had asked you to take the lead on this field school project for me, but I think this excavation would be a good master's thesis for Katie. Also, if David wanted to focus on wild tuber intensification for his dissertation, he could fold the work from this summer into a few more field seasons and produce a great piece of scholarship."

Jennifer looked at her mentor and admitted, "That sounds reasonable. I wasn't looking forward to writing this one up. As you know, my interest is more for stone tools, and we primarily found organics here."

"I was hoping you would say that, Jen," replied Riley. "When you get back to Pullman, can you feel Katie and David out on this? If either or both are interested, I'll meet with them later."

"Sure," said Jen. "Is there something else?"

"I know you are keen on those large bipointed tools from the burial at Central Ferry. The time frame matches exactly with your other collections from the end of last Ice Age, doesn't it?" inquired Riley.

"Wow!" said a smiling Jennifer. "I was hoping you would say that. They look a lot like those Sluiceway points Professor Rackerman from Penn has been finding in Alaska. Unlike any of the Alaskan materials, these are from a pristine, perfectly preserved burial. I'm hoping they represent some of the oldest stone tool technology in North America. Oh, my god, I can't believe it! This could be the missing link in understanding how the North American continent was first colonized! Massive points like that may be associated with megafauna hunting, too." Jennifer Henderson was practically jumping up and down.

Professor Riley held up her hand. "Let's not assume too much here. After you talk with Katie and David, why don't you meet with Claire and begin looking at the bipoints. It would be nice to get a protein analysis done on them soon and have them 3D scanned. I don't know how long we are going to have them before the Army Corps will want them returned."

Riley looked over to the waiting vans and trucks. "Okay, you guys, get out of here. I'll do the last walkover for the final site security and be right behind you," said Riley. The vehicles pulled out one at a time with students waiving and taking final pictures of the camp and site. Her university pickup truck was the only vehicle left. It became instantly quiet as it always did when she remained at the site on "take-off" day. Riley began her routine of walking over each of the backfilled excavation unit blocks, taking photographs and covering exposed datum points with additional rocks to protect the reference markers. Her team had already secured the markers, but she added a few more rocks out of habit. She made the hike up the ridgetop for one last time to collect any messages from the office and to make required telephone calls. As she neared the ridgetop, her cell service linked up and she noticed a flurry of messages related to a fire in Pullman. The previous day, Joe had sent a handful of messages, all with roughly the same horrific content. He noted that Peter Maddington's house had sustained some significant fire damage and that he was still missing. A text from Claire indicated that Deak Allen had stopped by yesterday and told her that someone had broken into her house, but that she thought Allen would give her the firsthand details himself. There was a message from Deak Allen that said to call him immediately and not to talk with any strangers. The message was from the previous day, and he indicated that he had a few things to do, but he was headed toward her camp and should be there by the afternoon the following day. Riley looked at the time on her cell phone, and it showed a couple of minutes after noon. She didn't know what was going on but thought she better head back down the ridge to see if Allen had arrived in camp.

As Riley came off the ridge, she stopped short when she noticed a white SUV parked in front of her pickup truck and two men peering into the truck. She would have rushed down and given them a piece of her mind about snooping, but she noticed one was holding a pistol behind his back as he peered in the window. She slowly backed up, not taking her eyes off the men. Without looking at the ground, she stepped on a loose cobble that rolled out from under her foot, almost causing her to fall. The cobble rolled down the ridge and crashed into the bushes. She froze and both men looked in her direction. They noticed her immediately and began calling, "Dr. Riley, we need to talk to you." Riley turned and sprang back up the trail towards the ridgetop.

The man farthest from her yelled, "Don't let her get away! Bring her back here!" The second man tore off after Riley. As Riley approached the top at a sprint, she was tiring from the uphill run. Her pursuer was closing in, but she could tell he, too, was getting winded from the sprint straight up the ridge. Riley left the trail and dropped off into the north facing slope where the timber grew the thickest. She had spent thirty days on the site and had a good feel for where the timber roads were. She was sure her pursuer was less familiar with the terrain. Riley flew down the mountain thrashing through the dense timber, losing her balance several times but able to catch herself. She saw her pursuer make his way down the slope just above her. Riley increased her speed and sprang deeper into the timber, dodging trees but getting slapped by low lying limbs. She could hear the guy just yards behind her by the snapping of the tree limbs as he ran. "Stop!" he shouted.

She pushed harder, heading for the older growth where there was more room to maneuver in the open understory. If she could put some distance between them, she was sure he would get lost and must turn back. To the right was another steep drop-off. She raced toward it and slid down the slope sideways on her feet and landed at a small ravine. She took it downhill, running as fast as she could. Riley heard the man tumble down the slope and crash at the bottom. She glanced over her shoulder and saw no one following her. She stayed within the small ravine, hoping it soon intersected with a logging road. Riley kept running but her strength was depleted. Her face and body were covered with small cuts and scratches. Her calf muscles throbbed, and her shin bones were swelling from direct hits. Her clothing was shredded from the underbrush.

Suddenly, the ravine opened onto a well-used timber road. Riley reached the road and started jogging steadily. Slowing down to catch a breath, she could hear a vehicle engine. She ran faster toward the sound of the car. Then she saw the vehicle coming down the road and stopped. Riley waived her arms over her head, then stopped waiving. It was the white SUV.

Riley jumped off the road and headed back to the ravine. As she entered the forest, two loud booms cracked over her head. "Stop or I will shoot you!" She paused a split second, then kept running. She ran up the ravine and looked to see if she was being chased. Nobody in sight. She turned to run and slammed straight into the original pursuer, who grabbed her tightly. She struggled and kicked him and broke away from his grip. He grabbed the collar on her shirt, almost tearing it from her. She continued to struggle, and he smacked her across the face, and then again. The second impact dazed her. Everything blurred. He shoved her down the ravine towards the logging road where his partner stood. Riley fell and hit the ground roughly. She didn't try to get up.

"Bring her here, Nick. Let's get her in the car and check her for the keys." Nick grabbed Riley by the hair and forced her up and led her to the passenger side rear door.

Alexander got in the driver's seat. Nick was about to toss Riley into the car when someone seized him by the back of the head and slammed his face into the side of the SUV hard. Alexander twisted to see Nick fall to the ground. He reached for his holster. As he swung his right arm around to aim toward the rear of the vehicle, Deak Allen grabbed his wrist with his left hand. With his right hand, he snapped the barrel of the pistol down and away, breaking Alexander's index finger. Still gripping the shooter's hand, Allen leaned in and slammed the butt of the pistol into his temple. He slumped down in the seat, out cold. Allen turned quickly to make sure the first assailant was still down and out.

He reached over to help Riley up. The two smacks had stunned her badly. The left side of her face had puffed up and her eye was almost completely closed. As Allen gently pulled her up, she recognized him with her functioning eye, and it began to tear up. "Is it really you? I was so frightened." She wrapped her arms around his neck, and he pulled her up off the ground. "Who are these people? Where did you come from?"

"You are going to be just fine, Samantha. I don't know who these people are, but I plan to find out. But first let's get you someplace safe." Allen collected both guns and their identification. He pulled the laces out of their shoes and tied their hands behind their backs and trussed their feet.

Riley was still not totally lucid, so he had her sit in the SUV while he made the quarter-mile jog back to the site area along the dirt road. He returned driving Samantha's pickup. Allen put her in the passenger seat and clipped the seat belt. He made a final check on the knots binding the two men. They were just beginning to come around. "Law enforcement will untie you two very shortly."

He hopped into the driver's seat of Riley's truck and drove past the excavation site, leaving his rental parked at the site area.

"A lot has happened in the past two days. Things are getting dangerous. I think you may have something somebody wants. Let's go to my friend's cabin and get you patched up. We can develop a reasonable plan from there. Okay?" said Allen.

"Deak, did you beat up those two bastards with your bare hands?" stammered Riley.

"Not really. The car door and the butt of a gun helped."

"My vision was pretty blurry. It was difficult to tell what was going on. It felt like you showed up out of nowhere and stopped those guys."

"Didn't you get my call? I left you a message that I was coming by the camp today to meet you," replied Allen.

Riley's head began to clear as they drove. "I think those guys said something about looking for keys. Maybe they were looking for the same keys to the vault Maddington was after," she speculated.

"I've been wondering about that too. That might be the reason someone broke into your house as well. Let's get to the cabin and review things. Maybe all this will make more sense after comparing notes."

After a few minutes of negotiating the two track timber roads of the forest, Allen pulled the pickup truck onto a paved county road and headed toward St. Maries.

Once they got cell service, Allen pulled over and called Jack Mills and explained the situation. He gave Jack the serial number of both guns, as well as the names and driver's license numbers of both. "Call the Idaho State Police and have them round up these fellas," said Allen. "I left them next to their vehicle, a white SUV, just past the site area. I'm going to text you a photograph of the site location map. I'll be available later to help fill in the gaps. Let the police know I'm in the middle of an operation and I may not be able to do a face-to-face meeting immediately."

"Okay, Deak. We should be able to clear some of this up from this end, but I'm sure you will have to report to some-place to make a formal statement," said Jack.

"Will you relay information to me as this thing devel-ops? For a fishing vacation, I'm feeling a little overworked and running out of time."

"I think your vacation is over and you're back on com-pany time."

Allen hung up and pulled back on the road. He looked over at Riley. "How are you doing? You appear to be fairly lucid."

"I think I'll make it."

Within minutes, an SUV coming from the opposite di-rection turned off the county road and into the forest. The driver moved the SUV slowly, not wanting to get lost in the maze of smaller tracks that intersected with the well-used track he was on. Mirsky instructed Pasha to go left at the next inter-section as he glanced from the map to the forest road they were navigating. "This can't be the road," complained Pasha. "There are no signs. We should have waited longer at the pic-nic area for them to show up."

"They were already an hour and fifteen minutes late. They are probably back near the site area stuck with a broken axle. We have no cell service. And there was no other turn.

This must be it." Mirsky pointed at the dirt road in front of them, "See, there are recent tire tracks using this road. They are down here, somewhere."

After almost twenty minutes Pasha and Mirsky were having second thoughts about their location. They had made turns when the road forked. The tracks they were following had steep switchbacks. They hadn't found a soul or vehicle anywhere. "Should we to turn around and go back?" suggested Pasha. "We have better roads in Russia."

At that moment, their vehicle jounced into a deep rut and the wheel spun without grabbing. Pasha gunned the engine several times but was unable to move the vehicle. "Don't spin the tires. Switch into four-wheel drive," instructed Mirsky. Pasha shifted into four low and rocked the vehicle back and forth and slowly pulled the SUV out of the rut.

"The road is getting narrower," complained Pasha. "We'd better pull off and try to turn the vehicle around before it is impossible."

"Perhaps you are right," conceded Mirsky, as he concentrated on the road ahead. "Wait, I see something."

They proceeded along the road. The object was a vehicle. "Stop here. I believe that car is right here, on the map," pointed Mirsky. "We are at the site area. Slowly drive by as if we are passing through."

They drove by the Subaru and kept slowly moving along, scanning the area as they went. They followed the logging road past the site area, where it narrowed even more. "How far are we going to go? They are not here," said Pasha.

"Look! There is something up ahead. Keep driving. It looks like a white SUV." Soon they could see Nick and Alexander on the ground next to the vehicle.

"This is close enough," said Mirsky. "Stop here." He scanned the area for anyone else around, then got out. "Go back and check that car parked back there, Pasha."

Mirsky walked over and released the trussed men. "Where is Riley?"

Nick's forehead was caked with dried blood. He massaged his wrists and answered, "We had her before we were attacked."

"Attacked?" asked Mirsky in a calm but quietly furious voice.

"I don't know," said Nick. "They came up from behind and bashed me before I could see them."

"How many?" asked Mirsky, as he looked at Alexander.

"It was hard to tell. They broke my finger," explained Alexander.

"What do you mean you don't know? Didn't you have your eyes open?"

"Well, there was Riley and another one, well, at least one other, who came out of nowhere," said Alexander.

"Just one?" yelled Mirsky. "Why didn't you shoot him?"

Alexander and Nick felt for their empty holsters and didn't need to reply to Mirsky.

Mirsky appeared calm as he looked at the two but was fuming on the inside.

They turned when they heard Pasha coming back to the SUV.

"There is nobody in or around that car. I circled the perimeter outward for almost fifty meters. But there is something else. I think that vehicle was parked in Riley's garage."

"Are you sure?"

"It is very similar."

Mirsky looked at Alexander. "What did this man look like, who attacked you when you weren't looking?" demanded Mirsky, sarcastically.

"He was strong. He had a mustache and dark hair. It all happened so fast."

"Was he tall?"

"He was tall. Maybe approaching two meters. It was hard to tell."

Boris Mirsky paused and thought about the man he had encountered at Riley's. "Mr. Allen," he said out loud. "Mr. Deak Allen."

"We need to go back to Pullman and find Riley. You two, watch Riley's house. Report her every move to me. Do not approach her and do not let her see you. Pasha and I will watch the university laboratory. It is vital that we get both Riley and her skeleton."

The four climbed into their respective vehicles and began negotiating the drive out.

CHAPTER 26

ST. MARIES, IDAHO

The tires of the pickup truck rolled slowly to a stop in the gravel driveway. Deak Allen turned to Samantha, "How's the head?"

"I feel okay, just a little fuzzy." Riley squeezed the door handle, stepped out and was able to walk into the cabin without help.

Once inside Allen looked at her with concern. "Let's get some ice on that eye to reduce the swelling," suggested Allen. But first he poured her a hefty snifter of brandy found on Walt's liquor shelf. He handed her the brandy and began preparing a couple of ice packs.

Riley was slouched down on the sofa. After thirty minutes of icing and nursing her second drink, Riley admitted to feeling almost human. "Why don't you hit the shower, and I'll see if I can find something for dinner. I put your bag in the spare bedroom."

"Thanks, but I don't I have any clean clothes in that pack. I didn't have time to restock in Pullman and those are my field clothes from the past two weeks," explained Riley.

"Check the drawers and closet in the main bedroom. You look about the same size as Windy. I'm sure she wouldn't mind."

The warm water from the shower poured over Samantha's head replenishing her awareness. After scrubbing herself dry, she searched the closet for clothing. Samantha emerged from the bedroom wearing an oversized button-up fishing shirt. The shirt must have been Walt's because the tail hung almost to her knees. Barefooted, Samantha dried her hair with a towel. "Wow, that had to be one of the top three showers I've ever taken. I've got a hundred scratches, cuts, and bruises and my left eye is going to be a real shiner, but I feel pretty good right now."

"Welcome back to the living. I better get a shower, myself. Make yourself at home. I'll just be a minute and we can talk about dinner."

While Deak showered, Riley explored the modest knotty pine cabin. It was L-shaped with a great room and bedrooms off to the side. The great room included a full kitchen separated from a sitting/lounge area by an island. It also had a large circular table and chairs off to one side, opposite a sofa, stuffed chairs and a fireplace along the other wall. Pictures, shelves with minerals, fossils, ceramics, stained glass, and books were everywhere. A pair of binoculars rested at each window. The cabin expressed contradiction. It was packed full and at the same time spacious, functional but elegant. It was the definition of feng shui. Samantha went to a set of French doors that opened onto a series of decks overlooking the lake. The spectacular view overlooked the southern end of the lake and followed a river valley up the mountains. There were layers of different hues of green as mountain ridges receded, growing paler with distance.

Riley heard Allen rustling in the cabin and went back inside. "Deak, this view is amazing. How did your friends ever find such a place?" A shirtless Allen was combing his hair.

Riley walked up behind Allen, then noticed extensive scarring on his right side. They were a combination of scars from sutures and healed over burns. "Are those your military wounds?"

Allen felt uneasy about his injuries and just nodded. Riley studied his scars, following them from Allen's rib cage as they curved toward his front and disappeared below his belt line. She wondered how extensive his injuries were.

Allen couldn't take his eyes from her.

"What is it, Deak?"

Riley was covered with scratches, bruises, and had a swollen eye. But Allen thought she looked beautiful. "Nothing, really. You just look incredible."

"Why, thank you."

Samantha faced Deak. "I never thanked you for what you did today. You probably saved my life. And just who are you, really?" They stood there trying to read each other's thoughts. Neither spoke.

To lighten the situation, Allen spoke, "You might be suffering from a concussion. Head impacts cause people to say and do things they normally wouldn't."

Riley leaned in and slid an arm around his back and drew him toward her. "I don't have a concussion."

She pressed her lips into his and they embraced. Allen gently pushed Samantha back, "Samantha, you have a concussion. Please sit down, I'll get you some more ice and a dose of ibuprofen for your swelling. I've found some salad fixings and some sliced turkey. You need to eat."

The next morning, Allen was in the kitchen on a telephone call and inventorying breakfast possibilities. After a decent night of sleep, he had called Jack Mills. "Are you sure they went to the right spot?" asked Allen. Mills had already talked to the state police, who found no SUV and no trussed men.

"Absolutely," replied Jack. "They saw your rented Subaru and drove past that."

"I don't suppose the serial numbers and IDs turned up anything?"

"The guns were reported stolen from a pawn shop in Seattle last year and the names on the licenses were people who died a few years ago," said Jack.

"Did you get anything on Rackerman?"

"I'll send you an attachment later today. He's an archaeologist at the University of Pennsylvania."

"That's why I remember the name," said Allen. "He did some work with early sites in Alaska, as I recall."

"I've got the details in the report for you. Hey, Deak, I have you scheduled for a nine-thirty meeting with James Ross at the University of Montana tomorrow morning. He seems to be slammed for time so this might be the only opening for some time."

"Okay. Add it to my calendar. I'll drive up this evening."

"Good. I have you booked at the Double Tree Hotel next to the university," said Mills.

Allen looked up and saw Riley leaning against the door frame. "I must go, Jack. Keep digging on the Utkin company and let me know what you find." Allen hung up.

He grinned at Riley. "Look who finally crawled out of bed. How do you feel?"

"I'm starved. Anything to eat around here?"

"We have toast and peanut butter, butter, untoasted bread, and more peanut butter. We do have coffee and V-8."

"You really know how to stock a kitchen," joked Riley. "I'll have toast and peanut butter."

He poured her a mug of coffee. "Juice?"

Riley nodded. "Deak, I need to get back to Pullman and make sure my students are safe and find out what's going on with fires and break-ins."

"I understand," said Allen. "But you need to know that those two guys from yesterday somehow got away. When the police showed up, they were nowhere to be found. They were rescued by someone. I know they couldn't have untied themselves. Their SUV was also gone."

"Were they the same guys who broke into my house?"

Allen thought for a second. "No, but it seems too coincidental, your house burglary and the assault yesterday. I suspect they all know each other. My guess is they are trying to get at your ancient friend. Or it's related to the burial recovery in some way."

"Well, that means I need to get to the university that much quicker. That skeleton is putting my students in danger."

"It's daylight at a busy university," said Allen. "I notified campus security, and they are increasing surveillance around Woods Hall. So, you can finish your toast. I've got to go to Missoula this afternoon for a meeting tomorrow morning."

"What's happening in Missoula?"

"I have a hunch about climate change and Bryozoans. There's a guy over there doing the research."

"Boy, you do cast a wide net. Bryozoan research? I'm not even sure what they are."

"I'm just trying to follow up on an idea that might help our climate change project." He went to the window overlooking the lake. Riley followed. Allen pointed across the lake. "I was fishing over there and noticed the gelatinous organisms all over the place."

"Gelatinous organisms?" she questioned.

"They look like a jelly fish colony attached to subsurface materials," replied Allen.

"I think I may have seen something like that near the site in Helmer. But it was during the spring when the valleys were flooded. Like clusters of single celled goop?" said Riley.

"That's what they look like."

Allen's voice switched to a tone of absolute seriousness. "Samantha, I think you are in a very dangerous situation. I know you need to go back to Pullman and take care of your students, but you were just viciously attacked. Your house was broken into and searched. When I get back from Missoula, I'd like you to stay here with me until this gets cleared up. I'll call you as soon as I finish my meeting tomorrow and we can meet back here."

Riley pondered his proposition. "You're probably right, Deak. I'll ask Joe to make me a reservation at the University Inn in Moscow for tonight. Jennifer and David can go with me to my place, and I'll pack a bag. Give me a call tomorrow and we'll meet here." She looked at her toast and peanut butter. "No offense, but I'll cook dinner."

"Samantha, can you give me a lift to Helmer on your way back to Pullman? I left my rental back there."

Riley continued to gaze out over the lake without responding.

"Hey, Samantha, are you okay?"

She turned to him with a thoughtful expression on her face. "Do you mean because of my concussion or my advance on you yesterday?"

Deak cracked a crooked smile. "Best kiss I've ever had."

Samantha almost beamed, "And yes, I can give you a lift to Helmer." She walked to Allen. "And don't-ya-know, my concussion is gone."

Allen smiled and took her in his arms. Samantha pulled him in tightly. He whispered, "I'm very happy to hear you've recovered."

A few hours later Allen and Riley were at the archaeological site area near Helmer. Allen stepped from the pickup truck and walked to his rental.

For Riley, the area emanated an uncanny atmosphere. She waited to make sure Deak Allen's rental car started and her thoughts and introspections drifted back to the previous day and her narrow escape. For the first time, she felt afraid.

After starting the car, Allen got out and studied the area as he walked a short circle. He hoped to spot a clue as to how the two thugs had escaped. After a few minutes Allen looked up and returned to the pickup. "I'll follow you out to the main road," he said. "Don't stay at your place tonight and I'll call you tomorrow on my way back from Missoula, okay?"

"Thanks, Deak. I'll be fine," replied Riley.

CHAPTER 27

PULLMAN, WASHINGTON

Samantha Riley drove straight to Woods Hall. She wanted the details about the events from her department colleagues and students. She dropped into the departmental office before heading upstairs and immediately caught Joe's attention. "Hey, Joe, any more news on the fire? Has Maddington returned from wherever he's been hiding?"

Joe began to respond, then stopped dead, "What happened to your eye?"

"Someone tried to kidnap me yesterday as I was leaving the site in Helmer. Did everyone else in the field school make it back safely?"

"As far as I know, everyone made it back. What do you mean someone tried to kidnap you?"

"It's a long story. The police are already involved. I'm going up to my lab to see if any of the students are around."

Joe replied, "Dr. Riley, I booked you a room at the University Inn for tonight, like you asked."

"Thanks, Joe." Riley rushed out the door and headed up to her lab.

Joe stopped her with another yell, "Wait, you have a message here from Jonathan Higgins at the Walla Walla Army Corps District. He would like you to call him as soon as possible."

"Thanks, Joe."

Riley walked into the isotope lab before dropping her bags in her office and found the lab buzzing with chatter. All four of her graduate students stopped talking in mid-sentence and stared with looks of surprise, concern, and questions. Jennifer blurted out, "Where have you been? We've all been so worried. You were supposed to be right behind us yesterday," in a tone that was mildly scolding.

David DeRue tapped Jennifer on the arm and motioned with his head toward Riley. Jennifer looked up and studied her advisor's face. "Oh, my god. Were you in a car accident? We should have driven back to the Helmer after you didn't show up at the lab yesterday afternoon."

Claire jumped in, "Are you okay?"

Katie added, "This morning the rumors have been flying that Professor Maddington's body was found in the burned rubble of his home. You were missing and Maddington dead. None of us knew what to think."

Riley put her bags on the lab table and held up both hands. "I may have a black eye, but I am safe and well. Are you guys okay, and how about the field school students?"

"We all made it home safely," reassured Jennifer, still staring in semi-shock.

"All of the gear is unpacked and in the storage room," contributed David. "We were able to unpack all the artifacts yesterday afternoon. They're in the compactor ready for inventory."

"This morning most of the field school students took off from Pullman or Spokane to their homes. The local students are probably celebrating a successful summer semester," said Jennifer. "We are all safe."

Katie asked, "Tell us about your black eye, Dr. Riley. What happened?"

"Yeah," said David. "And where have you been for the past twenty-four hours? There's so much unexplained stuff happening around here."

"Alright, I'll start from the beginning, but first you have to tell me about the fire at Professor Maddington's house," said Riley.

"Claire knows the most about that. She was here when it happened," said Katie. "Claire, tell us again. It was a big deal here in Pullman."

"The truth is, they still don't know what caused the fire, but it happened four nights ago. The same night your house was broken into. I know it was the same night because I talked with Dr. Allen the next morning and he told me about the break-in at your house. He was pretty banged up when I saw him the next morning."

"Hey, where is that guy anyway?" questioned Jennifer. "It seems coincidental that all this started happening after he showed up. I wonder if any of this is related to his visit?"

"Wait," said Samantha. "Let's stick to the Maddington issue first. He went missing?"

Claire began again, "Yes, after the fire he was missing. He still hadn't shown up. But today, there have been anonymous sources from either the fire or police department that his charred remains were found under his car. He was maybe working on his car in his garage, and it fell on him. He was probably under the car when the fire started. Sources say the fire started in the garage and then spread to other parts of the house. Most of the house is still standing, but it's gutted. I guess we won't know for sure until they complete the investigation, and the fire marshal makes a formal report or statement, or whatever they do in these cases."

Riley looked at Claire, "What do you mean Dr. Allen was pretty banged up?"

"He interrupted the intruders who broke into your house," replied Claire. "Apparently, they worked him over pretty roughly."

"How badly was he hurt?" asked Riley.

"I don't know for sure. He came into the lab the following morning. So, he could walk and talk but he showed signs of pain."

The four students became quiet and looked in the direction of their mentor. Riley looked back at them, a little confused. Jennifer raised her index finger and slowly traced the tip of her finger under her eye. "Oh, the black eye," said Riley. "So much has happened in the past twenty-four hours that my black eye isn't even high on my list."

"Well, it's at the top of our list," said Jennifer. "Were you in an accident? What happened?"

"Where have you been?" blurted Claire and Katie simultaneously.

Riley began. "After you all left the site, I began my usual routine of checking the datum markers and looking for anything that might have been left on site. I came down off the ridge and a couple of guys showed up and tried to kidnap me.

Riley paused as she thought about what had happened. It was a brutal assault, and it became apparent to her students, as they looked toward her, that the memory of the attack troubled her. They huddled around her protectively.

Riley looked up quickly. “I’m fine,” she said.

She went on about being chased through the forest and down the ridge and described how she struggled and was almost able to get away, but one of the bastards punched her and dragged her by the hair to their car. She described as best she could, the arrival of Deak Allen, and how he overpowered and disarmed the two assailants. “Apparently, Dr. Allen was trained in combat techniques when he was an officer in the Iraqi War,” said Riley. “He subdued the kidnappers and tied them up.”

“Dr. Allen was in the Iraqi War?” asked Jennifer.

“Wow, he doesn’t look that old,” added Claire.

“Iraq wasn’t that long ago,” explained Riley.

Katie looked over at Jen with a playful smile. “So, he’s not that old, Jen. Maybe just a year or two younger than you.”

Claire broke in before Jen could continue the banter. “So, where were you last night?”

Riley then explained that she stayed at Allen’s place on Lake Coeur d’Alene so nobody could find them, just in case they were still looking for her. She also emphasized that the two attackers had somehow gotten away and were nowhere to be found when the authorities arrived. “I dropped him off at the site this morning to retrieve his rental car and drove directly here,” concluded Riley.

Claire looked at Riley and said, “There is something scary going on here. Dr. Allen has informed the campus police and they've been coming around a lot. Do you think it has anything to do with the skeleton we excavated?"

David asked, "Where is Dr. Allen now? Is he in Pullman?"

"I don't know if the skeleton has anything to do with all of this, but it sure may be related in some way. And no. Dr. Allen is not in Pullman today. When I dropped him at the site for his car, he had business in Missoula, but should be back through here in a day," said Riley.

"You were lucky he came along and was able to rescue you," said Jennifer.

Samantha looked at them and thought about all that had taken place the previous day. "I may owe that man my life."

At that moment, Riley's cell phone began ringing and she checked caller ID. "Uff-da," exclaimed Riley. "I have to take this call." She grabbed her bags and walked toward her office.

Riley answered the call while unlocking her office door. "Hi, Jonathan, sorry I didn't get to you sooner. I'm just getting back from the field."

"I certainly hope you had a productive field season, Dr. Riley," said Jonathan.

"It was memorable."

"I hate to rush you, but I need the human remains from Central Ferry returned to Walla Walla as soon as possible. Some of the tribes are worried that their ancestors are being kept out of their resting place too long and they need to perform some ritual cleansings on the remains," said Higgins.

"They can perform those rituals here, Jonathan. We have a private place where tribes often come to bless the remains of their ancestors. It would be a simple matter to have tribal representatives come here."

"I know that Dr. Riley, but there is also concern that the remains may get lost," informed Higgins.

"We have a temperature controlled, locked vault here, Jonathan. You don't have anything like that in Walla Walla. Our department has invested in state-of-the-art curation facilities. The human remains are safer here than they are in Walla Walla."

Higgins' voice became impatient. "Dr. Riley, I need those remains returned immediately. I don't need the artifacts or sediment samples right now, just the human remains," he insisted.

"Of course, these remains are your responsibility, Jonathan. But I must remind you that I cannot produce a professional report without the remains, if you still want me to do the analysis."

Riley stopped, thought about what Higgins was asking, then blurted out, "Is that what this is, Jonathan? Are you going to hand the remains over to a different research team? Are you getting some pressure from one of the larger universities?" asked Riley.

Sternly, but with a touch of apology, Higgins spoke, "I can't go into all the details about this situation, Dr. Riley. You are right. This is my responsibility and I have to proceed in the way I feel is most appropriate."

"I'm sure you haven't talked with Dr. Allen about this, have you? Dr. Allen has asked that my team conduct a few more tests and that's what I hope to do. If you would like to discuss this with him, I'm sure he can confirm these tests."

"Well, okay," conceded Higgins. "How long will it take you to complete the additional testing, and when can you have the remains to me? I'll really need them as soon as possible."

"We'll work today and tomorrow, and I'll transport them over to Walla Walla myself in two days. Jonathan, I hope you know what you're doing. I excavated these remains. I know the specific context of this recovery. I have worked with the indigenous groups in this area for several years and have a positive relationship with descendant communities. And you know, nobody does archaeological forensics as thoroughly as I do." Riley hung up the phone, bristling. She couldn't believe that Higgins would hand the project over to someone else.

Riley dialed Jennifer's number. Jennifer answered after a one ring. "Everything okay?"

"Can you come to my office, Jennifer? I need to go over a few things with you."

"Sure, I'll be right over."

Jennifer walked in carrying a stack of computer printouts. She settled into her usual chair across from Riley. Then she smiled and shook her head. "I can't get over your shiner, Samantha."

"It should dissipate in a few days." Riley got right to business. "Walla Walla wants the skeleton returned soon. Did you get a chance to talk with David and Katie about the Helmer project?"

"I did. They are both interested in working on the field school materials. Katie thought the site report would make a great master's thesis, and David would love to use the organics for his subsistence dissertation project."

"Good. You are then relieved from doing the site report. I'll have Katie do that and David can help."

Riley continued, "Walla Walla will soon be asking to have all the artifacts and samples returned as well. Did you get the bipoints imaged with the 3D scanner?"

"I just started getting them ready for scanning," said Jennifer.

"Make sure you get that done first so we have a record of every measurement and flake scar on their surfaces before we lose them. I'd like you to run a trace element analysis on them and run a sample of any large flakes found with the skeleton. Do the protein analysis last, okay, Jen?"

"Got it. I've been trying to contact Tom Rackerman at University of Pennsylvania, but his office says he hasn't checked in for a while. I think he would be a good outside person to sit on my dissertation committee, if he's willing. What do you think?"

"I don't know him personally, only of his work, but I think he would be perfect," replied Riley. "You might even be able to use some of his collections to complement your study."

"It would be great if I could get access to a comparative collection from Alaska," said Jennifer. "You look tired. Can you get some rest? We can handle the lab without you around for a day."

"That's the other thing I wanted to ask you about," said Riley. "Can you and David come with me to my place so I can collect some clothing? With the break-in, I'm staying in Moscow tonight. I plan to meet Dr. Allen at his lake place tomorrow."

"Sure," said Jennifer. "I'll ask David now." She smiled at Riley, "You and Dr. Allen seem to be developing a friendship."

"Thanks, Jen. Now, go do some artifact scanning before your new dissertation samples disappear into Army Corps warehouses."

Riley followed Jennifer back to the isotope lab to talk with Claire. "Claire, how much of the laser ablation scanning have you completed?"

"I've finished the oxygen and carbon isotopes. Those have been scanned, but the analysis can take a while. Haven't had time to do the strontium that you asked for," said Claire.

"Don't worry about analyzing the carbon or oxygen scans. We have the scan and can analyze them later. Focus today and tomorrow on getting the strontium scanning done. We'll need to have all the human remains boxed up and ready to ship by tomorrow night. Will you come with me to Walla Walla the day after tomorrow to transfer the collections?"

"They already want the collections returned?" questioned Claire.

"Just the human remains. We'll be able to continue working with the artifacts and geological samples. We have plenty of data already and you'll get the remainder we need today and tomorrow, right?"

"Alright, a road trip!" exclaimed Claire. "I love going to the wine capital of Washington."

"Good," said Riley. "We'll use the drive time to review where we stand with the analyses and what we can shoot for in a final report. Plan on an eight-thirty departure, day after tomorrow. I'll have a university vehicle at the loading dock that morning."

Riley returned to her office and began reviewing what had taken place. She opened her laptop and typed in University of Pennsylvania, Anthropology Faculty. A list of faculty profiles came up and she jotted down the contact information for Tom Rackerman. Riley composed a quick note introducing herself, mentioned the ancient human remains, and some of the recovered bipoints. She included her cell number and sent the note to Rackerman's email address.

CHAPTER 28

MISSOULA, MONTANA

It was a crystal clear Missoula morning. Deak Allen had checked into the Double Tree Hotel just after dark the previous evening. The campus was a short walk across the Clark Fork River by footbridge from the hotel, so he opted to make the hike to his appointment. Allen halted on the bridge to inspect the bubbling and tumbling water and the surrounding ridges that ringed the city.

The Clark Fork had been dammed by ice at the end of the last glacial maximum, when the continental glacier advanced southward and blocked the river. The ice dam blocking the Clark Fork created a giant Pleistocene lake, Ancient Lake Missoula, about half the size of current Lake Michigan. As the continental glacier receded northward about 15,000 years ago, the ice dam was breached and released a catastrophic flood over the interior Pacific Northwest. It scoured the land down to its ancient basalt bedrock, forming what is known as the scablands covering much of what is now eastern Washington State. The city of Missoula sits at the bottom of the ancient lakebed, surrounded by the ancient lake shores rising above the city. The Clark Fork River today is a world-class trout fishery.

Holding his still tender rib cage, Allen advanced up the steps at the Molecular Biological Sciences building for his morning appointment. He turned the door handle and stepped into the outer office with a large glass window looking into an inner office area, where a receptionist sat typing into a computer. "Hello, I'm Deak Allen. I believe I have a meeting with Dr. Ross." The receptionist checked a printed sheet and said, "Yes, Dr. Allen, he is expecting you in his office, room two fifteen. You can go right up."

Allen paused in front of the old wooden door, checking the office number. He knocked gently and heard a cheerful voice respond, "Please, come right in. The door's open."

Allen was met by a clean-shaven, short man, with thinning gray hair and an inviting smile. Ross had clear blue eyes behind tortoise shell glasses. "Hello, Dr. Allen. I'm James Ross, but please call me Jimmy."

"It is a pleasure to meet you, Jimmy. I go by Deak. I hope my assistant provided some context to this short notice visit?"

"I have found that good assistants of all types make sure the rendezvous is confirmed and leave the details to those attending. I remember him saying "Bryozoan, Department of Defense, and Dr. Allen. What can I do for you, Deak?"

"I'm dealing with two projects now that you might be of help with. I'm a minor player in a study dealing with climate change and its impact on human and natural resources. The other project I'm more involved with deals with archaeological materials that may suggest some people were living for a fairly long-life span at the end of the Pleistocene."

"That's right, your assistant said you are an archaeologist by training," replied Ross. "What makes you believe some people were living longer back then?"

"We have some human remains that indicate as much," said Allen.

Allen went on to explain the context of the finds, how they were dated, some of the initial information about the potential diet, and finally his discovery of Bryozoans in the watershed.

"I see," said Ross. "What a fascinating story. You archaeologists get involved with some of the most interesting things. Significant archaeological discoveries, like most scientific discoveries, are the result of an unanticipated find or an overlooked fact. We are so happy when we anticipate something and then it is confirmed, but the most interesting things are discovered when our anticipations are wrong."

"You are so right about that, Jimmy. And as you say, this is true for almost all scientific investigations. But once we are alerted by the surprise discovery, we can often focus our efforts and make some progress understanding it," said Allen.

"But back to the Bryozoans," continued Dr. Ross. "We do know that Bryozoans prefer warmer climates, and they need water to live and thrive. I shall speculate that you believe there was a Bryozoan population peak at the end of the Pleistocene because the climate was warming, and water tables were rising as glaciers were melting. If that is what you believe, I can tell you that you are absolutely correct."

"I must confess that I didn't have all of that quite put together," replied Allen. "Also, it is important to remember that continental glacial melt may have caused rising sea levels along the coasts, but it also produced drought conditions in the interior of continents."

"Oh, yes," said Ross. "Glacial melt is directly related to global warming. Flooding in some areas. Drought and fire in others. In the end, it is the unpredictability of climate that changes the composition of flora and fauna."

"Are Bryozoans edible? They don't appear palatable for humans, and I doubt they provide many of the nutrients we need for survival."

Ross's huge smile erupted, and he said, "I'll answer one question at a time. First, they are edible, but primarily for some fish, and some mollusks and gastropods. You are correct also that they are not palatable to us. However, food preferences are culturally determined, so the palatability issue may be debated. Having said that, I would also add that people living off the land on wild plants and to some extent wild animals that were found in the same watershed as Bryozoans were probably consuming them without knowing it."

Allen looked a little surprised and said, "I've seen these large gelatinous masses, Jimmy, and I would know if I were consuming them. Please explain."

"True. These are single-cell organisms that live in colonies. Each individual from the colony is an independent organism called a zooid. The zooids are hermaphrodites, so they can reproduce without another individual zooid, but when they are in a colony, they switch to sexual reproduction. The same is true of all hermaphroditic organisms."

"Are there times when the zooids are not in colony form? I mean, do they ever live in a form outside the colony as single individuals?"

"The short answer is yes," replied Ross. "However, this really is the short answer. Some species of Bryozoans produce statoblasts. These are reproductively viable "pods" that often go dormant, either seasonally or when the water they are living in retreats or evaporates. The statoblasts allow the Bryozoans to go dormant for many years. For instance, when the climate changes drastically and cold weather stays for long periods, say for years."

"You mean, maybe like a short ice age? There have been short fluctuations in climate over the eons of time. Bryozoans have apparently been able to survive?" asked Allen.

"True. You are correct again, Deak. They are among the oldest living animal organisms on Earth," said Ross.

"So, what's the mechanism by which humans consume Bryozoans, Jimmy?"

"Oh, right. During environmentally stressful times, the statoblasts are broadcast all over and settle into the environment. They become attached to aquatic roots and other plant structures. If humans eat those roots or leafy components they will be eating the Bryozoans in miniature dormant form."

"I have been told that Bryozoans may help to cure cancer. Does that rumor have any truth?"

Ross again smiled. "That is what I am interested in, Deak. I have been working on this topic for over a decade," replied Ross. You should know that Bryozoans carry bacteria that live in a symbiotic relationship with the Bryozoan. The bacteria gain a home and get food from the Bryozoan. The Bryozoan gets a foul-tasting chemical from the bacteria that wards off predators. Remember, I told you that some fish, mollusks and snails feed on Bryozoans. Well, those Bryozoans with the bacteria undergo less predation because they have this foul-tasting chemical, we call bryostatins."

Ross paused. "To make a long story shorter, the bryostatins are chemical compounds that act as antibiotics. This particular kind of antibiotic can alter cellular activity, such as the uncontrolled division of abnormal cells, like cancer cells. They may even alter the growth of other cell division, too, such as moles and other kinds of dermatoses. Bryostatins might even help maintain a youthful appearance or extend the longevity of some organs. We don't know exactly how they interact and if they interact differently with different types of cells. But I'm working on that piece."

The two men talked about Bryozoans for another hour or more. Finally, Allen stood to say goodbye and to thank Professor Ross for sharing his insights and the results of his investigations. "You are doing some amazing research here, Jimmy. I doubt that my assistant told you, but one of the goals of our Interagency Institute is to promote new research. I think your investigations may intersect with some of our projects. I hope we shall meet again."

"Thank you for your kind words, Deak," replied Ross. "I have yet to ask you my question that surfaced as we've been talking. Do you have a few more minutes?"

"Shoot," said Allen. "I've taken up a great deal of your time asking you questions. It is only fair that you ask me a few in return. I hope I'm able to answer them half as intelligently as you have addressed mine."

"You came here and began by telling me you were connected to two projects. One associated with climate change and the other associated with old, aged humans. I haven't yet determined where those projects relate to our conversation.

How do Bryozoans relate to either of those projects?" asked Ross.

"Unfortunately, I cannot answer that question, Jimmy. I can't because I don't know how, or even if, Bryozoans are linked to either topic. I do believe that glacial melt at the end of Pleistocene was responsible for drastic climatic shifts. I was curious how Bryozoans responded to those shifts. I also think we have been witnessing some recent climatic changes and perhaps some of those recent changes have affected Bryozoans," said Deak.

"Certainly, I have turned to Bryozoans in my research because they have recently been sighted all over the interior of the country," replied Ross. "We have known about bryostatins for some time, but my attention to them has only recently been piqued because of the increase in attention given to Bryozoans.

"Like I said, I am currently collecting and digesting all of this information," said Allen. "I don't know enough to answer your questions now. I just know enough to ask you more questions. Incidentally, the researcher working on the old, aged humans is Dr. Samantha Riley at Washington State University. I hope you two will be able to meet sometime in the near future. I am just a facilitator in the scientific mix. It is people like you and Dr. Riley who are doing the actual scientific research."

Allen paused and reached into his pocket to fish out a card. "Jimmy, this is my contact information. My assistant is Jack Mills. I was serious when I said earlier that my agency promotes promising research. If you should find more significant information that Bryozoans and bryostatins may be related to human health, please contact me. I would love to know more, and the Institute can help with additional research funds."

"That's certainly fair enough, Deak. Our discussion has been extremely valuable. I'm sure I'll be thinking about Bryozoans from a new and different perspective as a result our exchange. Have a safe journey back, Deak."

The two men shook hands. Allen left the building and slowly walked back over the Clark Fork and tried to put the pieces together. He again stopped on the bridge, wondering if he had enough time to cast a fly. Allen had already checked out of the Double Tree, but his bags and vehicle were still there. As much as he craved the opportunity to stay and fish the river, he had planned to meet Samantha back at the cabin, and he still had to finish the Afghanistan report. He gave the river one final yearning look, turned and walked to his car.

Allen drove for several hours straight to downtown Coeur d'Alene and swung the rental into a gas station. While refueling he texted Riley, letting her know he would be at the cabin in about forty-five minutes. Just before getting back onto the highway a sign for a wine shop caught his eye and he remembered that Riley had promised to cook dinner. Allen pulled across the street and entered the wine shop. He browsed the rows and after some thought, selected a South African *Pinotage*. After a few more minutes of indecision, he opted for two bottles, paid, hopped into the rental, and headed south to the cabin.

CHAPTER 29

PHILADELPHIA, PENNSYLVANIA

The University of Pennsylvania is embedded within the city of Philadelphia. It is a magnificent campus occupying over three hundred acres. Beginning in the 1740s, the campus now contains over one hundred eighty buildings. Forty of those buildings are listed as Certified Architectural Structures on the Philadelphia Register of Historic Places, and seven of those buildings are on the National Register of Historic Places. The campus itself includes over a hundred acres of gardens and green spaces.

Tom Rackerman was sitting in the registered building that housed the Dean's office, his usual dapper appearance gone. His eyes were sunken, and the whites were laced by tentacles of red veins. He pleaded with his Dean, Wilford Harrington. "You must be able to do more, Wilford. They were going to kill me. Can't you call the U.S. State Department or the FBI?"

Wilford Harrington wore a brown tweed jacket with tan leather elbow patches. His blue striped tie blended into the background of his pressed blue shirt. He was an elfin man with gold wire rimmed glasses. He spoke deliberately, but chose his words carefully, worn out by the repetition. "Tom, as I've previously stated, the authorities have been contacted. They have reached out. Right now, it seems that the group of criminals you encountered in Vladivostok were a gang of muggers. I'm sorry this happened to you, but muggings occur all the time over there, particularly to Americans travelling by themselves."

Rackerman had been in transit for close to sixty hours, Vladivostok, Anchorage, Seattle, Philadelphia, and was trying to explain the threatening experience he had undergone. He had hit a stone wall with Harrington. "This is horseshit, Wilford. They weren't muggers. They were trained assassins looking for research information. Like I said, they were interested in recently discovered indigenous human remains of individuals that lived to be over a hundred years old, from both Siberia and here in the U.S. These weren't muggers or hotel thieves."

"Please, Tom, the investigators here have talked to your contacts in Vladivostok and nobody over there knows anything about the ancient human remains you have described."

"How about Dimitri Kozlov? I bet nobody has talked with him. He'll confirm the ages of the human remains and back my story," shouted Rackerman.

"Tom, you have had a terrible experience. That everyone can see, and we have no doubt that there were some thugs in your room. But it was simply a robbery. They took your wallet, cell phone, and laptop. You are safe and unharmed, and we are all grateful for that. The authorities will continue to investigate the situation."

Rackerman spat out again, "This is horseshit. I'm going to the provost about this, if I have to."

Wilford held up his hands and looked calmly around the room. "Tom, Dimitri Kozlov emphatically denies any knowledge about these ancient remains except to say that they have uncovered an early site dated to the end of the Pleistocene with human remains and an assortment of stone tools, that he says you examined. There was no evidence or report of a one hundred twenty-year-old person."

"What! That's nuts!" Rackerman stood, pushing his chair away from the table almost knocking the chair over backwards. "Harrington, you are a bureaucratic ass. I intend to pursue this." Rackerman turned and stomped out of the room.

Rackerman unceremoniously marched across campus toward his office in the Museum of Anthropology and Archaeology, not making eye contact with anyone. He was clearly upset. Reaching his office, he slammed the door and thumped into his desk chair. He had left Vladivostok without seeing Dimitri Kozlov or getting to make a final examination of the stone tools associated with the burial. Kozlov had become unavailable. Rackerman left Vladivostok the following morning. During his extended trip back to Pennsylvania he attempted to call Kozlov several times and was unable to get through to him. Maybe Harrington was correct and that everything possible was being done. He took out the new cell phone and punched in Peter Maddington's office number. No answer from him either.

Rackerman touched the mouse on his desk and his computer screen came to life uploading various alerts and email messages. He began deleting the endless string of junk mail coming to his address. Even though the university used advanced sorting programs to recognize and partition junk mail, tons of junk always made it through. He paused when he spotted a legitimate message, a note from a Dr. Riley at Washington State University. He clicked and read the message. A spurt of adrenalin ran through his veins. Was this real? This was exactly what he needed to help convince Harrington that Vladivostok was more than just a mugging. He reached for his cell phone and dialed the number listed in the email.

First one, then two, and interrupting the third ring was a woman's voice. "Hello, this is Samantha Riley."

"Hello, Dr. Riley, my name is Tom Rackerman. I believe I just recently received an email from you regarding, how shall I put it, a unique archaeological discovery."

"Thanks for getting back to me, Dr. Rackerman. One of my graduate students has been attempting to contact you for several days now and your office hasn't been able to get the two of you connected," replied Riley.

"I've been out of the country and then lost in transit for the past few days. What can I do for you?"

"Like I mentioned in my email, we have a late Pleistocene burial that contains large bifaces that resemble some of the bipointed specimens that you've reported on from Alaska. I have a senior graduate student working on these for her dissertation and I'd like to get you two connected. Perhaps she can have a look at some of your specimens and maybe you could compare yours to what she has?"

"Early bipoints in Washington?" asked Rackerman. "How big are they?"

"Her name is Jennifer Henderson. I'm sure she can speak to you more informatively than I can since she is taking all the vitals on them, but some look to be in the twenty-centimeter range, maybe larger."

"How wide and thick are they?" pursued Rackerman.

"Again, Dr. Rackerman, you might want to ask Jennifer specific questions like that, but they are substantially large bifaces," explained Riley. "Jennifer tells me they are not preforms or early-stage bifaces. She says they are abnormally large, finished points."

"Do you have any idea of the raw material type?"

"Some type of chert or flint. You'll need to discuss that with Jennifer," replied Riley.

"You say they are from a well dated context?" asked Rackerman.

"They are from a well dated burial."

Rackerman paused before continuing. He didn't want to appear too anxious, but he had to know, given what he'd seen in the St. Petersburg report that apparently no longer existed. "This burial, where the bipoints were found, wouldn't be associated with an individual of unusual age, would it?"

Now, it was Riley's turn to be cautious about what she chose to reveal. "Perhaps, but let me ask you first if you found an Ice Age burial that contained an individual well over a hundred years old at the time of death, what could account for such a long life?"

"That is a good question, and it just so happens I've been thinking about this recently. I've read a report of an individual who died at the age of one hundred twenty found in Siberia and who lived during the end of the Pleistocene. The only thing that makes sense to me is that these Ice Age people may have a slightly different genetic composition, perhaps for cold weather adaptation. It would be a trait selected for, perhaps, in the heterozygous form, similar to the sickle cell trait."

"Wait, you've been working with human remains aged at one hundred twenty years old?"

"I'm interested in the artifacts associated with the human remains. My colleagues in Russia have been working with the bone," replied Rackerman.

"You mentioned the sickle cell trait? Explain your thinking about that," asked Riley.

"In heterozygous form, the sickle cell trait prevents malaria. Those with the trait survive, thus perpetuating the trait. Overall, the population survives and is biologically successful in a malarial environment. This was found to be the case in West Africa with the genetic mutation for the sickle cell trait getting passed from generation to generation, because those with the trait could survive malaria. Of course, those with the trait in homozygous form would contract sickle cell anemia and die young."

Rackerman paused again. "I'm no human geneticist or physical anthropologist. However, an extreme, cold weather adapted trait might have successfully spread throughout a human population as well," he suggested. "In much the same way as the sickle cell trait."

"Particularly, during the last Ice Age?" interjected Riley.

"Exactly," said Rackerman. "Such genes often have other unanticipated effects. Perhaps a slightly longer life span? We'll never know without conducting a genetic profile on a skeleton preserved from the last Ice Age."

"That is a very interesting theory, Dr. Rackerman. I'm sure you could talk about this for days with my graduate student Jennifer Henderson. Can I have her call you to discuss those bipoints?"

"Absolutely. I look forward to talking with her and with you more on this topic," replied Rackerman. "And please, call me Tom."

"Very well, Tom. I certainly look forward to exploring this topic in greater detail with you."

"This is fabulous. I'll bid you farewell until we talk again," said Rackerman.

After switching the phone off, Rackerman was reminded of Maddington's condescending comments about Samantha Riley. She seemed levelheaded and reasonable. He would have to meet her to gain a real sense of her character. In the meantime, rest and then reassessment of the Vladivostok situation.

CHAPTER 30

ST. MARIES, IDAHO

Allen negotiated the rented Subaru cautiously into the cabin driveway. A dark blue Tesla was parked in front of the stairs leading down to the cabin door. Allen cursed himself for not asking what kind of car Riley drove.

Stepping purposely but lightly, Allen moved to the door and tried the handle. It was unlocked. He opened the door, peered in then called out, "Hello, anyone home?" There was no sound or movement on the inside. He waited a few seconds and called out again. Finally, there was an answer from the lower deck. "Hello. We're down here. Is that you, Deak?"

Windy came around the corner from the lower deck, all smiles, looking up at him. "I thought you were still here. We saw all your gear. Walt and I are coming right up. We were just down at the water collecting some things for dinner."

"What a great surprise," responded Allen. "I didn't think you guys would be back for a while."

"We didn't think so either, but we were in the San Juans and thought we just couldn't miss you, given that it's been so long, so we moored the boat and drove over," said Windy.

"Great. Let me collect stuff from the car and I'll meet you guys on the deck."

Allen walked back to the Subaru grinning as he grabbed his backpack and the wine. He hurried back through the cabin and out to the main deck overlooking the lake. Windy was fussing with a basket full of green shoots and berries. She smiled up at him. "It's so nice to see you again, Deak. Walt has missed you. You're like a son to him. It's been about four or five years, hasn't it?"

Allen thought and then nodded his head. "Must be about that long. Amazing. I guess it's the sign of lasting friendship. Seems like we were just together a week or so ago. Where's Walt?"

"He's down on the dock. Should be here in a few. You look good, Deak. How are the old injuries? I assume you are well healed by now?"

"I'm stronger by the day."

Windy turned and looked him square in the eye, so she could read him. Have you found someone, Deak? Please don't tell me you're still looking for love in all the wrong places?"

"Windy, you sound just like my mother." But he skipped the answer.

They could hear footsteps ascending the deck stairs and Walt appeared. "I see you had an opportunity to use the boat. Your fly rod is still in the rack. How are you doing, my friend?" Walk and Deak embraced. "What can I get you to drink?" inquired Walt.

Before Allen could answer, they all heard someone coming through the door onto the deck and turned. "Ah, Windy and Walt, this is my friend, Dr. Samantha Riley, from WSU." Allen walked over and put an arm around Samantha. "We've only known each other for a few weeks but it seems like a short lifetime given all that has happened."

Windy immediately walked over with an outstretched hand. "Any friend of Deak's is always welcome in our house. Windy Steward." She pointed across the deck. "That's my husband, Walt."

"Deak has told me so much about you two. I'm glad we can meet so soon."

Walt broke in, "Hey, how about I mix up a pitcher of margaritas to celebrate old friends and new?"

"That sounds great," responded Windy, taking Riley by the hand and guiding her to a chair. "Can't wait to hear about how you two met and how a few weeks can be like a short lifetime."

With that, Riley and Allen relayed the story about the burial discovery and the preliminary report, how the Inter-agency Institute got involved, and the attempted kidnapping.

"My goodness!" exclaimed Walt. "Assault, kidnapping, maybe the death of your colleague, and the oldest person to ever have lived on Earth. You two have lived a lifetime in the past couple weeks."

Riley changed the subject. "Walt, Deak tells me you two have been retired for about five years. How can that be? You both are so young." It was true. Windy could have been Samantha's sister. Windy and Walt had both turned sixty earlier that summer. But Windy looked at least twenty years younger than her age.

"I can't tell you how my wife has retained her youth. I guess I'm just lucky," said Walt.

"You look young as well. You can't be of retirement age," pressed Riley.

"After a career as a researcher and V.P. for research at the University of Wyoming, where Deak worked with me on his dissertation, I took the provost position at Western Washington University. I spent almost six years there. Windy moved her veterinary practice to Bellingham and life was good. We had just turned fifty-five and decided to turn the page and start a new adventure while we were still healthy. She still has an interest in her practice, and I still do some cultural heritage consulting. They're fun, but they don't run our lives on a day-to-day basis anymore. We mapped out what we wanted to do, ran the numbers, and realized we had an opportunity that not many have. I don't know. Maybe early retirement helps postpone aging," said Walt.

"Thanks, Samantha," said Allen. "I've never asked Walt why he didn't stay in his lab until a ripe old age like most academics. You meet him for half an hour and know more about him than I do."

"The woman speaks her mind, Deak," said Walt.

"I hope you two like salmon, water potatoes, wild rice, and wild green salad?" asked Windy. "We have plenty."

"That sounds great, Windy, but I don't believe I've ever had water potatoes," admitted Samantha.

"Windy has been out collecting in the shallows again. Water potatoes are the tubers found under a variety of water plant that grows around here," said Walt. "One of the other reasons we came to the cabin was to resupply the boat with some fresh wild foods. We are traveling back to the west side tomorrow morning."

"What are your plans, Deak?" asked Windy. "Are you going to be in the Northwest much longer?"

Riley gave her full attention to Allen. "Yeah, Deak, what are your plans?"

"Listen, you are welcome to use the cabin for as long as you need," informed Walt. "We are based out of our place in Anacortes when not on the boat."

"Thanks, Walt. I still have some things to do here. By the way, I ran into a park ranger while fishing. What's his name?"

"Probably Rick," responded Walt.

"Yes, Rick. He informed me that Windy's photos were selected in some kind of contest."

"I finally won!" responded Windy joyously.

Allen's phone vibrated and he left the deck to address it. It was Jack Mills. "Hey, Deak, I just wanted you to know that we still have no clue about those guys you hog-tied near Helmer. Also, Jimmy Ross from the University of Montana called looking for you. He indicated he's got an update for you on the freshwater Bryozoan you two discussed. You should probably give him a call."

"I'll call him tomorrow. Can you contact his office and set that up for ten in the morning my time? Also, I think his work may be some of the most cutting-edge research on new human health leads. I'd like to ask him to submit a proposal through our research foundation," said Allen.

"Have him send it to me and I'll process it," replied Jack. "Anything else?"

"Yeah, there is one other issue. Can you ask General Ortega to contact his old buddy Colonel Blankenship in Walla Walla. I'd like the Institute to remain connected with the recent burial recovery at least until there is better resolution and a clear direction of analysis."

"Okay, Deak. You know General Ortega will probably put you on that project if Blankenship agrees."

"I know," replied Allen. "I just have a feeling there is something special going on with this ancient burial."

"Will do, Deak. I'll send confirmation texts for both issues."

When Deak walked back, Windy and Samantha were preparing dinner, chattering away in the kitchen like two close sisters who hadn't seen each other for a year. He looked over at Walt, who was pouring both another margarita.

"That's a good woman, Deak. You better not let her get away."

"Hey, we've only known each other for a couple of weeks," responded Allen.

"Sometimes that's all you need, particularly given what you two have been through together."

Samantha called out, "Hey, you two, cocktail hour is over. Dinner is being served in here, with a lovely South African wine."

The four sat down and toasted again, celebrating each other's company. The dinner was delicious and unusual. The water potatoes were steamed and sprinkled with sea salt and first pressed oils. Samantha studied the green salad. "What an interesting combination of vegetables. Tell me again what's in here, Windy?"

"Those are arrow leaf stems, a species of *Lomatium*. Those greens there are a form of balsam root shoots." Moving her finger to another species, "fiddlehead fern tips, thinly sliced Chanterelle mushrooms, and everything is on a bed of wild rice and covered with huckleberry sauce."

"Isn't it a bit late for fiddleheads?" replied Samantha.

"A bit. I know a steep north facing slope with a cold spring coming out. The direct sun doesn't hit it until mid-June. I keep the ferns cut back all spring so I can harvest some in the summer. This is probably the last batch."

"I bet this is wild salmon, eh?"

Walt responded, "We just harvested a few salmon from the coast before driving here. I hope you like fresh Coho."

Deak remarked, "It is rare for modern people to eat all wild foods, at least on a regular basis. It is just not available reliably anywhere around the world."

"True, domestication is a mark of modern humanity," said Walt. "Domestication of plants and animals hailed from the Neolithic Revolution and stimulated the birth and growth of modern civilizations everywhere--wheat and barley in the Middle East, rice in Asia, corn in North America, potatoes in South America. Population densities jumped when domestication became our way of getting food."

Samantha replied, "Yes, but in some ways, it was also a curse. I've been looking closely at human diet over time, and yes, populations did dramatically increase during the Neolithic Revolution, but shortly afterwards, all over the world there was a population crash. I believe, as do other researchers, like Nathan Goodman at Harvard, that early domesticates were actually almost all wild foods, then gradually as they became more and more domesticated their genetic diversity drastically declined, which is the definition of domesticated foods. With that decline in biodiversity, human populations also began showing signs of poor health, causing the post-Neolithic population crash."

Allen added, "So we modern people are stuck. Ninety-nine percent of food is domesticated, and we need to eat but it's not as healthy and nutritious for us as the wild foods our distant relatives ate."

"It is not clear how nutrients and vitamins from foods, particularly wild foods, interact with our bodies and minds," continued Samantha. "Many nutritionists today say most vitamin supplements are useless when compared to vitamins absorbed by the body in food form. Wild foods contain an amazing number of complex compounds that we just don't know that much about."

"So here we sit," commented Walt, "eating a rare, delicious, and mysterious, meal."

As dinner was ending, Windy spoke, "It's getting late." She looked to Samantha, "I assume you are staying here tonight?"

Windy noticed some eye contact between Riley and Allen. "Samantha, you can have the guest room and we'll put Deak down in the man cave suite."

"The man cave suite?" inquired Samantha.

"There's an extra bedroom down there with a deck overlooking the water and an adjoining room with fly tying gear, flat screen TV, and a refrigerator full of beer. I call it the man cave."

"I accept. It sounds like Deak will be right at home down there. I must be in Pullman tomorrow morning at eight to transport some materials to Walla Walla. Deak, I'd like to talk with you about the human remains if you have time in a bit?"

"Sure, how about meeting me on the man cave deck this evening," replied Allen.

CHAPTER 31

The lower deck faced east, across the lake looking up the St. Joe River Valley and its layers of mountains. The clouds that gathered over the eastern horizon at dusk were ignited with color. This reverse sunset or eastern sunset was caused by the sun in the west illuminating the skyline over the eastern mountains. Allen poured Samantha a glass of the *Pinotage* as they watched the sky shimmer and then darken over the water.

"Higgins has requested I return the human remains. That's why I'm going to Walla Walla tomorrow," informed Riley. "Needless to say, we were just beginning the analysis before he called."

"Did he give a reason?"

"He did not. I'm afraid he's getting pressured to shift this project to a larger institution with a bigger forensics or osteology lab. It's just a one-woman show at Washington State."

"This is partially his responsibility. I'm sure he is just getting too much heat from the local tribes and perhaps his own superiors," replied Allen. "My bet is that he will change his mind and you'll be able to complete the analysis."

"I sure hope so, but he really wants those remains by tomorrow. He sounded like a guy under a lot of stress when I talked with him the other day."

"I'll make contact with him and find out what he's thinking," replied Allen.

"Thanks, Deak." Riley raised an eyebrow, "Seems like that that dinner I keep promising you has a way of getting delayed or cancelled."

"Maybe after you get back from Walla Walla," responded Allen. "I'm going to stay here tomorrow and attempt to finish that Afghan report."

"I've been thinking about the age of our friend from Central Ferry," said Riley. "The other day I had a conversation with a colleague from the University of Pennsylvania who thinks that perhaps Ice Age people may have had a genetic mutation that helped them survive cold conditions and that one of the side effects of the gene was potentially a longer life span."

Allen turned his head toward Riley. "You wouldn't have been talking with Tom Rackerman, would you?"

Samantha gave Deak a puzzled and suspicious look. "Now why, how would you know I might be talking with Tom Rackerman?"

"You mentioned Penn and I know that Rackerman was just over in Vladivostok dabbling in some Ice Age assemblages," replied Allen. "He also called Maddington from there about a week ago."

Samantha continued to scrutinize Allen as she spoke. "Yes, Rackerman was the colleague I talked to. I still don't see how you could have possibly pulled that name out of the air."

"Like I said, it wasn't random. My assistant did some sleuthing. And what did Rackerman say about genetic mutation?"

"He likened it to the sickle cell trait in West African populations," replied Riley.

Allen thought, "That certainly is a possibility. Humans have great genetic diversity. The potential to live longer because of genetics may certainly be held by some people, and it's just a matter of context for that potential to be expressed. In fact, many researchers believe differential heritage to be the primary factor for some people living longer than others."

"True," said Riley. "But if it happened in the way Rackerman postulates, the mutation probably only relates to cold weather survival. There is no reason to suppose that such a mutation also increased longevity. And like the sickle cell trait, which has no advantage outside of malarial environments, the proposed cold survival trait has little advantage in warmer climates or after the invention of warm clothing," said Riley. "As more people obtain the trait the greater probability of homozygote transmission and the elimination of the trait from the gene pool."

"Have you expressed this opinion to Rackerman?" asked Allen.

"Of course not," replied Riley. "I want him to work on Jennifer Henderson's dissertation committee. And besides, he may be partially correct even if I, and you, are skeptical."

"It is an interesting possibility," repeated Allen. "Genetic differentiation has to be one of the leading contenders for an explanation of the differences in human life expectancy."

"Yes, but that is not necessarily the same thing we are talking about," countered Riley. "We are talking about the oldest person to have ever lived on Earth as far as we know, and that person lived over thirteen thousand years ago. That's a bit different that Uncle John dying at sixty-five and Aunt Jane dying at eighty-five."

"Agreed," replied Allen. "Do you have any other ideas?"

"I'm working on it. I think it relates to diet, but it will be difficult to nail down if I can't continue the isotope analysis on the man from Central Ferry," said Riley.

"Understood," said Allen. "What are your speculations with diet?"

"Again, I lean toward the wild food hypothesis. There are so many complex compounds in wild varieties of plants. Any single or combination of compounds may have enormous positive impacts on human health. That diversity is exponentially reduced when domesticates dominate our diets. So, my bet is with the complexity of wild foods," replied Riley.

Allen responded, "Doesn't Claire still have samples to process that could be informative?"

"She does. But there is so much more we can do. She just collected a few nondestructive sample isotopes. And Jennifer is still in the early stages of her stone tool analysis. She hasn't had any time to begin the protein assessments or blood residue analysis."

"Well, like I said, I think Higgins will come around."

Samantha stretched. "It's getting late, and I've got an early morning and a long day tomorrow."

"May I interest you in a tour of the man cave suite?" invited Allen. "Apparently, it's a relatively new addition to the cabin."

Samantha grinned slyly. "I'll take a rain check. My schedule calls for an early up and out of here. Give me a call tomorrow afternoon, okay, Deak?"

"You did promise me a dinner. So, I'll pester you again tomorrow. When do you think you'll be back from Walla Walla?" he asked.

"I'm not sure what to expect from Higgins. We're targeting an early start so I'd estimate we should be back in Pullman by early afternoon," replied Riley. "Maybe two or three."

"I'm going to have one more short glass of wine and listen to the lake wildlife before I retire. Are you sure I can't interest you in a second drink?"

"That sounds tempting, Deak. But it also sounds like it might derail my plans for an early morning. I'll catch you tomorrow, eh?"

"I'll call you in the afternoon. Good night, Samantha."

She leaned over, kissed him on the mouth, and hurried up the stairway.

CHAPTER 32

PULLMAN, WASHINGTON

The morning air held the scent of rain. It was an inordinately cool and overcast day. The typical summer weather for the Palouse was sunny and dry, but this was a relief since the last rain was thirteen weeks ago. The dark sky portended an ominous change.

From his vehicle Boris Mirsky watched with binoculars as Riley and Claire put the last box into the trunk of the university vehicle and slammed it shut.

Their trip to Walla Walla was planned to be a one day, there-and-back excursion. They planned to get to the Army Corps office by 11:00 a.m., eat an early lunch in town, and drive back to Pullman by early afternoon.

"Let's hit the road," said Claire, holding a large thermal container of fresh coffee. Samantha got into the driver's seat and pulled out from behind Woods Hall. She turned the vehicle onto the main campus drive and headed toward downtown Pullman. Both Samantha and Claire felt a slight sense of adventure as they turned onto the state highway to drive through rural eastern Washington. The trip to Walla Walla would take them across the rolling dunes of the Palouse, down into the bottom of the Snake River canyon, back up the other side, and on to the edge of the Blue Mountains.

Riley and Claire didn't begin talking about the isotope analysis until they had been on the road for over an hour. Instead, they reviewed the events of the past few incredible days. Finally, Claire asked, "What kind of a report are we going to be able to build without doing a comprehensive analysis of the remains?"

"We have some tests done, and we have all the context for the excavations. One of our responsibilities is to make sure we report what we found, where we found it, and when we found it. Nobody else can report those things, only the researchers who performed the excavation. We can provide details and results from the analyses we were able to conduct. We need to be clear on how we determined age at time of death, as well as the age of the site, and any of the raw data from our isotope analyses. When we meet Higgins, I'll ask him what other types of analyses are being planned for the skeleton."

"We already have a bunch of isotope scans done, so there is a great deal of analysis ahead of us, even if it's all laser ablation," said Claire.

"It's a nondestructive isotope technique. We need to be respectful to heritage values," said Riley. "We also have all the artifacts that need analysis. Jennifer is working on that as we speak."

Despite the ominous weather, the morning ride was splendid, and both driver and passenger were enjoying the remote scenery and relaxed time together. One-on-one time was something that Riley tried to provide all her graduate students. It was not something that all students got from their mentors.

Riley's cell phone was linked to the university vehicle's blue tooth receiver, and she noticed the incoming call from Jonathan Higgins. She touched the information screen and accepted the call. "Hello, Jonathan."

"Hello, Dr. Riley. I assume you are on your way."

"I am," responded Riley. "I have Claire Anderson with me. She has been the one working on the isotope analysis and helped with the osteon counting."

In a persnickety voice, Higgins asked, "I hope you were able to complete all of the preliminary analyses you had been planning."

Claire rolled her eyes as she listened in.

"We rushed through everything we could, in the little time we had," replied Riley.

"I do have a change in my schedule today, Dr. Riley. I am currently outside of the Walla Walla office in Dayton and won't be back to Walla Walla until late this evening. Perhaps we could meet at the Winehard Hotel in Dayton to transfer the collection. You should be driving right past it on your way to Walla Walla," said Higgins.

"Jonathan, I wish you had called me last night or earlier today. We could have brought the remains up tomorrow and had an extra day to work on them."

Again, in a polite tone, "I am sorry, Dr. Riley, but this works out for the better since I need the collections sooner rather and later," responded Higgins.

"We'll be in Dayton in about fifteen minutes," said Riley.

"You can't miss me," said Higgins. "I'll be standing in the parking lot out front."

The rendezvous at the Winehard Hotel was not comfortable. Clearly, Higgins was in some distress. As Claire and Samantha loaded the curation boxes into Higgins' car, he shuffled about nervously, and speciously apologized for the short timeframe and change in plans.

Before parting, Riley again asked, or rather warned, "Jonathan, I hope you know what you are doing. By most measures, I should be working with these collections, and you damn well know it. What do you intend to do with these remains?"

"As I have stated, this is my call and I've made my decision."

"Jonathan, you haven't heard the last from me on this matter," said Riley.

Higgins was anxious and remained silent. He turned and lifted the car door handle, slid in and pulled out of the parking lot.

Samantha and Claire stood flat-footed, as they watched his car roll away and turn the corner. Within seconds it had disappeared, along with the collection they had been working tirelessly to better understand. "What a creep!" pronounced Claire. "He sure isn't justifying his position in any logical or even professional manner."

"My guess is that he is having flashbacks from his Clarkston Mummy days," responded Riley. "He's panicked. I've never seen him like this before."

"Was he the one who managed the Clarkston Mummy fiasco for the Corps?" asked Claire. "I remember watching it on the national news, with all the protests."

"In all fairness, he was in a no-win situation. The Corps, with him as one of the primary administrators, were sued by over a dozen of the most respected scientists in the nation. Fortunately, most, but not all, the local tribes were supporting the Corps position. I hope he's learned something. Let's go."

CHAPTER 33

ST. MARIES, IDAHO

Allen had been restless the entire night and rousted early to begin his Afghan report, but his mind kept drifting back to his discussion with Riley the evening before. Could the Central Ferry remains really be one hundred thirty-eight years old? How could that be possible? Could those remains have clues to a longer life? He kept returning to Samantha's comment about diet and the conversation around the dinner table with Walt and Windy regarding domesticated and wild foods. Then he'd mentally ponder Rackerman's genetic mutation proposition and Samantha's rebuttal. It was about eight in the morning when Walt and Windy interrupted his musings and said their farewells.

"Deak, we'll be in Anacortes for a few days if you need anything," said Walt. "After that we'll be on the boat. We'll spend a few days in the San Juans then cross over to Salt Spring Island on the Canadian side."

"Deak, you be sure to come and visit now that you are on this side of the country. We have plenty of room on the boat. And bring Samantha, too," added Windy.

"Okay, okay," replied Allen. "You two drive safely. I'll tell Samantha she's been invited for a cruise."

Walt and Windy left and Allen kept pecking away at the report until his phone alarm sounded and reminded him to call Professor Ross in Missoula.

Jimmy Ross picked up the call almost immediately. "Hello, this is Dr. Ross. To whom am I speaking?"

"Hi Jimmy, this is Deak Allen from Interagency Institute. Good to hear your voice again."

"Deak, thank you for getting back with me so promptly. I wanted to give you a heads-up on our work with bryostatins--the compound produced by bacteria with a symbiotic relationship with Bryozoans."

"What have you discovered, Jimmy?"

"The work is still preliminary, but it seems that we do indeed find that bryostatins attack and destroy alien cell growth in some types of tissue. We have a handful of positive lab tests, and we are thinking about expanding the diversity of samples to look at a variety of cell types for different organs."

"This is great news, Jimmy. Remember from our previous conversation I indicated that the Institute could solicit proposals from promising research? Well, I'd like you to submit a proposal on this topic," informed Allen.

"How does that all work with your Institute?"

Allen briefly explained, "It is essentially a fellowship with a stipend and research funding. You can buy out all or part of your time with the fellowship and the research funding can be used for lab staff, graduate assistantships, or supplies.

Everything must be less than two hundred and fifty thousand per year and it can be renewed for two additional years."

"Fantastic," said Ross. Where do I send the proposal?"

"Send it to my assistant, Jack Mills. You have his address on my card. The fellowship does require a six-month progress report and an end of the year final research report along with a face-to-face presentation in D.C. The presentation will be in front of a review committee."

"How about indirect costs and university overhead?" asked Ross.

"You'll have to deal with your institution on those issues for supplies and lab assistants. The fellowship is stand alone, directly to you."

"I'll send Jack Mills a draft proposal and copy you on it," said Ross.

"Great, Jimmy. I can't wait to work with you on this project. Let me know as questions start emerging."

"There is one other thing, if I can pick your brain?" asked Ross.

"Sure. What is it?"

"I've been thinking about your Ice Age human, and I keep thinking about how it might relate to changing environments today," said Ross. "I'm a firm believer in human-induced contemporary global climate change, but from what you said the last time we met, there was dramatic climatic change at the end of the Pleistocene. I'm a microbiologist, but I can't believe that was caused by ancient people. Seems like you were saying the environment is naturally dynamic and changing all the time."

"True," said Allen. "I did say that. The terminal Pleistocene witnessed extreme climatic change. Thousands of plant and animal species were extirpated. However, that climatic episode occurred gradually in human life terms. Of, course, there were dramatic localized climatic events caused by earthquakes and volcanic eruptions, but those were isolated events. Late Ice Age extinctions took place over a twenty-five-thousand-year period."

"But that is a relatively short period of time in geologic terms, isn't it?" asked Ross.

"Yes, and remember, I'm not talking about some regional climatic change that occurred in one specific place. I can't tell you the number of times I talked with some old timer who remembered when the so-and-so river froze all the way across, back in 1947. Those kinds of local climatic events are continuous. I'm talking about global climatic episodes."

"But the end of the Ice Age was a global phenomenon, wasn't it?" asked Ross.

"It was," said Allen. "However, there is a big difference between contemporary climate change and Pleistocene climate change. Ice Age climate change was continuous over the course of more than a thousand human generations. Contemporary climate change is occurring over two or three human generations. We may not have time to adjust or adapt to significant perturbations."

"Interesting," replied Jimmy. "Most of us remember our grandparents or great grandparents. And some of us remember our great great grandparents, but those ancestors are only four human generations back. You are talking about over a thousand human generations. That is a difference that I never really considered," said Ross. "I'd better let you get back to your work and I'll begin writing my proposal."

It was just before eleven when Allen put the still-unfinished Afghan report away. His phone buzzed and he picked up. "Hi, Jack. What do you have for me?"

"I hope you talked with Ross today?" said Mills.

"Sure did. He's going to be sending you a draft proposal related to his Bryozoan research," replied Allen.

"Great. Deak, Ortega met with Blankenship via Zoom yesterday and apparently their old friendship has been rekindled. Blankenship must have been impressed by you because he agreed to keep the Institute on the human burial piece, but he wants you and the Institute to take responsibility for the project."

"It sounds like the political situation must be heating up around these remains?" inquired Allen.

"That's my read as well," said Mills. "He wants his office to relinquish responsibility just in case this thing blows up."

"Where does Higgins fit into the mix?" asked Allen.

"He'll be the Walla Walla point of contact for the project, but the Institute will have management responsibility."

"I didn't want this to happen. It's so important for the regional centers to maintain management control of these kinds of projects," said Allen.

"Understood, but that's Blankenship's deal. And another thing, Deak, you are going to have to spend most of your time on site because of the amount of in-person contact this project is generating."

"Well, any other news for me?"

"Not now. I'll talk to you as things develop," said Mills, and signed off.

Allen was unable to reach Riley by phone to stop her from delivering the human remains to Walla Walla. As the new project manager, he thought it was best to allow Riley to continue her isotope research. He decided to drive straight to Pullman to visit with Riley when she returned to give her the news.

CHAPTER 34

GARFIELD COUNTY, WASHINGTON

The trip back to Pullman was silent most of the way. Samantha and Claire hadn't yet crossed over the Snake River and were in Garfield County, descending into the Snake River canyon. An SUV came up behind them and signaled to pass them. The canyon road was full of turns, but occasionally had a clear window for passing. The SUV passed them on the first opportunity it had, and disappeared in the distance as it sped around curves. Within minutes another SUV appeared behind them and approached at rapid speed. "What the heck," said Riley. "That car is riding my tail." She sped up a little to get the vehicle off her bumper. The SUV closed the gap and remained at her rear without slowing down. Riley peered through her rearview mirror at the driver of the offending vehicle. "Oh, crap. Claire, dial 911." Riley floored the gas petal and pulled away from the pursuing SUV. She slowed only slightly, taking a sharp curve and then sped up again.

"What is it?" asked Claire. "I'm only getting one bar. We must be in a dead zone out here."

Riley quickly explained, "The guys that tried to kidnap me are in the SUV behind us. Keep trying to get through and I'll try to lose those bastards."

Claire turned around to see who was following them. "They're catching up to us."

"I know. Make sure your seat belt is secure." Riley pegged the gas pedal again and her tires squealed as she took a curve, much faster than was safe. She recovered as the road in front of her straightened. Her car rocked as she again took another tight curve as they descended the canyon. As she brought the car around the curve, Riley slammed on her brakes and her car fishtailed. The SUV that had passed them had slowed down and was driving in the middle of the road.

Claire was busy with her phone. "I'm texting and sending out messages. If we hit some cell service, the messages should go out."

"Good going, Claire." Riley looked into the rearview mirror and could see the SUV from behind, closing the gap. She leaned on the horn and swung the wheel to pass on the left side of the vehicle in front of them. She quickly pulled back behind the lead SUV as it swung to the left to block her way.

The lead SUV had progressively slowed down and the rear SUV was now right on their bumper again. Riley picked up speed and crowded the front vehicle and then swung the wheel to attempt a pass on the left. Again, it pulled to the left to block her. Instead of swinging back behind the SUV, Riley sped up and turned into the rear side panel of the front vehicle. The front SUV skidded and almost turned completely sideways, but then corrected. It was now fully over into the right lane and Riley pulled up even with the SUV. Before she could pass the vehicle, it slid left and smacked into her passenger side. "They're trying to run us off the road," yelled Claire.

"Hold on, Claire." Riley slammed on the brakes and the SUV on their side shot forward. The trailing SUV crashed into their rear bumper and jolted them forward. The rear vehicle was not expecting them to brake and fell back. They were coming up to another tight curve in the road and Riley floored the gas again. Just before entering the curve, she hit the brakes and swung the wheel as hard as she could. The lead SUV disappeared around the corner as Riley's car skidded and spun one-eighty. The trailing SUV was now headed straight for them and hit its brakes. Riley stepped on the gas and aimed the car straight for the SUV. They sped toward each other, an impending head-on. At the last second, both vehicles swerved to their right. Riley shouted, "Brace yourself! We're going off road!"

Riley slammed on the brakes as hard as she could, but the edge of the road was mostly loose gravel, and the vehicle only slowed a fraction. She released the brakes as the car left the shoulder and shot down the hillside. The canyon road was in a treeless zone with patches of rabbit brush, bunch grass and wild sunflowers. Riley tried to hold the car straight as they barreled down. The car was not slowing, and Riley anticipated a head-on impact with the facing hillside once they reached the bottom. She turned the wheel before making impact, so the side of the car would slide into the hillside, or they would roll into it. "Brace!" she yelled. The front of the car curved left, but the force of their momentum kept them racing down the hill. They were skidding sideways on the passenger side wheels and fanned up a spray of sediment and dust. The steep angle of the hill caused the car to tilt. The driver's side wheels left the ground as they approached the bottom of the ravine. The car continued to hurtle down the steep ravine sideways. The passenger side wheels caught a patch of rabbit brush, and the car flipped all the way over and settled upright on its four wheels.

The SUV had run off the road as well, but they were able to sideswipe the steep roadside cut and come to a stop. Nick, with a large white bandage on his forehead, was driving. He slammed the steering wheel in anger and backed the SUV off the road cut and shouted in Ukrainian, "Crazy cyka." He turned the SUV around and drove to where the university vehicle had left the road. Both men stepped out of their vehicle and examined the crash site from the road.

"There is some movement," noted Alexander, as he pointed with his bandaged index finger. The second SUV pulled off and Boris Mirsky stepped out of the passenger side.

"Where is it?" he demanded. "You didn't let her get away again, did you?"

"Down there."

Mirsky looked down from the edge of the road. The vehicle appeared to have flipped and rolled at least once but it was now sitting on all four tires wedged into the bottom of the ravine, the trunk facing them. Suddenly, they could hear someone trying to start the car engine. "What are you two waiting for?" bellowed Mirsky. "Get them!"

Riley realized that the car wasn't going to start so she stopped cranking the engine. She unbuckled her seatbelt and reached over to Claire, who was turned toward the passenger door. "Claire, can you hear me?" Claire rolled over. "Claire, do you have any pain?"

Claire, in shock, "Are we still alive?" she asked.

Riley was running her hands down Claire's legs and then her arms. She brushed the hair from Claire's face to look into her eyes. "Do you think you can get out of the car? We need to get out of here."

Claire began to collect her bearings. She felt around and unbuckled her seatbelt. She tried to open her door, but it was jammed shut from the roll. "I can't open this door."

"My door is cracked open," said Riley. "Do you think you can crawl over to this side and get out?"

Riley forced her door wide open with loud pops and grating metal sounds. She stepped out of the car and tested her own legs by shifted weight from one foot to the other. She looked up and saw the two men making their way down the ravine. "Give me your hand, Claire. I can help you out."

"I can't find my cell phone."

"Don't worry about it. Leave it here so someone can find this car." Riley helped Claire untangle from crawling over the seats and gripped a hand on each of her shoulders as Claire stood in front of her. "We must run, Claire. Can you run?"

The men began sliding down the hillside faster when they saw both women outside the car. Claire noticed the dust cloud created by the men flying down the hill. It seemed to snap her out of her malaise. "Let's go!" she yelled.

"Follow me," instructed Riley, as she headed down the ravine, away from their car. Claire took one step and crumpled as her right knee gave out. Riley stopped immediately when she realized Claire could not follow. The two men were upon them in seconds.

Nick pulled Claire up roughly. "I have you."

"Get your filthy hands off her, bastard," yelled Riley.

Nick released Claire and walked menacingly toward Riley. "You need to be taught a lesson. I am going to make sure you can never run again." He reached into his back pocket and pulled out a switchblade and flipped it open. "I'll show you," he uttered in a low voice.

An imposing voice behind them yelled, "I said she was not to be harmed." Mirsky was standing next to the car. "Dr. Riley, it's so nice to finally meet you," said Mirsky, in an exerted, calm voice. He looked at Nick. "Put that away, idiot."

Pasha had now made his way down the hillside as well. Riley stared at Mirsky. "Any other morons up there? Who are you and what do you want with us?" she demanded.

"Dr. Riley, I need your assistance with examining some ancient human remains. My company will pay you handsomely, and in a short time, you can go about your business as usual."

"Business as usual? You could have killed us. What makes you think I would help you after what you've done?" She pointed to Nick and Alexander. "And these two cretins are already wanted by the police. You should send then back to Romania or wherever you found them and find some fresh simpletons." She stared at Mirsky. "I have no intention to help you with anything except a long jail sentence."

"I am sure we can convince you to help," replied Mirsky.

"Pasha, tie her hands and help her up the hill and into my automobile."

Alexander asked, "What shall we do with this one?"

"Help her up the hill and get her some water. I believe we can find a use for her."

Once they reached the SUVs, he instructed Nick, "Stay close behind. That one will be in your car. When we get into cell range, I will call the pilot to have the transport ready. Dr. Riley will be with us." Mirsky directed his comment to Riley. "And Dr. Riley, if I have any trouble from you, I will have Alexander cut your friend's throat and dump her along the road for the coyotes. Do you understand?"

Horrified, she gave a slight nod of her head. "Where are you taking us?"

"You'll see. Soon you will be joining our research team."

The two SUVs pulled out and headed north. After about an hour on the road the vehicles had cell service. Mirsky dialed his contact in Spokane to prepare the corporate jet for takeoff that day. When he was told the jet was no longer available, he commanded, "Listen to me. I need that jet back here immediately. It needs to be fueled and ready today. You will text this telephone number as soon as you find out when the jet will be ready."

As the two dented SUVs approached the outskirts of Spokane, Mirsky received a text informing him that the corporate plane would return to Spokane but, at present, the time of its return was unknown. Mirsky thought furiously about how to handle the situation. He would have to call Utkin, but that required a secure line. He was getting more and more frustrated with the Utkin personnel in Spokane. Mirsky called the trailing SUV. "We're driving to the company warehouse. I need to make a secure call. We'll have to wait for the jet. I'm sure there is a protected location for our guests at the facility."

The eastern section of Spokane near the Spokane River was a large expanse of manufacturing buildings, warehouses, a railroad yard, and fenced in lots. The area was referred to as the East Spokane industrial park. The two SUVs turned off the highway at Mission Avenue, which paralleled the railroad yard. They came to a fenced gravel yard littered with broken bricks, old railroad ties, assorted metal, and unrecognizable rubble. Both vehicles turned through a gate into the yard on a cleared track, leading to an old, corrugated metal warehouse. One side of the warehouse had three truck loading bays, lining the full width of the building. The SUVs drove past the loading bays and circled around to the front of the warehouse. They rolled by a relatively clean parking lot outside a signless office door. The SUVs pulled to the far end of the lot away from the office door and parked in front of a gray knobless steel door. It appeared to be a fire escape exit but had no markings. Nick got out and inserted a key into the door lock and pulled the door open. He looked in and switched on a light, and then he motioned for the others to follow. Alexander assisted Claire, and Pasha walked Riley. The group was trailed by Mirsky, who closed the door behind him.

The area inside the steel door had been structurally isolated from the remainder of the warehouse and office. The door opened into what looked like a small lounge or waiting room, with stuffed chairs, coffee tables, and a conference or dining table with chairs tucked around it. There was a partition that segregated a kitchen. A hallway led from the waiting room to a set of stairs to the second floor. Along the hallway there were doors that opened into two bathrooms and a darkened meeting room. The place was clean enough, but there were no windows to the outside.

CHAPTER 35

SPOKANE, WASHINGTON

Boris Mirsky was irritated but determined. He was on a mission as he entered the warehouse. He assiduously put his duffle down and pulled out his laptop, making for the stairway and his secure telephone call.

Alexander called after him, "Where do you want these two?"

Stopping just for an instant, "Lock them in the conference room." Then Mirsky bolted to the second floor.

Alexander reached for Riley's arm, but she pulled away from him, "How about a bathroom!" she snapped. "You criminals don't have to be uncivilized."

Mirsky overheard this and, looking at Riley from the second-floor landing, nodded to Alexander. "Show them. Then show them to the conference room. Nick, go make sure the vehicles outside are locked."

"What do you guys want from us? My student is injured. She needs medical attention."

Mirsky looked down at Riley again. "So, you wish to talk?"

Riley looked back, considering her options. "Okay," said Riley. "As soon as we freshen up."

Mirsky smiled, turned and went into an upstairs room to make his call.

Riley and Claire moved to the bathroom door indicated by Alexander. Just before closing the door, she warned, "You touch that doorknob, and I'll break your other finger." She slammed the door and locked it.

Both Riley and Claire were disheveled and badly shaken. As they cleaned up, they quietly talked. "Who are these people and what do they want from us?" asked Claire.

"I don't know for certain, but I think it's all about the human remains from Central Ferry. I'm not sure what they want from us. Something about helping them with research. However, we may just be collateral," mused Riley. "If we can find out a little more about what they want with us, we might figure out how to work it to our advantage and get out of here."

"Should we act like we'd seriously consider whatever it is they want from us?" suggested Claire. "It might be better for us?"

"You might be right. We should play along. How is your knee?"

"It is a little sore, but I can walk fine, and maybe even run," said Claire.

"Good, but don't let them know that. Keep favoring your leg. They may give you a longer leash, thinking you can't get very far."

Riley and Claire were in the bathroom for over fifteen minutes savoring just being away from the goons, when Alexander pounded on the door. "It is now time!"

"Just another minute," Riley called out to him.

When Riley and Claire came out, they were a little less battered and grungy. After making a few different calls, Mirsky was just coming down the stairs. "Can we get some water and food?" asked Riley.

"So, you wish to talk and eat as well?" said Mirsky.

"We haven't had anything to eat since this morning. We've been in a significant car crash, and we think you may have the wrong people," suggested Riley.

Mirsky handed Riley two bottles of water. She took them and gave one to Claire. "You are Dr. Samantha Riley, are you not? And you are the one who found the ancient skeleton?"

Riley consumed the water thirstily, and said, "That is correct, but why are you looking for me? I don't own the skeleton. I have yet to analyze the skeleton. In fact, my student and I were returning from Walla Walla after having conveyed the skeleton to the U.S. Army Corps."

"But I saw the report you wrote with one of your students, maybe this student?" Mirsky was pointing at Claire. "What is your name? No, wait, you are Claire Anderson, are you not? Your name is on the report."

Claire limped over and sat down in one of the stuffed chairs. "Yes. I am Claire. Why are you doing this to us? We have done nothing. Those two tried to kill us. I don't trust them."

Nick looked up and began to object but was stopped when Mirsky held up his hand. "You are correct, Claire."

Mirsky handed them more water. "The actions of these two has caused a great deal of misunderstanding. They were supposed to introduce themselves and ask Dr. Riley to meet with me. Instead, they attempted to abduct her. That was never my intention," explained Mirsky.

"We'll talk to you," said Riley. "But I don't feel comfortable with those two. Can we talk privately?"

"Of course. But please explain to me why you gave the skeleton back to the Army. Is the analysis complete?" asked Mirsky.

Riley answered, "The skeleton was recovered from lands managed by the Army, and they want to take over the analyses and care of the skeleton. We did some preliminary analysis, but the complete study will take months. I won't discuss anything with those two in the room."

"Don't listen to them, Boris. They are just…"

"Quiet!" yelled Mirsky, "Why don't you two go outside and have a smoke."

Alexander and Nick stood looking. "Leave now," insisted Mirsky. The two men stomped out of the room. Both gave Riley savage looks as they walked past.

"Those two beat me up pretty badly," Riley angrily stated.

"Believe me, they were not supposed to lay a finger on you. Only introduce themselves and set up a meeting. They will not hurt you again."

"So, if we are being honest with each other, what is your name and who do you work for?" asked Riley.

"I am not at liberty to reveal my employer at this time."

"And you go by?" asked Riley. "One of them called you Boris."

"My name is not important. My employer wishes to hire you and your assistant to do human bone analysis on ancient skeletons."

"What kind of analysis?"

"I am afraid I am unable to answer that question, Dr. Riley."

"For someone who wants to hire some highly trained researchers, you don't seem too willing to share even the basic components of an agreement."

"You misunderstand me, Dr. Riley. I cannot answer the question because I do not know enough to tell you the type of analyses needed," explained Mirsky.

Claire asked, "When you say you are willing to hire us, what are we talking about? Is this a short-term agreement, long-term, just to conduct specific kinds of analyses?"

"My employer is involved with a massive project that may significantly change what we know about how people age. We are looking for people with the right kind of training to help direct the project toward completion," said Mirsky.

Claire and Samantha looked at each other, wondering where to take the conversation. A phone rang. "Excuse me. This is my call. Pasha, look after these two ladies and don't let those idiots near them!" Mirsky pulled out his cell phone and walked up the stairs.

At the top of the stairs, he turned to his left and walked along a row of windows overlooking the warehouse interior and then entered an office. The dock doors were open, and trucks were being loaded on the docks. He kept the door open as he loaded his laptop and plugged his cell phone in. He was soon connected and spoke to his superior.

Nicholai Utkin talked faster than usual, revealing his impatience. He had expected Mirsky to deliver the skeleton several days before and had recalled his corporate jet to transport him from his yacht in Varna to Vladivostok. With the delay, Utkin stayed in Varna and sent the corporate jet back to Spokane. "Do you finally have the skeleton and the woman?"

"The skeleton will be here within the next few hours, and I have the woman," replied Mirsky. "We have some rather incompetent people working in Spokane. They were unable to seamlessly transport Dr. Riley to me, and delayed our exit," explained Mirsky. "I will begin a detailed review of our operation here after returning to Vladivostok. There are many things here that lead me to believe our operations could be run much more efficiently."

"The aircraft is on the way and will be in Spokane at 9:00 p.m. your time. There is a diplomatic bag on the aircraft. Use that to carry the skeleton."

"How shall we handle Dr. Riley?"

"Don't attempt anything different this time, Boris," instructed Utkin. "Follow the usual procedure. Hold her in the fuel truck compartment and bring her out after the customs inspector has left. Get her on the aircraft just before takeoff. Once in the air it will be safe."

"I have a second researcher as well," explained Mirsky. "It is one of Dr. Riley's graduate students. She helped with the initial analysis. I believe she might be useful, should Riley decide not to cooperate. There is room in the compartment for both. It will be an easy matter to make sure both are secure on board before we take off."

"Excellent, Boris. Bring my prizes home soon. I shall sail from Varna to Odessa tonight for a first-hand look at our year-old pharmaceutical plant there. The research team is ready in Vladivostok awaiting your return. Have them begin the work before my return. I feel that we have finally collected what is needed for the Centenarian Project to succeed."

Mirsky hung up. He was not a fan of doing work in the U.S. Utkin Chemicals had enormous power in Russia and in other former Soviet countries. There, he could make a call and law enforcement would gladly accommodate him. Here, he was always trying to cover his tracks, and felt as though he was only a step ahead of the authorities. The hounds were baying at his heels here, triggering him to make quick and risky choices. He had also concluded that many of the company employees here were incapable of doing what was required. The American laborers and truck drivers were not his concern. None of them knew what the company was actually doing. Mirsky's ire was aimed at those whom he had stationed here from Russia. Maybe they were becoming too American. For the future, he decided to maintain a fresh team in Spokane, and rotate employees in and out over shorter periods.

Mirsky looked out over the busy warehouse. Still thinking about the Spokane operation, he turned and hurried down the stairs. Dr. Riley and her student sat at one of the tables eating sandwiches. Nick and Alexander were back inside, observing the women and talking quietly. Pasha stood just outside the small kitchen watching everything.

At the bottom of the stairs, Mirsky's cautious demeanor relaxed as he settled into one of the chairs around the table. He was in a better mood. He had a clear direction. He had Riley. The skeleton was on the way, and he knew he would be in Russia before morning.

CHAPTER 36

GARFIELD COUNTY, WASHINGTON

Bill Mitchell and Dick Bender swung their pickup truck off the gravel road coming to a stop. It was over a month before the opening of pheasant season, but this was their first opportunity to work their two young wirehaired pointing griffons. The dogs were kenneled in the back of the truck. They were brothers from the same litter, eleven-months old. Bill and Dick had been training them at home, but this was their first field trial with real wild birds.

"Should we work one dog at a time or put them both out?" inquired Dick.

"Let's start them both at the same time. After they get the hang of it, we can rotate them," suggested Bill.

The men wore bright orange and carried shotguns to allow the dogs to get accustomed to the gun report after flushing a bird. They opened both dog kennels and leashed the eager bird dogs.

"Let's move over to the base of that draw and then release the dogs," said Dick, as he pointed toward a tight brushy canyon.

They walked about twenty yards from the vehicle and had the dogs sit while they unclipped leashes. The dogs were antsy and wanted to break but both men repeated the stay command several times and the dogs remained sitting, with the occasional whine. Each man stood next to his dog facing up the canyon. Bill with Commander and Dick with Chief.

"Well?" said Dick.

"Let's give it try."

Both men pointed and commanded, hunt! The dogs leaped forward and began working through the brush, noses up, searching for a scent. Bill and Dick watched for a few minutes and then began walking, following as the bird dogs lead the way. They kept vigilant eyes on the dogs, sometimes calling and pointing to the left or right to move the dogs into different corners of the draw.

They had been working the canyon for over twenty minutes before Dick shouted, "Where's your dog, Bill?"

"I saw him just an instant ago up ahead. He must have locked up," replied Bill.

"I don't see Chief now either," responded Dick. "They both must be on the same bird." Both men hurried up the canyon toward the last place they spotted movement. They climbed up to a level bench within the canyon draw that opened into a fan-like surface covered with rabbit brush and sage. No dogs were visible, but the brush was high and thick, easily concealing a dog or two.

"Damn, where are they?" huffed Dick.

"Spread out. They must be up here," replied Bill.

"Should we call them?" asked Dick.

"No. They could be on point. This could be their first wild bird point. We need to release them and command them to flush. If we call them back now it might just confuse them for next bird," said Bill.

The two men looked out across the flat bench. From their vantage point they could see the highway above them as it curved in toward the canyon. "Shall we keep moving up?" suggested Dick.

"Sure," replied Bill, still looking up the canyon. "What's that up there?"

"Where?"

"Up there near where the road comes close to the draw," pointed Bill.

"It looks like an old, abandoned car."

"Let's go have a look."

The car was not old. It apparently did not negotiate the curve in the road and tumbled down into the draw. The two men approached with caution thinking perhaps there may be a body or an injured person in the vehicle.

"Nobody in the vehicle," said Bill. "Maybe the driver was thrown out. Let's look around some."

"Hey Bill, look at this. The plates are official state plates. This is a state-owned vehicle of some type. Can you check the glove box?"

Bill reached in through the passenger side window and opened the glove box. There was a Washington State University motor pool registration along with a gas card in an envelope. "We better call somebody. This looks recent," said Bill. "This is a WSU vehicle."

"Where are the dogs?" Dick scanned the draw looking for the two griffons. "I think those dogs might be on some more birds," said Dick. "Should be go after them?"

"Whistle them back in, Dick. This looks like a recent accident. We need to get into cell range and call the state police or the sheriff's office. Someone could be missing or injured."

Reluctantly, Dick pulled out his dog whistle and gave three sharp calls. No dogs appeared. He waited another minute and repeated the return command. The dogs came barreling toward him out of nowhere, obviously having run a long distance. Both were panting heavily. Dick and Bill rewarded Commander and Chief with affection, leashed them and headed back down the draw toward their truck.

CHAPTER 37

PULLMAN, WASHINGTON

Deak Allen arrived on campus a little before 1:00 p.m. and headed to the isotope lab. He could see Riley's graduate students working busily. He knocked and entered. "Hi, Jennifer, David, and is it, Katie?" They looked up and welcomed Allen.

"I was wondering if Dr. Riley has returned from Walla Walla?" he said. "I tried calling her earlier and didn't get an answer."

Jennifer replied, "She might have been out of cell range. She and Claire drove to Walla Walla at the crack of dawn to drop off the human remains from Central Ferry. I believe they were supposed to drop them off at the Corps office around eleven this morning. Did you try her more recently?"

"No. Let me give her another try." Allen left the lab to check her office and walked down the hall as he called. After getting no response he called Jonathan Higgins in Walla Walla.

The call went through, and Higgins picked up. "Hi, Jonathan. This is Deak Allen. I'm in Pullman right now."

"Good morning, Deak. I hope all is well in Pullman," said Higgins.

"I understand Dr. Riley and one of her graduate students dropped by earlier today to hand off the Central Ferry materials. Do you know if they are still in Walla Walla?"

Higgins corrected Allen. "She was supposed to drop off the collections this morning. I waited, but they never showed up. I called her number about an hour ago but got no answer. You know what I think…." The sentence ended with an abrupt interruption.

"Let me make sure I heard you clearly," said Allen. "Neither Dr. Riley nor her graduate student visited you this morning, but they were scheduled to drop off the collections to you?"

"That is correct, Deak. And Dr. Riley promised she would have those materials to me. She neglected to follow through. Furthermore, she was a bit rude when we spoke over the phone a few days back. I should have…." Allen cut him off again.

"Jonathan, Dr. Riley is not in her lab or office and has not been answering telephone calls. She and Claire did leave for Walla Walla early this morning. I'm going to check her house. In the meantime, can you call some of the hotels in Walla Walla to find out if she has checked in at any? Call me as soon as you find something. I hope they weren't in an accident, or worse," said Allen.

Allen walked back to the lab and informed Riley's students that she and Claire never made it to Walla Walla. "I'm going to check and see if she is at her house with a broken phone," said Allen. "Can one of you run over to Claire's house and see if she is there?"

DeRue responded, "I'll call her first. If she doesn't answer, I'll run over and check. She lives a few doors down from me."

"Can you meet back here in thirty minutes after checking on Claire?" asked Allen.

"Sure," responded David.

Jennifer and Katie had stopped working and were looking concerned. "What should Katie and I do?" asked Jennifer.

"Why don't you and Katie build a timeline with as much detail as possible. When they left, when you last saw either, when you received the last positive communication from either. Be sure to check with Joe in the main office, and call Higgins at the Army Corps to get specifics from him." Allen grabbed a pen from the lab table and jotted down a number from his cell phone. "Here is the direct number to Higgins' office in Walla Walla. We'll all meet back here," ordered Deak.

Thirty minutes later they assembled in the lab. Riley and Claire were not at their respective homes. Neither were answering calls. Jennifer and Katie went through the timeline. Allen called 911 and reported two missing persons.

When officers arrived, the four of them provided a detailed review of the situation. Allen insisted that they get the state police involved since Riley and Claire might be injured or stuck in one of the counties outside of Pullman police jurisdiction. The officers went into immediate action and followed protocol for missing persons in imminent danger. "We'll take it from here," they said, and left the lab.

Allen and the three graduate students went over the timeline again and then discussed hypotheticals. After a long discussion, Jennifer stood up and paced. "What can we do now?"

"Wait and see mode now," said Allen. "Try to get back to your work until we hear from them."

"Who knows how long that will be?" said Jennifer. "I've been waiting for a guy from the University of Pennsylvania to call me back for about a week now. He seems to be missing, too."

Allen looked at Jennifer. "That wouldn't be Tom Rackerman?"

Jennifer looked stunned. "Why, yes, yes, it would be Rackerman. How did you know that?"

Allen considered explaining his logic but instead opted for the shorter response. "I just guessed," said Allen. He looked over at the spread sheets Jennifer had in front of her. She preferred reading data on printed pages as opposed to the computer screen.

"Is that the trace element data and chemical compounds from your stone tools?" he asked.

"It's just the raw data I've downloaded from the portable XRF gun. It hasn't been sorted or tabulated. It's only a sample of the tools Dr. Riley wanted me to start with. Preliminary analysis will take a week, and that will be very preliminary. Here. Take a look."

"Jennifer, can you send me a copy of that data. I'd like to make a more detailed review."

"Sure, I'll send you an attachment right now. What's your email address?"

Allen pulled out his card. "Here, send it to this address." He felt his phone vibrate in his pocket and registered the number. "Excuse me, I have to return this call." Allen left the room and walked down the hallway and speed dialed Jack Mills.

"Hi, Deak," said Mills. "I have some news. That Utkin Chemicals Company telephone, from the L.A. call, was traced to their plant and office complex in Vladivostok."

"Utkin Chemicals has offices in Vladivostok?" asked Allen.

"They have a chemical plant and research facility there, as well. It's an open water port twelve months of the year. Russia doesn't have too many of those," said Mills. "Perfect location for Utkin Chemicals to ship their materials out. It is one of their main corporate offices. They have a research and development complex on the opposite end of the city as well. There's more, Deak. They are associated with a warehouse used as a distribution center in Spokane. The warehouse itself is owned by another company but that company appears to be owned by Utkin Chemicals."

"Is it a well-known fact that a Russian chemical company has access to a warehouse in Spokane?" asked Allen.

"It is not very well-known, nor is it clear what might be going on there. Our IT team was able to keep a trace on that Vladivostok cell phone that called from L.A. It has been pinged from Spokane and Pullman in the past four days," informed Mills.

Allen looked up the hallway and saw Jennifer running toward him. "There you are."

"Hang on a minute, Jack."

"They found Dr. Riley's car and they found Claire's cell phone. They were in a crash in the Snake River canyon."

"Are they okay?" asked Allen.

"No!" exclaimed Jennifer. "They're gone! Someone took them."

"Wait, Jennifer. How do you know they were taken? They could be hiking out of the canyon."

"They found Claire's cell phone in the car and brought it to the Garfield County sheriff's office. They found a text to Joe in the office on her phone. It said someone was trying to run them off the road. It said it was the same guys who tried to kidnap Dr. Riley before. The skeleton from Central Ferry is gone too. It wasn't in the car."

"Let me finish this call and I'll meet you in the lab. I'll be right there," said Allen.

He went back to his call with Mills, who spoke first. "I heard it all, Deak. Sounds like you have your hands full. If there is nothing else, I'll let you take care of business there."

"Thanks, Jack, but I think we need to move quickly here, and I'll need your help."

"Let me have it, Deak."

"Send me a profile of Utkin Chemicals with any specifics related to their operations in Spokane and Vladivostok. I want a flow chart of senior personnel from each facility."

"When do you need the report on Utkin Chemicals, Deak?"

"Send me the address of the warehouse immediately and keep feeding any other information as you get it. Can you forward a copy of that cell phone number? Also, I want you to call Walla Walla and let them know that the remains have been stolen. Then call the FBI to get them involved."

"Isn't this outside their jurisdiction?"

"Those remains are federal property. That falls within the jurisdiction of the FBI. Let them know we have two kidnap victims associated with the theft, so they'll bump this up to high priority."

"What are your immediate plans, Deak?"

"I don't have any detailed plans, but I'm driving to Spokane as soon as you send me an address."

"Will do. Anything else?"

"Nothing at the moment. Keep feeding me intel as it comes in."

Jennifer, David, and Katie were waiting in the lab. Joe, from the main office, was also there. Allen was introduced to the department chair, Geoff Gainesville, who had joined them. They talked about next steps. Gainesville emphasized that the situation was now in the capable hands of law enforcement, and the best thing to do was to let them do their job. All agreed.

Gainesville continued, "The fire marshal has completed a report of the Maddington fire. Unfortunately, they found the charred remains of Peter Maddington. He was apparently working on his car in the garage and was also cooking on his grill. It appears the grill was not well lit, but the propane was turned on. There was an explosion that knocked the car off the jack and pinned Maddington. The fire increased in intensity and ignited the car's gas tank. The fire spread to the rest of the house. The car and Maddington's body were almost totally incinerated." Gainesville paused. "It was a careless accident."

Allen looked at the others around the table. "I'm sure that is one possible scenario for the fire. It just doesn't add up for me."

"What are you getting at, Mr. Allen?" asked Gainesville. "It's all here in the report."

"Who cooks with a propane grill in their garage, in the summertime, on a clear evening?"

"Maybe he wanted the grill close to where he was working in the garage?" suggested Gainesville.

"That could be," said Allen. "But even if that were the case, the garage door would have had to be closed to produce a large enough explosion to kick a car off its jack. And who uses only a jack to support a car when crawling under it? Most people support a raised car with something considerably more secure. This just doesn't make any sense to me."

"Well, I'm just relating the facts from the official report," replied Gainesville.

"There is another detail," began Allen. "Those human remains are federal property and I think the recent break-in at Dr. Riley's house, the fire at Maddington's house, and the attempted abduction of Dr. Riley at her site in Helmer are all related. I've had my office notify the FBI."

Gainesville looked nettled. "Are you sure that's a good idea?" he asked. "Don't you think you might be overreacting?"

"I hope that I have over blown the severity of this situation and that we find Dr. Riley and Claire Anderson hitchhiking or walking some back roads near the Snake River," returned Allen. "However, I would hate to underestimate the severity of the situation and find out later something terrible has happened to either or both of those women."

Gainesville stood. "I'm sure the authorities can handle this. I, for one, trust they will do a fine professional job. Come on, Joe. We've got work to do."

Joe paused and looked around. His look expressed an amount of agreement to what Allen had suggested, but he rose and followed Gainesville.

After Joe and the chairman left, Allen told Riley's students he had another project to attend to, but he would return in a day or two. He wrote his cell number and Jack Mills' contact number on a piece of paper and asked that they call him or Jack immediately if Dr. Riley or Claire were found. Allen wanted to tell them where he was going, and that Samantha and Claire would be safe. Unfortunately, he knew he could tell them neither.

Instead of going straight from Pullman to Spokane, Allen decided to drive to the cabin on the lake. The cabin was a little out of the way, but he needed to retrieve some items to put his plan into action.

Allen drove to the cabin in record time. He bolted from the rental, and once inside grabbed his backpack and began gathering what he needed. Mills had sent him the location of the Utkin Chemicals company warehouse and the number of the Utkin Chemicals company cell phone. Deak dropped the address into his cell phone mapping program to locate the warehouse. The program situated a warehouse next to the East Spokane industrial zone.

Allen switched from the map display to the satellite image display. It was a rectangular building with loading bays facing toward the south. The eastern side had a parking lot and what appeared to be a front door. The two remaining sides had no evidence of a door. The north wall of the building faced the railroad yard, and the west wall of the building was against the property line with a chain-link fence. The adjoining property to the west appeared to be a vacant lot covered with miscellaneous debris.

Allen scurried down the stairs to the basement where he found a wall with hanging tools. He shoved a pair of heavy-duty dikes with thick rubber coated handles into his backpack. He added a small flat-bladed pry bar. Allen grabbed a roll of duct tape sitting on a shelf, then he headed down to the dock and Walt's boat. Allen rifled the glove box for a flare gun, which he found along with a three pack of flares. Allen sprinted back up to the cabin and searched in the kitchen. He found a small Bic lighter, checked it, and put it in his pocket. He picked up one of the several pairs of binoculars Walt and Windy had around the cabin.

The mapping program showed the shortest route to Spokane from the Coeur d'Alene Indian Casino through Rockford, Washington. This shortcut saved thirty minutes. He grabbed the backpack, jumped into his vehicle, and headed out.

CHAPTER 38

SPOKANE, WASHINGTON

Allen was glad to be driving a nondescript car that needed a washing. He slowly cruised through the industrial district of Spokane, looking for the location of the warehouse. Now heading down Mission Avenue, he passed warehouses, railroad buildings, garages, and a variety of other unremarkable structures. Then, from the road, he could see the Utkin warehouse. The warehouse had no posted sign. It stood on the far end of a fenced lot. There were three trucks backed into loading bays that were being actively loaded or unloaded.

After driving past the warehouse, Allen idled on the side of the road for a few minutes and then turned the car around. He drove past and scrutinized the warehouse again. There was a gravel track that crossed the railroad yard. He took it and approached the warehouse from the opposite side of the rail yard. He slowed even more and came to a halt. With his attention focused across the rail yard he rummaged through his backpack for the binoculars. From this new position, he had a clear view of the front door and parking lot. There were a few cars and pickup trucks parked closer to the front door and several others parked in the lot. He assumed most of the cars belonged to warehouse workers. Allen sharpened the focus of the binoculars after he noticed two white SUVs parked on the far side of the lot in front of a gray steel door. They reminded him of the SUV at Samantha Riley's house. He slowly lowered the binoculars from his eyes with the realization that the two men who attempted to abduct Samantha at her excavation site were also driving a similar SUV. He was now convinced more than ever that both teams were working together.

As he mulled potential options, a line of railcars was pushed between him and the warehouse. The railcars were being switched to another track and hooked to a different line of cars further down the track. As the engine pushing the cars passed, he again had a clear view of the warehouse. It was the top of the hour at 5:00 p.m., and several men emerged from the front door carrying lunch coolers and headed to the various cars and pickup trucks. They pulled out of the parking lot one at a time. Others emerged and within a few minutes the lot contained only a car, a pickup, and the two SUVs.

As Allen watched, the train began jamming boxcars into their locked position with thundering bangs and squeaking wheels on the rusty sidetracks. Allen closed his windows to keep out as much external sound as possible and reached for his cell phone. He checked his text messages from Jack Mills and found the telephone number for the Utkin Chemicals cell phone that called had Maddington's office from L.A. Allen keyed in the number and waited. After four rings, Allen frowned, knowing that his number was not recognizable and would probably not be picked up. On the fifth ring a man answered. "Who is this?" The voice had a slow deliberate cadence with a distinctive Russian accent.

"I'm sorry," replied Allen. "I thought I was calling Utkin Chemicals. I must have dialed the wrong number."

"Where did you get this number? Who am I speaking to?"

Allen wanted to keep the man on the line as long as possible so he could listen for boxcar-loading noises in the background. "My name is James Waxman from DuPont Chemicals in New York," lied Allen. "I thought I was calling Utkin Chemicals in Vladivostok."

The mention of Utkin Chemicals and the Vladivostok office gave a sense of genuine error. But what were the chances this number would be called. Boris Mirsky replied, "I believe you have the wrong number, Mr. Waxman," and the phone went dead.

Allen clearly heard the railyard sounds through his earpiece during the brief conversation. He was now positive the Utkin cell phone was in the warehouse across the rail yard. He was also positive the voice on the other end was the man who broke into Riley's house. His guess was that Samantha and Claire were also in the warehouse.

Allen assumed the front of the warehouse contained the office area with access to the rear loading docks. The warehouse workers probably punched timecards in the main office on their way out. The door with the two SUVs in front might connect to the office area. His bet was that Samantha might be held in that part of the building. He started his vehicle, turned around, and drove back across the rail yard. He turned again and drove past the fenced yard facing the loading docks. There was still one truck in the end bay loading. The other two bay doors were closed. Allen had to move quickly. He feared the workday was coming to an end and the last bay door would be closed as soon as the truck was loaded.

Allen maneuvered his rental into the adjacent lot and parked it behind a stack of railroad ties. From the car, he searched for security cameras mounted on the roof and sides of the building. This side of the building had no doors or windows, and Allen didn't spot any security cameras. Allen again reached for his cell phone dialed Jack Mills. Jack was at a dinner party but broke away to take Allen's call. "What's up, Deak?"

"I'm at the Utkin Chemicals warehouse in Spokane. I suspect that Dr. Riley and her graduate student are being held inside. Notify the FBI and have them raid the warehouse."

"They'll want to know why I believe Riley is in there," responded Mills.

"Yea, that's why I thought the call would be better coming from the Department of Defense than from me. Let them know that I recognized the SUV driven by the guys who tried to abduct Dr. Riley."

Jack's voice projected a sense of caution but no hesitation. "You mean the SUV that wasn't where you said you left it, with two tied up would be kidnappers?" asked Mills. "I'm not sure that will be enough for a search warrant and a raid."

"We have two missing women," Allen reminded him. "They are already on the case, looking. Let them know I've seen the SUV, and they should at least drop by to ask the occupants some questions. Another thing, I called that Utkin Chemicals number that originated in L.A. The person answered from the warehouse."

"How do you know it was from the warehouse?" asked Mills.

"It's a long story. Just take my word for it," replied Allen with a touch of urgency in his voice.

"I'll make the call," promised Mills. "But it may be some time before they show up. Where can they find you?"

"Dr. Riley and her student may not have much time. I don't imagine they are being treated like royalty. I'm going in," said Allen. "Let the authorities know that one of the good guys will be inside."

He hung up the phone, pulled the backpack from the passenger's seat and cautiously walked toward the rusty chain-link fence. There was a small alley between the warehouse and the fence that contained old wooden pallets and assorted debris. Allen retrieved the wire cutters and made an incision from the ground up to about five feet, a perpendicular cut about three feet long, folded the fence back, and stepped through. He replaced the wire cutters and retrieved the flare gun. The flare gun had an orange tube for a barrel with a pistol grip. It resembled a water gun. Allen pressed the cylinder release and the barrel folded down. He gently picked up a flare and inserted it into the chamber, then folded the barrel back into place. Allen tucked the gun into the back of his waistband. He pulled the backpack straps over his shoulders and crept along the edge of the warehouse. He could hear the truck still being loaded. He moved closer to the edge of the building and peered around. The truck was backed all the way up to the loading dock, and a forklift was carrying full pallets of sealed cartons into the truck. The loading dock had a set of cement stairs about five feet from where Allen waited. The truck was about five feet beyond the stairs.

“That’s the last one,” yelled someone from the warehouse. The forklift driver backed away from the loading dock and shut down the engine. He hopped down and walked over to the truck and shut up the back of the truck.

The truck driver came over and checked the rear truck doors as well. “I’m out of here,” he announced to no one. He stepped out onto the loading dock and came down the stairs just feet from Allen and went around to the driver’s side.

Allen could hear the driver get into the truck. The location of the forklift provided a shield for Allen when he entered from the loading dock door. But he didn’t know where any warehouse workers might be. The truck driver slammed his door. Then the electric motor on the steel bay door engaged. Allen could hear the sprockets pulling the chain as the door slowly and steadily began to fall. Allen waited another few seconds to see if the truck was going to pull away. The truck engine started. The dock door now had about four feet before it would hit the cement dock. Now or never, Allen ran up the stairs, tossed in his backpack, and rolled under the heavy door an instant before it slammed tight to the floor.

Allen waited behind the forklift, hoping nobody would come to move it. The closed dock door reduced the lighting inside the warehouse, but internal ceiling lights provided plenty of visibility. Allen saw that the forklift driver was the one who operated the steel door. He was busy threading a padlock through the hoist chain and attaching it to a metal bar on the door frame. The back of the warehouse was piled with pallets full of cardboard boxes wrapped in plastic. One side of the warehouse had a floor-to-ceiling internal wall that had a door to where Allen figured the office was. The lit up second floor windows overlooked the loading area, near where the SUVs were parked outside.

Allen could see only one other man in the warehouse. He stood next to the pallets and marked something on a clipboard and seemed to carefully inventory one pallet, and then the next. He finished and hung the clipboard on a nail yelling over. "Let's go."

The forklift driver yelled back. "Let me move this fork and I'll meet you in the lot." He began moving in Allen's direction.

It was a small forklift and there was no way the driver would not see Allen if he got into the driver's seat. Just as he was about to climb on, his buddy yelled back across the warehouse, "Just leave the damn thing. It's already after hours. They don't pay us overtime. Let's go! We were supposed to meet the guys fifteen minutes ago."

"I'm on my way," said the driver. He turned, leaving the forklift where it was and headed across warehouse. His partner, next to a control box, reached up and pulled down four levers to turn off the overhead lights. The two men exited.

CHAPTER 39

Mirsky's relaxed mood was beginning to cleave as he checked and rechecked his watch. His contact was running late, and he couldn't afford another setback. Mirsky was now unsettled. He figured his capricious nerves must be from working in this forsaken country with imbeciles. Riley and her student were quiet. Pasha was poking around in the kitchen and the two Ukrainians were behaving at the moment.

The sun was beginning to set and soon night would settle over the industrial district. Most people working in the rail yard had quit for the day and it was progressively quieter. While waiting in the quiet, Mirsky began second-guessing his plan. Perhaps he should have sent the Ukrainians to make sure everything went as he wanted. No. The Ukrainians had become less and less reliable. Given the circumstances, he finally was convinced he had made the right decision. Everyone had a price. Then a faint sound caught his attention. Mirsky heard a vehicle rolling up the driveway, crunching gravel. "Alexander, see who that is. Pasha, stay with the women."

The car came to halt and a slim man stepped from the vehicle and walked toward Alexander. They shook hands. Mirsky left the door open a fraction of an inch and carefully monitored the outside conversation. The two talked politely. The conversation remained civil. After a few minutes, Alexander walked back toward the door, motioned for Mirsky to join them.

Before stepping through the door Mirsky directed Pasha, "Don't take your eyes off these two," and exited the building.

Alexander stood within arm's reach of the visitor as Mirsky approached. "What can I do for you, Mr. …"

"I believe we've talked several times on the telephone. Higgins. Jonathan Higgins. I am confident I possess something you are very interested in."

"Yes, Mr. Higgins. What a pleasure to finally meet you," said Mirsky in as pleasant a voice as he could muster. "I trust you have the remains with you?"

"I trust you have my payment," snipped Higgins.

"Well, of course, Mr. Higgins, but first let me see the remains."

"The three curation boxes are in the trunk of my car." Higgins reached into his pocket for the fob and popped the trunk. "Be my guest."

Without another word, Mirsky stepped to the trunk, pulled out his knife and snipped the zip ties securing the hinged lids on each box. Several long minutes passed before Mirsky returned.

"How can I be sure these are the correct samples?" questioned Mirsky.

"You read the report. You know that there are two boxes with bone fragments and one box with a complete skeleton. All with Washington State University labeling. That is what's in the trunk," responded Higgins. "I'm not sure I can do anything else to facilitate identification."

Mirsky nodded, "Very well." He turned to Alexander and ordered, "Put the boxes in my SUV."

"And my payment?" inquired Higgins.

"Come this way." Mirsky held out his hand toward the door. "We should complete the transaction inside, away from curious eyes."

Higgins paused for a brief instant before heading toward the door. Short of the door, he stopped, "Let's make this quick. I need to get back."

"I have urgent business as well."

Mirsky raised his open palm again and motioned toward the door.

Higgins walked through the door and stopped, flabbergasted to see Samantha Riley standing in the room. She, too, was dumbfounded. Neither said a word as they assessed the situation. Claire thought and privately hoped that they were being rescued.

Riley finally addressed Higgins in a less than hospitable manner. "I figured you for more of a pusillanimous jerk. But I stand corrected, Jonathan. You are totally without integrity and have the honor of a thief."

Riley couldn't keep the distain from her face. "No wonder you didn't want to make the transfer in Walla Walla. Did you plan to blame me and Claire when the remains didn't show?"

"I've busted my ass for this profession all my life and all I get is blamed when something goes wrong. I have always followed the rules and in the end, I get nothing. Unless a fall guy is needed. Then I'm the only one that gets recognized. Not this time."

"Jonathan, when this is over you are going to get more recognition than you have ever wanted or asked for. You are a common criminal and you belong behind bars," spat Riley. "Have you forgotten everything your training has taught you? What are you getting out of this? A few bucks? A year or two of salary? Is it worth it?"

"When this is over it will be you who lost the remains, not me. Remember, you never delivered them, and I have records asking you for them repeatedly. This time I won't get tagged for something I had no control over," said Higgins.

"What are you talking about? Are you still reliving the Clarkston Mummy fiasco? Do you think this is a repeat and you must change the outcome? Well, you certainly have created a different scenario. The Clarkston Mummy was a bad situation but you're turning this into a catastrophe. These people you're working for may have already killed. Who knows what they intend for Claire and me."

"I was left to fend for myself the last time. The academic community spearheaded the lawsuit against us. After all we've done for you. I won't let that happen again."

Higgins turned to Mirsky. "I believe I've heard enough from this female barbarian. I'll take my payment and get out of here."

"Absolutely, Mr. Higgins," smirked Mirsky. He reached in his jacket and casually extracted his silenced 40 caliber and pumped two rounds into Higgins' chest. The bullets punched him backwards. He was dead before his body slammed into the floor.

Mirsky ordered Alexander and Nick to put him in the back room. “After dark, dispose of him.”

Claire and Samantha simply stared in shock, unable to digest the scene.

“Did you have to shoot him?” stammered Riley.

“He is now one less potential obstacle,” said Mirsky.

The two Ukrainians were still staring. “What the hell are you two waiting for? Put him in the back room until it gets dark,” repeated Mirsky.

The murder increased the silent tension within the building.

CHAPTER 40

Allen carefully scanned the lighted second story windows, looking for signs of movement. In the darkened warehouse, he could move about relatively easily and see if anyone came to one of the windows. He worked his way over to the door leading out to the office area, and silently tried the knob. The reinforced door was locked, and his mini pry bar was useless.

Allen surveyed the warehouse, searching for a potential diversion. Silently he made his way to the forklift and studied the dashboard. He climbed up into the driver's seat and flipped the switch to warm the diesel plugs. The light on the dash glowed red and finally the indicator light switched to green. He pushed in the clutch and pressed the starter button. The forklift came to life. Allen shifted it into first gear and released the clutch. The forklift pulled forward and banged into the loading dock door. Grabbing the pry bar from his backpack he jammed it between the throttle and the seat. The forklift strained to move forward but was stopped by the metal door.

Allen quickly moved to a stack of pallets near the office door and felt inside his backpack for the flare gun. He shot a flare all the way across the warehouse and into the stack of pallets on the far corner. The flare embedded itself into the cardboard boxes. Within seconds one pallet begin to smoke and a flame appeared at the point of impact. The flames flickered larger as the plastic wrapping caught, acting as a propellant, and ignited more of the boxes. The fire gained strength and spread to an adjacent pallet and then another.

On the other side of the wall everyone had frozen. "Was that sound coming from the railroad yard?" asked Alexander.

Nick ran up the stairs to the observation windows and shouted, "It's in the warehouse!" A few seconds later, he yelled, "One of the forklifts is jammed against the loading door, and there's a fire in the warehouse."

Alexander started toward the door and Nick followed. "Where are you two going?" yelled Mirsky.

"That lift will break through the door if we don't shut it down," shouted Alexander.

"We need to extinguish the fire," yelled Nick, as he continued toward the door. Both men bolted out to the office door to gain access to the warehouse.

"Let's grab some wrenches from the office cabinet before opening up the warehouse door," said Alexander. "I'll go into the warehouse. You wait by the door. Let's move cautiously."

Pasha was moving to assist them. He halted when Mirsky grabbed his arm. Mirsky had seen enough and knew they were in a vulnerable situation. “Pasha, put these two in the car. We need to get out of here.” Mirsky turned and ran up the stairs for his laptop and a final sweep.

“Let’s go, you two,” said Pasha.

Riley sensed an opening, and asked, “How about an ice pack? Her knee is swelling, and we need to do something before it gets worse.”

Pasha looked over at Claire who limped to a chair.

Pasha frowned but went to the refrigerator freezer and began rustling around looking for ice trays. He spoke with his head buried in the freezer. “I see only one ice tray and a package of frozen vegetables.”

Riley quickly snuck beside him and slammed the door on his head, shouting, “Run, Claire!”

Claire was out the door, quickly followed by Riley. “Through the gate,” shouted Riley, and she took off in the opposite direction toward the rail yard.

Pasha was right behind her but paused, undecided which way to turn. “After the student,” shouted Mirsky, just seconds behind Pasha. “I’ll get Riley.”

Claire ran down the gravel driveway as fast as she could. Feeling no pain, she went through the driveway gate and turned down the road along the railroad track for ten, then twenty yards. She saw an alley between two buildings, turned and kept running. She was not thinking, just reacting as she came to intersections and forks in the alleys and paths she traversed. Soon twilight gave way to evening and night.

Claire glanced behind her as she ran. Nobody in sight. Nobody following. Her legs geared down and her sprint diminished to a jog and then to a swift walking pace. She sucked air like a deep-sea diver coming to the surface. Her head pounded from the lack of oxygen as she kept breathing deeply. Claire stopped for just a minute and put her hands on her knees and just sucked air. She began jogging again.

Claire was still deeply embedded in the industrial section of the city with its abandoned buildings and warehouses, all of which appeared black and sooty. She came to the end of the block and emerged from the buildings into a clearing. She could see distant lights from a major road or highway. Without stopping, she studied the lights. There were moving cars, stop lights, and perhaps gas stations or convenience stores. There was no direct route, so she kept jogging down the middle of the road hoping to flag a car as she descended as rapidly as possible. Her legs were wobbly as the terrain pitched downhill. Then she stumbled. Her momentum forced her down and forward, but her stumble prevented her feet from keeping up with her forward motion. Claire fell face forward and tumbled, then came to a stop. She lay there, exhausted and downright pissed for her clumsy footwork.

She kept inhaling deeply as she lay there. It was a relief to just lay there and not be running. Claire laid her head back and then faintly, but progressively, more powerfully, she heard and could feel the thump of footfalls getting closer. She sat up and stared up the hill where she had come and could see the silhouette of a man coming down the road toward her. Claire leapt to her feet and sprinted on the road, lifting one foot after another as fast as she could. She was getting closer to the lights and traffic below her. Yes, she could now recognize one of the buildings. Of all things, it was an ice cream parlor with bright lights and outdoor benches. Cars were in the parking lot and more vehicles were driving by. Claire accelerated her efforts from a jog to a sprint. The road came to a sharp curve, and she turned downhill picking up speed. She spilled out onto a larger road, paused, then turned left.

Just as Claire began accelerating, she was impacted by a body block and tackle. She crashed to the ground with arms around her. "Stop running before I have to hurt you," huffed Pasha.

Pasha was exhausted and could barely maintain his grip on Claire, but he held her with all his might. The tackle had knocked even more wind from Claire's lungs. Claire lay there in the middle of the road, unwilling or unable to respond. Pasha breathed hard, holding on to her but more interested in filling his own lungs. Without a word or warning, Claire simply turned, investigated the man's face, took aim and poked a finger into Pasha's eye.

It wasn't a direct hit but a glancing index finger that hit the inside bridge of his nose and slid into his eye socket. He screamed and let her go, holding both hands to his face.

Claire immediately stood and began to run again but Pasha snatched her by the foot, and she went down.

He rose to his feet before she could stand and yelled in Russian, "Stoy!"

Again, unwilling to obey his commands, Claire scrambled to her feet and Pasha kicked her legs out from under her. She hit the road again, but struggled to regain her footing, rolling away from him as he tended to his injured eye.

Claire attempted to run but Pasha reached over and grabbed her and pulled her back into his body. Pasha wrapped an arm around her neck. He shouted, "Stoy, or I will break your neck."

She attempted to pound her elbows into his side with backward jabs, but her efforts were weak, and he increased the pressure on her neck, pulling her off her feet.

Claire began to choke as he applied more pressure. Her struggle slowed and she gave up fighting, but he continued his strangle hold. Not knowing or not caring that she had surrendered.

CHAPTER 41

SPOKANE VALLEY, WASHINGTON

Becky Swenson and Tina Jackson were co-captions of the Gonzaga University Women's softball team. Becky was driving the lead passenger van and Tina was in the front seat. The team was returning from their Spokane Valley practice field, where they had just finished pitching and batting practice for their upcoming first round of the NCAA Women's Fast Pitch Playoffs. It had been a tumultuous year. First, a bitter Title IX lawsuit during the off season for better facilities and training equipment. A subsequent loss of almost a dozen players, including some of their best to other university teams. And now the team, with a new coach, had battled and scratched their way into the National Championship Playoffs. Becky and Tina were seniors, four years together, and they were good friends. Both were large athletic women, especially Tina. She was the team's first base woman and stood at least an inch over six foot. She carried over two hundred pounds of pure muscle.

There were six other teammates in the van and two additional vans were following Becky as she made a detour towards Sprague Avenue, heading into Spokane's industrial park.

"Where in the hell you are taking us, Becky?" griped Tina. "I know you said short-cut, but this looks like the middle of nowhere. There're no streetlights out here."

"No worries," responded Becky. "I know every back road in Spokane. I grew up in Liberty Lake just a few miles from our practice field. These roads are just fine, and this is the quickest way."

As the caravan drove deeper into the dark roads, they began to get some wise cracks from the back of the van. "Hey, do you two captains know where the fuck we are? This looks like Deliverance country."

"Listen." said another player. "Can you hear that? That sounds like banjo music."

Others began humming the tune for *Dueling Banjos*, causing general havoc throughout the van with comments, screams and laughter.

"Keep it down back there," shouted Becky. "Or I'll let you off right here and you can hitch back to campus. We'll be there in a few minutes, and I swear, this is the best ice cream in the entire Pacific Northwest. That includes Seattle and Portland."

The van wheeled around one dark corner after another, with lights on high beam to provide as much visibility as possible. Becky slammed the brakes hard. The van slid into the oncoming lane and Becky overcorrected, swinging the van back into the middle of the road. The van behind her had little time to react as it abruptly turned into the left-hand lane, tapped Becky's back bumper with its rear side panel and came to a stop, even with the first van. The third van drove up cautiously and pulled off to the right-hand shoulder of the road. The three vans came to rest blocking the entire road, including the oncoming lane, with headlights shining in the same direction.

"What the fuck. Do you see what I see?" said Tina with a tone of astonishment and a pinch of anger.

Some of the women in the back of the van were already crowding to the front and leaning forward, gawking and recording with their cell phones. "Oh, my god. Can you believe it."

The driver of the second van had already opened her door and was rushing out. Becky swung her door open, and others were stepping into the road from passenger side sliding doors.

Some of the students were already dialing 911, while others were looking through their field equipment for bats.

Pasha could only see slight glimmers of movement as figures crossed through the headlights. He could hear footsteps, but his eyes were blinded by the three sets of headlights a few feet from where he stood.

Claire could feel herself losing consciousness from the choke hold. Then her body collapsed to the ground as the bright lights pierced the air around her. Pasha had abruptly and unceremoniously released his strangle hold on Claire, and she dropped.

"Just step away, Buddy," said Becky.

"Don't think about running," said Tina. "We got you surrounded. If I was you, I would put my hands on top of my head and sit down. I mean now."

Claire was still crumbled on the road, exhausted but conscious. She shielded her eyes and raised a hand. "I need help," she croaked.

Pasha took a step backwards, turned to his left and then right. There were people behind him. He took another step back away from the glaring headlights.

"She said sit down," came a voice from behind him, poking him roughly in the back with a large aluminum softball bat.

A second voice from behind him also spoke. "She also said to put your hands on your head."

Then came a chorus of other voices from all directions around Pasha. Most using profanity, none with anything kind to say to the man standing over his victim. Pasha couldn't believe his rotten luck. There must have been twenty people surrounding him. Other cars began arriving from both directions and stopped, primarily because the vans had the entire road blocked. Soon the entire area was illuminated with car lights and milling people.

Pasha turned to see people near and far. The closest was a large woman with a metal baseball bat. She looked ready to use it. Pasha put his hands up to protect himself and slowly sat down, placing his hands on his head. Some of the softball players moved in and helped Claire to her feet and away from Pasha.

CHAPTER 42

SPOKANE, WASHINGTON

Allen lingered behind the stacked pallets as the forklift churned into the dock door and the fire spread to additional pallets on the far side of the warehouse. Nobody had come to check. The dock door began to buckle in front of the forklift, pulling the edges out of its tracks. Allen waited as smoke began to billow across the ceiling of the warehouse. He had second thoughts about starting the fire as he waited.

The office door finally creaked open slowly, and was then swung all the way, but nobody barreled through. A few seconds passed, then one of the men stepped through the door, a massive wrench in his hand, and walked sideways toward the light switch box. He pushed up the levers and illuminated the warehouse. Allen noticed the second man standing at the door. "Nick, get a fire extinguisher. I'll shut down the machine." The first man shut down the forklift and grabbed another fire extinguisher and rushed toward the far corner to help extinguish the blaze.

As both men desperately battled the fire, Allen slipped through the door and made his way to the front of the office. He stopped and ducked down when he heard footsteps running back toward the office. The first man was out of retardant and rushed to the emergency supply cabinet for another extinguisher. He was covered in greasy sweat, streaked with black. His clothing was burnt in places as he banged the door open and reached for another extinguisher.

Allen swiftly rushed the man and clubbed him with the butt of his flare gun, stunning him. Allen took the man to the floor, pulled out the roll of duct tape and bound him.

Allen stood up and could hear the first man shouting from the warehouse. "Nick, I think I've got it taken care of. Bring another fire extinguisher and mop up here and there. Nick. Where have you gotten to?"

Allen could hear mumbling and footsteps coming toward the office door. "Nick, what the hell are you doing?"

Alexander walked into the office and noticed Nick tied in front of the supply cabinet. He froze.

"I'm glad you were able to put that nasty fire out," said Allen.

Alexander began to turn. "No! Don't make a move until I tell you where to move," commanded Allen.

Alexander remained still but shifted his eyes back toward Allen. His demeanor changed slightly when he noticed Allen had him covered with an orange plastic gun. "Is that some kind of toy gun," mused Alexander.

"This flare may not kill you instantly, but it will puncture your face and fry your head so bad that you'll wish you were dead. Now face down on the floor."

Alexander was secured and Allen peered out from the main office door. The isolated gray door was left open and both SUVs were parked in front. He slipped out and trotted to the open door, flare gun in hand. Allen waited behind the door, listening for sounds from the inside. Hearing none, he stepped through the entrance and scanned the room looking down the barrel of the flare gun. First left toward the kitchen. Then right toward the hallway and stairs. He crept down the hallway opening each door as he went.

He opened the last door and was immediately struck by a prone figure lying in a pool of blood. Allen went to check for a pulse and was again stricken. It was Jonathan Higgins. He regrouped as quickly as possible, turned from the room and stepped up the stairway. At the halfway landing, he stayed low and then swiftly swung around the corner, gun first, and up the final few stairs to the second-floor walkway. Allen glanced out the first observation window and could see the forklift jammed against the door and the smoldering remains of the burned pallets in the far corner. He checked the first upstairs room just as he had done in the downstairs hallway. It was an office. Nobody there. The second door was another bathroom. Next door, a large storeroom. Nobody. Allen quietly came down the stairs and went to the door. He looked down the gravel road toward the gated entrance. Nothing. He searched the grounds in the darkening light and noticed movement about a hundred yards away between some of the rail cars.

Allen's cell buzzed and he checked the ID. "Hi, Jack."

"The FBI should be there soon. I can't say when, but they agreed to investigate the warehouse. I convinced some-one that you weren't a crackpot. They know you are there," said Mills.

“Thanks, Jack. I’ve tied up those same two guys I left in Helmer at the archaeological camp. They are here at the warehouse. The SUVs are here too. I still can’t find Dr. Riley. I’ve got to keep looking.” Allen hung up.

CHAPTER 43

Riley ran to the edge of the railroad tracks away from the warehouse. She had briefly watched as Claire sprinted through the gate and disappeared. She saw Pasha exit the building and take off after Claire. Mirsky immediately followed and looked toward Pasha and then in Riley's direction. She took off.

Mirsky watched as Riley ran down the tracks between different lines of box cars. He needed something to convince Riley to return or stop so he could get her on the corporate jet and leave the country. He trotted toward Riley's last position and hoped he was within voice range.

Riley determined that it would be absurd to try and outrun Mirsky. She also didn't want to abandon Claire if they captured her. She noticed several box cars with open doors and decided to hide in one or perhaps climb to the roof of one and wait. Mirsky and his henchmen wouldn't be able to search all the box cars, thought Riley. After passing a dozen more cars, she jumped up to the platform between two cars. Riley paused listening for footsteps. Hearing none, she climbed the ladder to the top of the box car and lay flat, waiting and listening.

Mirsky had lost Riley but continued moving away from the warehouse. "Dr. Riley, you must listen to me. You cannot abandon your student, Claire. You must come back with me, and I will release Claire." Mirsky had no idea if Riley was close enough to hear him, but he repeated his plea, again making sure to reveal his position. "Please, Dr. Riley, time is short. You must come with me."

Riley could hear Mirsky approaching the box car she was on top of. As Mirsky came closer Riley could hear his plea. "Claire is counting on you. I promise to release her if you come with me." Riley kept quiet, not making a move. She could hear him crossing several rail lines then all was quiet.

Ten minutes passed, then fifteen. She rose and searched the dark shadows of the rail yard. Nothing was visible and nothing moved. Riley quietly walked to the edge of the box car and carefully climbed down the ladder. She waited on the platform, listening and looking. Hearing nothing, she dropped to the ground and began trotting away from the warehouse. Riley slowed as she came to the end of box cars on her line. An open space extended out ahead of her. It was almost fifty yards before the next set of cars. She hesitated before making the dash across to the next box cars. As she began to move, she felt a tight grip on her arm.

"Dr. Riley, did you not hear me? I need your help. We must go," ordered Mirsky.

"Yes, I heard you. That's why I came out here to this opening, to surrender," said Riley.

"You were headed in the wrong direction, Dr. Riley. The warehouse is back this way." Mirsky swung her by the arm. He pulled his handgun and hurried her back to the warehouse.

CHAPTER 44

Allen found a heavy kitchen knife, went out and checked the interiors of the vehicles. He punctured the front and rear passenger side tires on all three. In the rear of one vehicle, he noticed three gray curation boxes. The doors were unlocked, and Allen opened the rear hatch and examined the boxes. They were marked with Washington State University labels. He opened the first box and immediately recognized the human remains Riley had recovered from Central Ferry. Allen closed the box and gently shut the rear hatch and put the butcher knife under the vehicle.

Allen had seen motion in the rail yard and headed that way. He was a distance from the warehouse when he heard a voice. Allen stayed behind box cars as he edged closer. He was close enough now to understand some of the words. Moving closer still he recognized the voice. The guy who had answered the telephone call he had made earlier.

Allen stopped moving and listened. It was the same voice. He waited motionless. No more talk. No more sound.

He moved cat-like up to the next box car, cautiously peeking under the wheels and behind doors as he moved. Then he heard a second voice, a female voice. Was that Riley's voice? The pitch of the voices changed. Allen could discern footsteps coming in his direction. He waited just briefly, listening, then turned and cautiously began making his way back toward the warehouse.

Allen went to the rear of the SUV for the knife. He opened the back door, got in and silently closed the door. Working quickly, he cut the rear seat belts loose and began fashioning them.

A loud voice broke the silence. "Pasha! Pasha where are you?" yelled Mirsky.

Allen just barely rose up to watch. Riley was held by the arm and guided toward the gray door.

"Pasha, we must go!" Mirsky opened the door, stepped through and pulled Riley behind him.

Allen now recognized the man as the one who broke into Riley's house. The dangerous man. The car alarm beeped once, locking the doors and then a second time as the door locks were opened. The guy had found the fob and was coming out. Allen carefully watched to see Riley being led out with her hands zip tied in front of her, followed by her captor with a duffle bag. They were heading straight in his direction.

Mirsky led Riley around to the rear of the vehicle and checked to make sure the curation boxes were there and intact. He laid his duffle bag next to them and slammed the door. He led Riley to the front seat. "Get in, Dr. Riley."

Mirsky disliked driving but Pasha hadn't returned, and time was running out. He got in and pushed the start button. The SUV fired up.

“Where are we going?” asked Riley.

“We are going to the airport and shall soon be out of this miserable country,” replied Mirsky.

“What, not waiting for your lackey, Pasha?”

“He can take care of himself,” snapped Mirsky, as he secured his belt buckle.

Mirsky put the SUV into drive and immediately felt the lopsided lurch of the vehicle. He hit the gas and the SUV swerved off to the passenger side. “Now what?”

He shifted into park and a thick webbing swept over his shoulders, followed by a distinctive metal clip sound. His arms and torso were pinned to his seat.

Mirsky attempted to twist and turn but Allen instructed, “Don’t make me put a belt around your neck. Might be very uncomfortable.”

Riley also turned. “Deak! He has a gun. He shot Higgins.”

Allen reached down into Mirsky’s jacket and extracted the pistol. “Just sit tight,” said Allen, showing Mirsky the pistol. He reached over and unlocked Riley’s door then stepped from the vehicle and helped her out. He freed her wrists with the knife.

Riley began rapidly talking. “I don’t know where Claire is. She took off running with the other one chasing her. And Higgins is dead. That bastard shot him. I wonder where those other goons are?”

“Slow down, Samantha. We’ll get this figured out. I found Higgins in one of the back rooms and the other two, your original kidnappers, are tied up in the main office,” explained Allen.

"This guy shot Higgins right in front of us. Higgins was working with them."

"What did you say?" asked Allen.

"Higgins sold the Central Ferry remains to these guys. He brought them here and instead of paying Higgins, they killed him," said Riley.

"Higgins told me that you never delivered the remains to Walla Walla," replied Allen.

"Higgins called us when we were driving and changed plans. Claire and I met Higgins in Dayton and gave him the remains. Then on the way back to Pullman, these guys ran us off the road and brought us here to Spokane," explained Riley.

"This is starting to make a little sense."

Allen looked up the gravel road toward the gate and noticed two cars slowly drive in toward the warehouse. The first one stopped near the gate and the second car drove up and parked behind the SUV, blocking it. The window rolled down and a clean-cut man in his forties asked, "Is this your vehicle?"

"You must be law enforcement?" replied Allen.

"That's right. Is this your vehicle?"

"No. Mine is on the other side of the warehouse where I cut a hole in the fence and broke into the warehouse looking for Dr. Riley and her student," said Allen. "This is Dr. Riley, and we don't know where her student is. There are two men tied up in the main office and a murder victim in one of the back rooms of the warehouse. The man tied to the driver's seat here is the murderer and I have his gun is in my waist band behind me."

The driver and his partner altered their behavior with the talk of a gun. "Keep your hands where I can see them."

"No problem. Did my colleague from the Department of Defense call you?"

"Are you Dick Allen?"

"No. My name is Deak Allen. I'm with DOD. I've been searching for stolen federal property and the two abducted women from Washington State University."

Riley broke into the conversation. "I have a young graduate student out there who is being hunted down by another one of these killers. Let's get moving before it's too late," emphasized Riley.

The driver calmly asked her, "Are you Dr. Samantha Riley?"

"I am. Do you have ID?" responded Riley.

The man reached for his credentials and held them for both Riley and Allen to view. "John Mathews, FBI."

A Spokane police vehicle turned into the gravel lot and drove toward the building. It was followed by the second car that waited at the gate. A policeman got out and walked up to the car blocking the SUV. "Are you FBI? We have a woman in the back seat who was found by some good Samaritans. She said she recently escaped from this building, and she is concerned about her friend who was also abducted."

Allen glanced at the police car and began to walk toward it. The policeman held out his hand to stop him. Riley ran past the policeman. The rear door swung open, and Claire ran to Riley and wrapped her arms around her.

Allen put his arm around Samantha and Claire and walked them toward the FBI car. The second agent and the police officer had already handcuffed Mirsky. The agents from the second FBI car had gone into the building to begin reconnaissance.

Allen turned the gun over to the agent and said, "I'll also need the three boxes in the back of that SUV. They are federal property and fall under my jurisdiction."

Agent Mathews was skeptical. "They may represent evidence in the homicide and kidnapping."

"They may or they may not. In any event, they are DOD property, and I will have them, if and when you need them."

The agent looked at him without giving an inch. "Let's see your credentials." Allen retrieved his DOD identification with "MILITARY" printed across the top. The agent examined it and then got out his cell phone and took a photograph of the ID.

"Call my superior, General Orlando Ortega, at the Department of Defense. You can use the number Jack Mills gave you. He will vouch for me."

"Where will these boxes be stored?" asked Agent Mathews.

"They will be housed at a Class 2 curation vault at Washington State University," replied Allen.

"Okay," replied Mathews. "Dr. Riley, we'll need to get a preliminary statement from you and Miss Anderson."

"I'll get my rental from around the back," said Allen.

Mathews looked over at his partner. "You better go with him."

After another hour of questions and paperwork, Allen drove Samantha and Claire back to Pullman. "Do you two want to get dropped at your homes or do you need something from campus?" asked Allen.

"A ride home would be great," said Claire.

"Take me to campus and I'll pick up my car. Claire, I'll drop you off."

"Does WSU have trauma counseling services?"

"I suppose we do, but I've never used them before," said Riley.

"You should call and set up a meeting with them as soon as possible," suggested Allen. "It's standard operating practice for anyone who has gone through what you two have."

CHAPTER 45

PULLMAN, WASHINGTON

By the next week, Allen had set up a temporary office in Walla Walla to manage the Central Ferry burial project. Riley was in her office on the telephone. "So, the FBI has reached out to you regarding your encounter in Vladivostok?" asked Riley.

"Yes, thank you so much for mentioning it to them after they raided the Spokane warehouse. I was able to identify the thug who assaulted me in Vladivostok. The same guy who kidnapped you," replied Rackerman. "He also kidnapped my Russian colleague's wife. Fortunately, the authorities were able to rescue her after our people contacted them about the arrest."

"Have you thought about sitting on Henderson's dissertation committee? She could really use your expertise. I specialize in archaeological forensics and isotopes, but she is a stone tool person like you."

"We have been corresponding via email," replied Rackerman. "It would be an honor to serve on any of your students' committees, particularly Jennifer's. That woman is brilliant. I believe she will have a significant impact on the profession."

"Tom, I must go. We'll talk later, eh?"

"You bet. Good luck on the analysis."

Riley downloaded the protein analysis report Jennifer Henderson had written for the large, flaked tools recovered with the Central Ferry burial. She sent a copy to her printer and a PDF to Deak Allen's email address. Riley picked up the desk phone and called Claire.

Claire entered the office and settled into her usual chair across from Riley.

"Claire, what do you have so far from the diet analysis?"

"The guy certainly ate camas and other tubers as a staple, probably as much fish as possible, but no anadromous fish, and no sea mammals. There probably wasn't a salmon run up the Snake River at that time," said Claire.

"So, nothing new until the strontium analysis is completed," asked Riley.

"That's all she wrote," responded Claire.

Riley's tone changed. "How are the sessions working out for you?"

"I'm doing well. If I hadn't worked in human anatomy and forensics during my undergraduate days, who knows how I would have reacted to the Higgins shooting. I've seen a lot of gory stuff," said Claire.

"Yeah, but it's different when it happens to you," responded Riley.

"I'm okay. No loss of sleep. In fact, just the opposite. What an exciting first year of graduate school. Found the oldest human to have ever lived. Kidnapped by Russians, and I have the coolest advisor ever."

Riley checked her watch. "Okay. Claire, I've got another meeting coming up."

Riley pulled Jennifer's report from her printer and sat down, going through it page by page, making marks with a red pen when questions surfaced. She needed to have the report digested before her meeting with Allen in fifteen minutes.

After reading the report, she picked up the phone and called Jennifer's office. "Hey Jen, nice job on the protein analysis."

"Great. Thanks Samantha. I have the spreadsheets with the tabulated raw data in my office if you need them. I couldn't put all the compounds in the report," responded Jennifer.

"I sent a copy to Deak Allen. He might have some questions for you."

"I sent Dr. Allen a copy of the raw data last week. This report might help him more easily understand those data."

"By the way, Tom Rackerman has agreed to sit on your committee. I think he would be more than happy to share some of his data, too."

"Really! This is amazing! Thanks for asking him, Samantha. I think this dissertation is finally coming together. Do you think I should email him right now?"

"Why not? Let him know we talked and then slam him with the details of what you're focusing on. See what he says. Make sure to mention the bipoints."

There was a knock at the door. "Hey, Jen, I've got to go. Talk to you later," said Riley.

"The door's open," called Riley.

Deak Allen entered the office wearing a white shirt with gray stripes, a WSU tie, and a jacket over his arm.

"Hey, look at you, all cleaned up," said Riley. "Did you finally get that Afghan report done?"

"All finished and sent to D.C.," said Allen. "It's been a few days. Are you doing okay?"

"I'm back to normal, with a touch of exhaustion. I've been chased, beat up, survived a car crash, worried about getting my project pulled by the Army Corps, and I've been on this pre-tenure grind. About normal. So, you're going to stick around for a while and manage the Central Ferry Burial project, eh?"

"That seems to be what they have planned for me," replied Allen. "I've been talking with the tribes. Sounds like you've been working with them over the past week as well."

"I got some DNA results back from the UC Davis lab on some sediments I sent them earlier to try and figure out what kind of organics were under the burial."

"What did you find out?" asked Allen.

"We got a hit on some bird species and a Pleistocene short-faced bear. There was also some human DNA. I compared the signature to existing genomes on file and it looks close to Pacific Northwest indigenous people. I called the Nez Perce, and it looks like we are going to conduct a joint study."

"A joint study?"

"It looks like this Central Ferry guy might be a direct ancestor to the Palouse Tribes. That would represent the longest definitive claim to lands any tribe has ever made with scientific evidence. It confirms what the tribes have been saying all along about their ancestral homeland. They want me to continue the DNA study and any other kind of nondestructive analysis on the remains," explained Riley.

"Great work, Samantha."

"I can bring you up to speed on where we are with the analysis quickly. We don't have very much new information," confessed Riley.

"Before we get going on that, I'd like to propose something," said Allen. "I've mentioned that the Institute sometimes requests fellowship proposals from researchers for promising scholarship. It's not much but it can help accelerate a research project."

"Are you inviting me to submit a proposal?" asked Riley.

"I'd like the Institute to help fund your research on the Central Ferry project. I believe it's important for everyone to understand how someone who lived during the last Ice Age was able to live to such a great age, and what that means for us today," said Allen.

"How opportune," said Riley. "Those are exactly the questions I'm interested in addressing."

"That's wonderful," said Allen. "I can brief you on submission details later. Today, let's discuss what is known so far and brainstorm some ideas and directions."

"So far nothing has changed with the isotope data. Complex carbohydrates from wild root crops, no anadromous fish or sea mammals."

"How about herbivores, elk, deer?" asked Allen.

"We're still waiting to complete the strontium analysis that should give us some of that information, but I can't see how we won't get a hit with artiodactyl diet."

"That makes sense to me given the trace element analysis," said Allen.

"Wait, what do you mean, that makes sense to you," asked Riley.

"We'll have to double check Jennifer's trace element analysis, but I'd bet her protein study indicates a large land mammal diet as well," said Allen.

"Do you mean the trace element scans she was making on the stone tools? How would they directly relate to diet? Everyone speculates that projectile points equate to hunting, and thus, animal protein. But that's old school archaeology, no direct evidence," said Riley.

"Well, we'll have to have a closer look at her report and analysis, won't we? There are just too many possibilities at play right now. I need a few more facts," replied Allen.

"Then I'll change the subject," said Riley. "How long have Walt and Windy had the cabin?"

"I'm not sure. Did you know Windy was a student at Washington State University?" said Allen.

"No, I didn't."

"She got her doctorate in vet med at WSU. I believe she and Walt were dating back then, a long-distance relationship. They used to head to North Idaho on breaks and fell in love with the area."

"Where did he do his graduate work?" asked Riley.

"He was at Binghamton University."

"That is a long-distance relationship."

"When he took the job in Wyoming and she finished vet school, I think they bought the cabin," said Allen.

"That would be over thirty-five years ago, right?" questioned Riley.

"I suppose. What are you thinking about?"

"I'm thinking Windy and Walt look way younger than their chronological age," said Riley.

"Listen," added Allen. "I think we've been looking at this from the wrong perspective. We've been searching for the silver bullet, the panacea, the one thing that will prolong the life of a human being."

"True. What's wrong with that? Maybe the genetic mutation Rackerman postulates is the silver bullet? We find that, propagate it, and humans live to a hundred sixty years old, right?" said Riley.

"What if there is no silver bullet? What if there is no genetic mutation? What if it's like most things in nature? What if it's the confluence of several indiscriminate things? When those align, they become greater by virtue of their synergy. The proof might be the ancient skeleton. The oldest human ever known just happened to live over thirteen thousand years ago."

"Okay, Deak. Let's look at the diet again. Claire's report shows consumption of root crops as a staple. Complex carbohydrates. Camas. We know the camas was from the headwater areas of North Idaho and not from the Snake River. The isotope study shows us that. But indigenous people have been eating camas as a staple for the past four thousand years in this area. And none lived to be over a hundred, as far as we know."

"That's why it's not just the camas. There is also something else, an additive," said Allen. "The two skeletons, one from Central Ferry and one from Siberia, lived during the end of the last Ice Age. You earlier indicated this was a time when the world was undergoing enormous change."

"Sure, defoliation, draught, super storms, massive extinction of animal and plant species. As lands recover, sometimes the same species would return, but there would be new species as well. They compete to fill the new niches," replied Riley.

"This region contains one species that's been around since before the Ice Ages and has survived them. It survives by hiding within other species. They are like seeds or hibernation pods. There is a special kind of bacteria living in organisms that are hibernating in these pods or statoblasts."

"Where is this coming from, Deak?" asked Riley.

"Remember when I went to Missoula? I talked with the expert on the bacteria, James Ross. Statoblasts are formed by Bryozoans when aquatic conditions are drying up or freezing. It's a way for the species to hibernate until conditions are good again. Another thing happens during those distressed times. The bacteria living in the Bryozoans excrete a foul-tasting chemical compound to help Bryozoan survival. Here's the kicker. That chemical compound has been found to be one effective way to fight the growth of cancer cells."

"You're suggesting that the production of the cancer fighting chemical compound is elevated during distressed times, such as the end of the Pleistocene," queried Riley. "You're also suggesting that the compound is associated with camas at the end of the Pleistocene, but not at other times, like four thousand years ago?"

"Correct, that's why those people eating camas as a staple, four or even a thousand years ago, were not living as long as people eating camas or some other aquatic root crop thirteen thousand years ago."

"Wait a minute, Deak. Why aquatic root crop?"

"The cancer fighting chemical compound, known as bryostatins, are carried by the bacteria living symbiotically with the Bryozoans, living in the water."

"Not a silver bullet! You're talking about a cure for cancer."

"Yes, but I'm also saying that cure is just one of a few things that need to be considered," said Allen. "So, if you review the causes of death in America, as assessed by the National Center for Health Statistics, what is the leading cause of death?"

"Cancer," guessed Riley.

"That's a close number two at 34.3 percent," said Allen. "Number one is heart disease at 36.1 percent. The next closest cause of death is preventable injuries, that includes all preventable injuries, and that's way down at 7.4 percent. All other causes of death are below that."

It then clicked for Riley. "So, the first two leading causes of death were mitigated in our Central Ferry skeleton by a consumption of wild foods or wild complex carbohydrates and a cancer reducing compound. Whether he knew it or not. And he probably didn't. How do we know for sure he was eating the compound?" asked Riley.

"Samantha, you are such a critical scientist."

"Isn't that the only kind?"

Allen opened his backpack and retrieved a printout. "Take a look at the raw data on trace elements from the stone tools that Jennifer generated and sent me last week when you were missing. See anything interesting?"

"How about a hint, Deak. There are hundreds of chemical signatures in these spread sheets.

"She has them in alpha numeric order. Look under the B section," suggested Allen.

"Wow, I see bryostatins. On the large, flaked tools, mostly. Some on the bipoints, too," said Riley.

"Our ancient man was using flake stone tools to process root crops that had grown in ground saturated with bryostatins. They probably got there from statoblasts or pod dispersal during drought conditions, like the last Ice Age. Do you buy it so far?" asked Allen.

"There's more?"

"Of course, there is no single silver bullet." Allen continued. "It can't be just aquatic root crops. There must have been other kinds of wild foods that helped. We know that domesticated foods, as convenient as they are, contain only a fraction of the biodiversity as wild food, from a genetic perspective. And of course, processed foods are even worse with the use of simple carbohydrates and sugars."

"From your perspective a broad spectrum of things lined up to prolong human life. Why couldn't there have also been a genetic mutation, as Rackerman postulates?" posed Riley.

"There may have been," said Allen. "We can't rule that out. However, like you so eloquently stated at Windy and Walt's place, there is no evidence that such a mutation has occurred."

"I like where you are going with this, Deak. What's next?"

"That's up to you, Samantha. You are the only one who has the data to put the various pieces together. Exactly which wild foods, and really, which compounds and how much of each. That's right in your wheelhouse. The cancer treating compound is an important piece, but only one in a longer sequence of items that will help us understand human longevity. I've asked Jimmy Ross at Montana to work on that piece and to collaborate with you."

Riley stood looking at Allen. "You are a bit of a manipulator, aren't you, Deak?"

"I asked Jimmy Ross why he never focused on the bryostatins before, but he didn't give me a straight answer."

"That's easy," replied Riley.

"Let's hear it."

"Over the past thirty years or so we've been having drier conditions all over the western U.S. Range and forest fires are common now. We even call it the "fire season." Those fires are defoliating the upper watershed in our mountainous forests, and Bryozoans, like the ones in the lake you saw and like I've seen around Helmer are stressed. Probably like the end of Pleistocene, and researchers are noticing them more."

"Wouldn't that mean that people who are actively eating wild foods from the region would be ingesting more of the compound and potentially living longer?" asked Allen. "But we don't see that happening."

"True, but there aren't too many people in this region eating wild food as a staple. Even most Native Americans in the area now only eat wild foods ceremonially," said Riley.

Allen nodded affirmatively. "That makes perfect sense, and it helps me understand something else."

"What?"

"Did you notice how young Windy looked?" asked Allen.

"Yes. Didn't I say that when you first walked in?" posed Riley. "She could easily pass for my sister and perhaps my younger sister," said Riley.

"Okay, now I understand why you brought that up," said Allen. "Anyhow, when I first arrived at the lake, I met the park ranger who thought I was Walt. I was in Walt's boat. He told me that Windy was a wild food nut, and that she collected wild berries and bushels of water potatoes from the edges of the lake. How long did we calculate they had the cabin? Wasn't it over thirty-five years?" asked Allen.

"She's probably been consuming regular amounts of bryostatins for more than half of her life. Not to mention the complex carbohydrates and whatever else wild foods provide," said Riley. "We know that complete human tissue replacement only takes seven to eight years according to isotopic studies."

Deak Allen gave Samantha Riley a long look. "There's really something important here related to the understanding and any cure for the two most common reasons for death in humans today, cancer and heart disease. By coincidence, the Central Ferry man probably reduced his susceptibility to both," explained Allen.

"Wow, now I'm even more convinced that those remains hold a clue to a healthier life and a significantly longer life span," said Riley.

"Human demographers say that the first person to live over one hundred fifty is probably already born. However, they don't know what kind of science will make that possible. And I think you already have most of it figured out," said Allen. "You are just the person to pursue this. There has never been a scientific lead like this before. This all needs to be carefully studied. It could change life as we know it."

Samantha nodded her head and sat back down. "There will be political, peer, and professional pushback on a project of this magnitude. I'm so damn tired. I need some time. This whole Utkin Chemicals attack has slammed me. Claire could have been injured or killed. It would have been my fault. I'm not sure I'm ready to put my students through this."

"Samantha, you might be the only person today who can handle this project."

"I'm not saying I won't take this on, but I want to make sure I'm ready," continued Riley. "This is what I got into archaeology for. This is potentially an amazing scientific breakthrough. And I have the students and the lab to tackle it. This is what I've lived for. But Deak, I need some time to recharge before I can switch gears and jump into such an apocalyptic project. I'm just not sure I can make this transition without a clear head and some time to really think this through."

"What are you thinking, Samantha? A month? A semester?" asked Allen.

"I don't know. So much has happened. I just need to go into this rested and with a good understanding of where I want to take it. I haven't had a week off in over five years and I'm starting to feel the repercussions. I need a few weeks to relax and gather my wits about what this means and how I might proceed."

"Samantha, I know just the place you can recharge. It has a great lake view," smiled Deak.

Riley's demeanor perked. "I do believe I promised to cook you a dinner."

EPILOGUE

WASHINGTON, D.C.

It had been almost a month since Russian troops entered Ukraine from the north on their march to Kyiv, and from the east, where their artillery was pounding Kharkiv. Russian mobile artillery, helicopter attack ships, and supersonic aircraft were unchallenged over Ukrainian skies and on Ukrainian roads. Ukrainian president, Volodymyr Zelenskyy was begging the West, particularly the United States, to help with modern ordinance to stall the Russian invasion.

Retired General Orlando Ortega had been called to a meeting by the Secretary of Defense. He carried with him a report from the FBI investigation of Utkin Chemicals Company. The report detailed how Utkin Chemicals sold and distributed opioids in the U.S., kidnapped two women in Washington State, and murdered two men in the same state. It included testimony from the two kidnap victims as well as testimony from an American who detailed his assault in Vladivostok. Additional testimony was given by two Ukrainian citizens living in the U.S. and working for Utkin Chemicals. Two other

Utkin Chemicals employees were being held in the U.S. as co-conspirators.

General Ortega was ushered into the room. Sitting around the table were Defense Secretary, Lawrence Houston; Secretary of State, Andrew Rinker; and FBI Director, Christine Bray. "Good to see you again, Orlando," said Secretary Houston, as they clasped hands. You already know Director Bray. I've asked Secretary Rinker to sit in on our meeting."

Orlando Ortega reached over and shook Bray's hand and did the same for Secretary Rinker. "It's a pleasure to meet you, Mr. Secretary," said Ortega.

"Please sit down. You may know that Ukraine has requested modern ordinance to halt the Russian invasion," said Lawrence Houston.

"Lawrence, I've only heard what has been reported in the news. And that's all I've heard," said Ortega.

"Orlando, we are giving the Ukrainian request serious consideration, but our intel suggests that we are going to have to support them with hundreds of stinger missiles for aircraft defense and maybe thousands of javelin missiles for anti-tank defense," explained the Secretary of Defense.

Rinker added, "This will more than likely continue for an extended period, costing American taxpayers hundreds of millions, maybe billions of dollars."

"I'm not sure how this relates to me and my team," said Ortega. "I thought I was called here to discuss a stolen property case."

FBI Director, Christine Bray spoke, "General, I trust you have read the FBI report on Utkin Chemicals. Your team was a prime player in acquiring those witnesses and building the case against Utkin."

"Thank you for the acknowledgement, Director Bray. But the case is yours. Yes, my team was involved, but it is an FBI investigation," replied Ortega.

"Well, General," said Secretary Houston, "we are about ready to extradite Nicolai Utkin and confiscate his assets that are not located in Russia. His yacht alone is worth over eight hundred million. That pays for all the javelins and most of the stingers for a year."

"The last I heard he was in Bulgaria," said Ortega. "I don't believe we have an extradition treaty with them."

"So, you have been keeping up on Utkin," said Houston. "Something tells me you were the right person to discuss this with. Ukraine has an extradition treaty with Bulgaria. And we are working on an agreement with Ukraine. You see where this is going?"

"I still don't understand what all this has to do with me," said Ortega.

"We want to have as much background as possible before pushing the button on this one," said Secretary Rinker. "There is nothing in the report about why Utkin had the Americans killed and why he kidnapped two other Americans. What can you tell us?"

"I'm sure the witnesses have, or will speak to that issue," replied General Ortega. "I'm not sure I can speak to why Utkin did what he did. I do know that both murdered Americans were archaeologists as were the two kidnap victims."

"All are archaeologists?" said Secretary Houston. "That isn't readily apparent from the report. At least I didn't pick it up."

"What could that mean?" asked Christine Bray. "Why were archaeologists targeted?"

"It could just be a coincidence. It might be related to a single event in Washington State. Or something else. I'm not sure what it means," said Ortega.

"Come on, Orlando. This is right up your alley. Your institute has half a dozen archaeologists on staff or on contract, and two dozen more specialized scientists and data analysts. Why would a Russian oligarch be killing and kidnapping American researchers?" probed Houston.

"If I told you, you won't believe it. I'm not sure I do," said Ortega.

"We have an opportunity right now, at this very minute, to arrest Utkin and seize his assets both in Bulgaria and Ukraine," said Secretary Rinker. "The Ukrainians are desperately waiting for the ordinance. Is there anything we should be concerned about with Utkin Chemicals before we act?"

"As far as I can tell, Nicholai Utkin is a psychopathic billionaire buddy of Vladimir Putin. I'd seize the assets and ship the missiles," said Ortega.

"Why did he kill and kidnap Americans?" asked Bray.

"The guy is crazy," said General Ortega, as he paused and pondered what he was about to say.

"Come on, Orlando, nothing can surprise me these days," said Secretary Houston.

Ortega gave a serious look around the room and shook his head. "Unbelievably, Utkin thought a rare archaeological discovery in Washington State contained the secret to the "Fountain of Youth."

"What?" replied Secretary Houston, incredulously.

"I told you. Nuts!" said Ortega.

Rinker peered into each face around the table, digesting the discussion. Without speaking he reached over, picked up the desk phone and pushed a preset number. He said just two words. "Project Green."

The *Krasivaya Ptitsa* was moored in Nicholai Utkin's favorite city, Varna, Bulgaria. It was early morning and Utkin was still asleep on board his yacht. He wore green silk pajamas, and his eyes were covered by tiny goggles. The rest of his face was entirely shellacked in a purple paste masking he had applied to moisturize his skin. Utkin's hair was lathered in a gel and covered with a shower cap.

There was a commotion outside his stateroom. First, it consisted of a loud conversation. That escalated to a shouting match between his security personnel and someone attempting to enter the stateroom. Soon a scuffle could be heard outside the door. Utkin, distracted by the noise, stood and grabbed a robe. Someone was going to pay for this intrusion, he thought, as he soaked a towel under hot water in the bathroom and began to wipe the paste off his face. Before he could finish, the door to his stateroom flung open and a Bulgarian military officer entered, followed by five or six heavily armed soldiers.

"What is the meaning of this?" shouted Utkin, with remnants of the purple paste clinging to his face.

"Nicholai Utkin?" asked the officer.

"I am. And whoever you are, you will soon wish you never met me," sneered Utkin.

"This boat is now the seized property of the Bulgarian government, and you are under arrest for drug trafficking and espionage." The officer motioned for his guards. They moved to handcuff Utkin.

"Take your hands off me or I will see to it that you and your families live the rest of your days behind bars."

The officer hit Utkin with a Taser. His body shuddered and he fell backward to the floor. He was cuffed and when he could respond, he was led off the boat. Waiting on shore were two men in gray suits and name tags hanging around their necks. The blue and yellow colors of the Ukrainian flag was obvious on the tags. They pointed to a waiting fleet of three official looking vehicles. Utkin was led to the one in the center. He was helped in, and the caravan left the harbor area and within seconds disappeared into the city known for its mystery.

Made in United States
Troutdale, OR
05/30/2026

49535052R00194